Poetry as Consciousness
Haiku Forests, Space of Mind, and an Ethics of Freedom

by Richard Gilbert

Illustrated by Sabine Miller

慧文社

Poetry as Consciousness

Haiku Forests, Space of Mind, and an Ethics of Freedom

By Richard Gilbert

Illustrated by Sabine Miller

Copyright, Richard Gilbert, 2018
Cover art: "Stupa," by Sabine Miller, 2017

Published by Keibunsha, Co. LTD.

ISBN978-4-86330-189-4
Printed in Japan

Poetry as Consciousness

*Haiku Forests, Space of Mind,
and an Ethics of Freedom*

CONTENTS

ACKNOWLEDGEMENTS 17

INTRODUCTION 23

    Poetry and the Beauty of Distance 23

    A Personal Journey 25

    Overview: Poetry, Sanctuary and the Space of Mind 27

I. SPACE OF MIND 29

    The Perception of the Unique 33

    Immeasurability 38

    Sunny-side Up in Space 41

    Soul 43

    Space is the Place 45

    The Specious Present: The Poetry-line & Haiku 55

    Between Meaning and Unknowing 57

I. SPACE OF MIND (continued)

Architectures to Inspire Dwelling 60

Properties of Thoughtspace 62

Six Notions Concerning the Psycho-poetic Landscape of Thought 62

Seven Properties of Thoughtspace 64

II. PHILOPOETIC VOLITION 67

Volition: Enactments of Personal Philosophy 72

Remembrance and Distance 75

III. THE SHAPE OF JAZZ TO COME 79

A Memoir 83

Inhabitation 84

In Review: And Why Haiku? 85

Secrecy 86

IV. PRIVACY MATTERS 89

    The Panopticon 93

    Time Slips Away 95

V. SANCTUARY 99

    Theatre of the Sacred 104

    Sanctuary, Temenos and Risk 108

    Beyond the Salon 112

    Anarchic Sanctuaries, Collaborative Worlds 114

        Q1. What for you is an anarchic sanctuary? 114

        Q2. Would you provide some examples? 114

        Q3. How would entering a virtual social world contrast with reading speculative fiction? 118

        Q4. Experiencing group-creative social & virtual collaboration, what are some benefits and contrasts? 125

        Q5. Is somatic physicality (being present in physical proximity) overrated as to social congress? 129

        Q6. How do you imagine the future, in relation to a positive sociality which values anarchic forms of sanctuary? 131

V. SANCTUARY (continued)

Where We Have Never Been 133

VI. HAIKU, AN ETHICS OF FREEDOM 137

Remystification 141

Analysis: Conceptual Architectures of Thoughtspace 142

Outline: 36 Qualities of Thoughtspace Derived from 7 Properties ... 143

1) SPACE *(Perception)* 147

1. Minimal Creation 147

2. Novel Worlds 149

3. Immeasurability 150

4. Unknown Unknowns 152

2) LANGUAGE *(Terminologies & Shared Communication)* 157

5. Concreta vs Abstracta 157

6. Conceptual Blending 159

7. Neologism (Unusuality) 161

- **8.** Possible Worlds **163**
- **9.** Inferred Narratives **165**
- **10.** Staging — Theatres of Story............................ **167**

3) <u>THOUGHTSPACE</u> *(Conditional Ephemerality)*........................ **171**

- **11.** Philopoetic Volition **171**
- **12.** Practice of Invention......................................**174**
- **13.** Spatial Thermoclines **176**

4) <u>METAPHORICS</u> *(Deformational fictions; 'to be as')* **181**

- **14.** Fantasy Imagery... **182**
- **15.** Paradox **184**
- **16.** Alternativity **185**
- **17.** Idiosyncrasy (Fallacy)..................................... **187**
- **18.** Crafting of Presentation **188**
- **19.** Mimesis ("Shadow of the Divine") **190**

5) ARCHITECTURES *(Design-intention)* **195**

    20. Design-architecture **195**

    21. World building, Construction **196**

    22. *Temenos* **198**

    23. Precincts **200**

    24. Construction — Sacred Construction **201**

    25. Notions of Anarchic Sanctuary **203**

6) SOUL *(Explorative Desire)* **209**

    26. Soul (as Core Value) **209**

    27. Remembrance and Distance **210**

    28. Grit, Guts **212**

    29. Desire, Passion **213**

    31. With Risk **217**

7) THE "THIRD" *("Hypothetical" Humanity)* **223**

    32. Distance **223**

33. Forms of Resistance **224**

34. Inhabitation (Dwelling) **226**

35. Place **228**

36. Consciousness — Revisions of World and Self **229**

CONCLUSION **235**

Permeability **237**

Poetic Force and Imaginal Space at Liberty **238**

An Ethics of Freedom **239**

VII. APPENDIX 1. 36 QUALITIES OF THOUGHTSPACE **243**

Verbose Description **243**

1) SPACE **243**

2) LANGUAGE **244**

3) THOUGHTSPACE **244**

4) METAPHORICS **245**

5) ARCHITECTURES **246**

VII. APPENDIX 1. 36 QUALITIES OF THOUGHTSPACE (continued)

    6) SOUL 246

    7) THE "THIRD" 247

VIII. APPENDIX 2. DISJUNCTION IN HAIKU — STRONG AND WEAK 249

    A New Definition 249

    Disjunctive Modes 250

    Haiku Exhibiting Strong Disjunction 251

    Haiku Exhibiting Weak Disjunction 253

    Critical Usefulness: Terminology 256

    Living Haiku 258

IX. APPENDIX 3. FORETHOUGHT 259

X. ENDNOTES 263

XI. REFERENCES 287

Illustrations

Floragrams, by Sabine Miller

1. "Poet and Temenos," 2016 — **21**
2. "Space-egg," 2017 — **31**
3. "Immeasurable Intangible Unknown," 2017 — **53**
4. "Spatial Thermoclines," 2017 — **69**
5. "Roses for Ornette," 2017 — **81**
6. "Imagination is Unclaimed," 2017 — **91**
7. "Theatre of Dwelling," 2016 — **101**
8. "Anarchic Sanctuary," 2017 — **123**
9. "Emily's Darlings," 2016 — **139**
10. "Rose in Time," 2016 — **155**
11. "Contiguous Spaces," 2017 — **169**
12. "Thoughtcraft," 2016 — **179**
13. "Amnion," 2017 — **193**
14. "Surface and Depth," 2017 — **207**
15. "The Spectral City," 2017 — **221**
16. "Volitional Formations," 2017 — **235**

Acknowledgements

From early days in junior high school through my first college years, several teachers recognized something in a strange, silent, kid and allowed him the freedom to experiment and creatively explore. A music teacher in seventh grade who (at some professional risk) allowed access to six tape recorders, two-story stepladders and microphones to compose musique concrète on an empty auditorium stage in the afternoons; a science teacher who gave course credit for attending Buckminster Fuller lectures and building geodesics; an anthropologist at a Community College who shared her research-field passion by taking students to a local Native American dig she led; a math teacher who taught calculus and combinatorics with compassion and insight all the while her husband dying of cancer in a hospital, up the hill.

At Naropa University, Barbara Dilley, a pioneering postmodern dancer/choreographer (later university president) taught innovative conceptual-performance practices of sacred space in dance, resulting in lasting contemplations, and Patricia Donegan imparted her knowledge of haiku studies, comparative literature and Japanese aesthetics—giving expert critical attention to student works.

In graduate school, a high point was training in contemplative psychology with Chogyam Trungpa, Rinpoche, and a group of experienced therapists eager to share their knowledge and serve as guides. In doctoral studies at The Union University, being given creative latitude to design my curriculum allowed for study with renowned psychological philosopher James Hillman, while continuing a clinical psychotherapy practice.

I acknowledge these teachers, and importantly the non-traditional institutional frameworks supporting them, in recognizing an alternative-learner's potential. As an educator myself now for some decades, I aspire to care for my students in a similar way. This book is dedicated to my teachers, mentors and the community of authors, artists, students, and clients who have illumined me through their books, collaborations and lives.

Over the last year, a talented group of editors have donated many hours to this manuscript: Stephen Bailey, Clayton Beach, Sabine Miller, Prudence Northrop, Victor Ortiz, and Michelle Tennison—from the bottom of my heart, thank you. My dear wife, Keiko, has also patiently supported the writing process, while providing earthly love and support.

Auspicious meetings with remarkable artists of poetic imagination remain a lifeline, nourishing aspects of the muse. Ovid writes, "Breathe your breath into my book of changes ... my soul would sing of metamorphoses." This work is an offering to those who have enlivened my days, and evoked blessedness in my life, deepening mysteries and intimacies of the heart. You know who you are.

The present work began some months into a sabbatical year. I thank my Department and Faculty for granting me the time, and given the current political climate note that academic tenure has provided the psychological space to research and contemplate in a non-distracted *temenos* of sanctuary—this work would not have been completed otherwise. I wish to express my thanks to all of the haiku poets cited, each representing excellence in the international genre.

This work has been supported by The Japan Society for the Promotion of Science (JSPS) Grant-in-Aid for Scientific Research *Kakenhi* 15K02755 (2015-2018). Book publication has been supported by a Kumamoto University Academic Publication Subsidy.

(Grant information in Japanese:) 本書は平成29年度熊本大学学術出版助成、および平成27～29年度採択日本学術振興会・科学研究費補助金基盤研究（C）「俳句の国際教育への活用とネットワーク構築：現代俳句の文化的多様性の双方向的発信」（課題番号：15K02755、研究代表者：リチャード・ギルバート）の助成を受けたものです。

Poetry as Consciousness

Haiku Forests, Space of Mind, and an Ethics of Freedom

1. "Poet and Temenos," 2016 [1]

*What can be said for poetry? In today's world, something
needs to be said, and we could be saying more.
How is it for a soul to find, for however brief a time,
novel orientations of landscape? And how many ideas change a life?*

Introduction

Poetry and the Beauty of Distance

Simone Weil wrote, "attention is the rarest and purest form of generosity."[2] When I think of poetry—works that reach through skin and bone, sparkling as rain, bringing elements that enhance the nature of psyche, I muse that what is most valuable in life—those notions which have sustained a life, may be least articulable. The question, "What drives us to poetry?" is similar to "What came before the big bang?" We may theorize, but it remains a mystery, poetry. So I wish to begin simply, with attention to the question of how mind creates space, poetically—to explore the depth of knowing as presented by metaphoric images in their arriving—and the extent via their reception and contemplation that we become more interior beings.

It's a strange situation that while good poetry is intelligent, and we too are intelligent, on the topic of the value and use of poetry we remain almost entirely mute. The closer we come to consciousness itself the more mysterious we are to ourselves, and there occurs a schism: these interior and intimate experiences are not easily articulated through language-communication. Consciousness researcher David Chalmers (1995) writes, "There is nothing that we know more intimately than conscious experience, but there is nothing that is harder to explain."

The starting point of this exploration is impelled by a certain frustration, which is also a goad: what can be said for poetry? In today's world, something needs to be said, and we could be saying more concerning which poems we praise. How is it for a soul to find, for however brief a time, novel orientations of landscape, to adopt new shapes and forms of imaginal space through novel surprises, discontinuities and sonorities?

And how many ideas change a life? For myself, only a few. One is that lacking psychic material, it is not possible to know oneself well—know the colors, textures, and sense of story: the make-up (*kosmētikós*) of psychic landscapes, including dream, fantasy and sentences. While one's psychic landscape is not necessarily the vessel or possessor of rational meaning, imaginative landscapes are the way psyche clothes itself in form. Lacking form, there can be no interior vision, no deeper interaction to be made visible, so as to *inform*.

There is no magic bullet in a poem. No sudden "a-ha!" of enlightened transformation. There are moments of recognition, a feeling of connection to something ineffable and numinous. It feels so much less loud, solid or sure, poetry. And yet there are gifts—one is the otherness of poetic landscapes, distant from familiar narratives. It isn't so much that I *need* to change the story of my life, or become something "other than"—but there is a deeper need, perhaps better described as a calling. Within a violent world, contemporary poetry ascertains, memorializes and reminds; poetry offers insight and cultural reflection, but this isn't why I read poems. I don't read poetry for answers, yet there are reasons, associated with ideas of freedom and sanctuary.

Each poem is inherently unique: behind the eyes *images speak*—re-describe earth on their own terms. In George Berkeley's epithet, *esse est percipi*: "to be is to be perceived": fresh images in a poem become origin-points creating imaginal worlds. Even if we may trivialize such "imaginations," nonetheless we arrive. *Being* in imagination is not only perceiving something "out there"—we are also perceived to be there in the first place, by what is other to us. That is, what arises in imagination isn't purely self-willed, consciously self-constructed. In this sense, as Berkeley points out, perceivers are perceived as from a distance of otherness (alterity), of strangeness, novelty. We see and *are seen* in imagination; this is an intimacy of seeing that occurs whenever we are jolted, moved or surprised by what shifts us out of habitual frames of concept and perception, within the space of thought. Another way to say this is that the ego is de-literalized via imaginative experiences. Worlds of imagination arise spontaneously and *autonomously*—poems re-construct being, hover and flit through the under and overground of consciousness. Each poem becomes a focus, a lens: a novel *cosmetics* of cosmos. Psyche *in*forms.

There is a sense of strangeness in the beauty of distance when looking across an ocean toward unknown shores, silvered waves rippling across the horizon. What happens within the space of thought? We do not possess the scientific understanding of *why* we are self-aware beings, why we each experience an ongoing "virtual video" (as Chandler puts it) in our heads, of the *qualities* of consciousness: the consciousness of consciousness itself. This sense of "unknown" or mystery frees us to speculate on the arising of such qualities.

By collectively sharing experiences of poetry it becomes more possible to verify notions of poetic creativity, why we enjoy its practices, and consequently what its value may be. Conversations in this vein clarify and validate the subjectivity of private perceptions and intangibles of landscapes that rise and fade in intimate distances.

Poems are not ores to be mined merely for meaning. The drive towards greater tangibility and greater knowing generally diminishes a poem's psychic force, the *faces* of its images. This is one of the conundra involved in attempts to present a personal and social value for poetry—significance may lie in the intangible—even in what eludes us.

While the desire for greater tangibility can diminish poetry, it isn't enough to claim that intangibility itself is inherently beneficial, and it remains to be seen as well which intangibles are of value. How to assay the landscape of thought as a poetics? This is the starting point of a journey.

A Personal Journey

Although the focus of this book concerns poetic imagination as a whole, haiku are presented as a means to illustrate how the space of thought may be activated or "performed" by both reader and composer—how certain phenomena of consciousness can be articulated with the barest minimum of text. Haiku often open us to this thoughtspace quite mysteriously.

I moved to Japan in 1997, in the next decade befriending and interviewing a number of haiku poets, notable authors abundant in personal warmth. Through their willingness to communicate I encountered jewels of the contemporary progressive-critical haiku tradition. My 2008 book, *Poems of Consciousness,* was a first attempt to articulate new perspectives for haiku in English. Its two main goals were to inform the English-speaking world concerning the modern haiku tradition in Japan, which had remained almost completely unknown to that point, and to divine critical approaches to illustrate expansive conceptions and techniques regarding haiku—and to share appreciations of haiku as a novel poetics of consciousness.

In the decade since *Poems of Consciousness,* an international revolution in haiku poetics has occurred, due to an evolution of critical approaches and the rapid development of social media and online poetry sites. Haiku has been exploding around the planet! On browsing through the *Living Haiku Anthology* online, one finds more than 8,000 haiku from 40-plus countries are represented.

Over the years, our Kumamoto University Kon Nichi Haiku translation group has published several books of haiku translated from Japanese, and developed online media at the *gendaihaiku.com* website (housing subtitled interviews of contemporary Japanese poetry and criticism); viewers worldwide can garner some of the verve and spirit of preeminent *haijin* (haiku poets) in the modern lineage.

As uber-minimal narratives, haiku are concentrated: focused linguistically, imagistically and emotionally, with exactitude. In doing so much with so little they are unique exemplifications of poetic imagination.

You need not be a committed "haikuist" to appreciate aspects of poetic imagination. That said, haiku often present novel dimensions of psychology, social commentary and spirituality, enriching the mysterious relationship between poetry and consciousness. Haiku are codes to what we are becoming.

Overview: Poetry, Sanctuary and the Space of Mind

The first part of this work views contemporary poetry through the lens of cognitive and literary linguistics, and depth psychology, focusing on two areas: enactments of personal philosophy and creative freedom. The practice and inventiveness of poetry is investigated as a form of resistance, and as an expression of secrecy and privacy. Related discussions touch on the need for "quality time" as well as "quality place"—both need to be fought for, being that *sanctuary* as space of mind cannot easily be defined (let alone defended) as "productive." To keep the discussion focused, annotations are given as endnotes.

In Chapter 1, "Space of Mind," *imaginative thought* as a fount of images is re-conceived as routinely poetic and spatially unique, possessing a philosophical-poetics spawning *novel worlds of mind*. The poetic space of mind is discussed in three ways: *spatially* as geometries and relationships of thought, *structurally* as architectures of thought, and last as houses of the "unhousable"—as poetic dwellings and *inhabitations* of psychic life. Seven properties of "thoughtspace" (the space of mind) are then determined. Chapter 2 unpacks the idea of "enactments of philosophico-poetic imagination," coining the term *philopoetic volition* to connote *activities spawned by poetic intention*. Chapter 3 offers a memoir of indwelling *poetic inhabitation*. Chapter 4 shifts from the personal to the social, discussing issues of privacy, distraction and freedom.

Chapter 5 glosses western-historical conceptions of sanctuary, introducing the term *temenos* to describe sacred place and space. The creation and significance of arts-collaborative *anarchic sanctuaries* is discussed, via a survey sent to poets responding to a six-part questionnaire. In Chapter 6, evolving from the seven properties of thoughtspace, 36 unique psycho-poetic qualities are associated to the seven "properties." Each quality is illustrated by a grouping of six haiku. These groupings elucidate the great diversity of qualities of the space of mind apparent in poetic creation, and make palpable routine experiences of poetic imagination which generally go unacknowledged. Through ample exposition, the aim is that a plethora of psychic spaces and the unique explorations they inaugurate may be appreciated and preserved.

Throughout the exposition, Sabine Miller's visual art, created in collaboration with this writing, brings dimensions of poetic volition to life through her "floragrams"—florals and verdure of the plant kingdom. Sabine works in San Rafael, California. These artworks open up expressive worlds that reveal nuances of emotion, as Sabine boldly addresses each of the main ideas presented. She has chosen quotes out of this text for her captions. (Sabine's "artist's statement" is found in *Endnote 1*.)

Haiku have been sourced from several recent anthologies, and an online international haiku archive.[3] For quick reference, Appendix 1 presents a descriptive outline, including text-references and short quotes which link the seven "properties of thought" with the 36 "qualities." Appendix 2 presents an explanation of disjunction in haiku and variations in disjunctive effect (strong/weak), as seen in a range of excellent haiku, and Appendix 3 presents a "Forethought," based on Simone Weil's essay, "Forms of the Implicit Love of God." My design-intention for this book began with a contemplation of her text, and a line-by-line commentary, as an origin-point of philopoetic volition. The flower bloomed returns to seed.

I. Space of Mind

2. "Space-egg," 2017

*Behind the eyes images speak —
redescribe earth on their own terms.*

I. Space of Mind

> *Recalling poetic feelings and lasting impressions of poetry, wishing to explore the beauty, mysteriousness and delicacy of the space of thought, what occurs entering poetic space, a created space more substantial than fantasy? Experiences are vivid, memorable—yet only partly of the literal world. How to consider this space?*

The concept of mind is in flux. Many scientists now eschew the term, preferring to consider "mind" as sums of cognitive modules: 'a set of cognitive faculties, awake states, perception, memory, thinking, judgment'—the so-called "easy problems"[4] of consciousness—implying that mind isn't a holism so much as an open drawer with its contents spilled out, with various parts yet to discover. "Mind" then as a typological placeholder for those modules it contains. It should be remembered these compartmentalized functions and network-relations remain speculative and little understood.[5]

What matters is how we see ourselves as conscious beings. How we connote our being—what could be more intimate? I would like first to discuss two perspectives on consciousness—uniqueness and immeasurability—with the goal of resisting such "moduled" typologies of consciousness.

The Perception of the Unique

What is unique is always available. There is nothing "non-unique" about us, or the world. It's not hard to argue this point, from snowflakes to faces: every *thing*, each action in this very moment is unique, and unrepeatable. That the objects and experiences of this world are unique seems obvious, but to what extent is the unique noticed and valued? How might we attend, become more attuned in awareness? Unlike novelty, uniqueness doesn't necessarily wear off. Persons and artworks can change our lives and remain unique over a lifetime, depending on how deeply we receive them.

Why bring attention to the perception of the unique? Though we may perceive uniqueness subliminally in a routine way, the perception of the unique can evolve into a pro-activist stance, including practices that move us deeper into what enriches us, psychically.

The *face* (appearance) of the unique is usually disregarded via conversion into a "type" of thing: a class (of objects), or an experience fitting into defined categories of meaning. This is done with persons as well. Typologies can certainly be useful: when the unique is reduced to type, as an act of simplification to aid in decision-making, a company might choose to hire a specific personality-type determined as more "visual-spatial" than "interpersonal." This determination has a basis in Gardner's eight-intelligences theory, drawn from cognitive science. Another common way of typing people is through the Myers-Briggs personality inventory, developed from Jung's typology of personality. Although the intention of his method was to more finely discriminate aspects of personality, such as character traits, Jungian typology has over time been converted into a basis for measurement. That empirical evidence is lacking for these theories has generally been forgotten. Because such tests and evaluations create measureable, ranked data, in consequence 'typed' data-point rankings and scores become stand-in substitutes for the human.

As it happens, qualities that differentiate us most uniquely remain unknown because they *cannot* be measured. Here are some examples of the importance of the perception of the unique, outlined by James Hillman, in three notable cases:

> At Harvard in the 1890's Professor William James had in his classes a rather wonky, stubby talkative Jewish girl from California. She was late for classes, didn't seem to understand what was going on, misspelled, knew no Latin—that sort of typical mess, the girl who couldn't get it together … William James let her turn in a blank exam paper, and gave her a high mark for the course,

helped her through to medical studies at Johns Hopkins. He saw something unique in this pupil. She was Gertrude Stein ... only ten years later far from Harvard, in Paris.

In a Southern small town a man named Phil Stone, who had some literary education at Yale, took under his wing as coach and mentor, a short, wiry, heavily drinking, highly pretentious lad of the town. This young fellow wrote poems, pretended to be British, carried a walking stick and wore special clothes—all in small-town Mississippi during the First World War. Phil Stone listened to the boy ... and perceived his uniqueness. The man went on to become the William Faulkner who was awarded the Nobel Prize for literature in 1949.

A third tale of the perception of uniqueness: In the year 1831 one of those marvellous old-fashioned scientific expeditions was to set forth; a schoolmaster named John Henslow suggested that one of his former pupils be appointed naturalist. The lad was then 22; he had been rather dull at school, hopeless in maths, although a keen collector of beetles from the countryside; he was hardly different from the others of his type and class: hunting and shooting, popular member of the Glutton Club aimed for the clergy.... Henslow saw something and persuaded the parties involved, including the pupil named Charles Darwin, that he make his journey.

What did they see and how did they see it? Is this sort of seeing a special gift, as some have held, or is it possible to anyone—providing nothing stands in the way of such perception, a perception which implies, in these cases, a deep subjective affection, a loving. (1980)

Who hasn't been in love? Recall those moments when you suddenly *saw* that person, felt the becoming of love. When to begin they were a man or a woman; wearing jeans or dressed in red; shoeless on a sofa or sitting across from you in a café; riding on a train or listening to music. Recall the strangeness: a deepening of dimension as if there were a different sense of "person" that suddenly arose—perhaps as a pool, or flowing-falling water; a hesitancy in moments—perception as its own fulfillment, with no further action required.

Everything about that person changes, yet much of importance changes for us, as well. How simple the perception of the unique is, yet how rare. The perception of the unique is "a perception which implies, in these cases, a deep subjective affection, a loving." I will use the term "attention" here to imply more than objectivity; there is also care. In acts of love, I becomes *Thou*.

Poems (those here) are waiting to be perceived. They "see you"; some may be too hot and need time to cool off to be touched (the poem resists the reader's desire for meaning). Others need warmth: the fires of insight behind one's eyes suddenly spark, sensing invitations to depth.

Our world is made of keys—cars, doors, logins, proper manners, forms of greeting, situational responses, making conversation. We judge and evaluate ceaselessly. We are often "typing" unconsciously. Perhaps gracefully as well, but aren't we missing something, socially? Within the egalitarian arrangements of our categorized "fragments" of persons, relations and things, are there wholes that remain invisible among our daily utilities?

To seek the perception of the unique is also to be sought. We seek participation and are lucky to encounter it, whether in a person or an artwork, and this dual perception is rare—a depth akin to aesthetic arrest: in whatever we find artful enough that the mind is stopped and the world for moments becomes holistic in perception. Untypeable into any schema, category, set of qualities, properties, gender or genre and impossible to divide into fact versus fiction. In such moments, what has hitherto been least tangible arises as matchless fulfillment of reality.

Our poem under purview may be arranged as furrows in a field, or brow, feel of a specific or timeless age, be born in some far country or written next door. We may note the identity, gender, age and such of the author, at some point. And all this will matter again soon, just as it mattered, if differently, before. But in the perception of the unique, as Wallace Stevens said, "the lion roars at the enraging desert."[6] This roar, incommensurate with any other, is everything we are. Without this roar, an impeccable cry of intimate, incomparable being, there can be no seeking of deeper truth—this is the roar of the heart's rage in

> The desert of modernity ... [when] the heart has no reaction to what it faces, thereby turning the variegated sensuous face of the world into monotony, sameness, oneness. What is passive, immobile, asleep in the heart creates a desert that can only be cured by its own parenting principle that shows its awakening by roaring.... The more our desert the more we must rage, which rage is love. The passions of the soul make the desert habitable. The desert ... is anywhere once we desert the heart.... The desert beast is our guardian in the desert of modern bureaucracy, ugly urbanism, academic trivialities, professional official soullessness, the desert of our ignoble condition. We fear that rage. We dare not roar ... we let the little lions sleep in front of the television... (Hillman, 1989, 304-05).

Rage here means that we are willing to fight for our need for depth and won't stand for less. Ginsberg's *Howl*. The perception of the unique unavoidably involves the recognition that we too often live within psychic wastelands—environments composed of fragments of things measured against each other, sliced, diced and categorized in various ways. Decent though our environments may be, and decent though we may be, concerning value, normative perception and normative consciousness are not enough.

To love is also to be loved in being perceived as unique—this experience also occurs within passions and obsessions (non-derogatory) of taste, activity and poetic craft. Consider those moments when knowledge falls away in rapture. It's not just being "head-over-heels," but the forgetting of self that's important: direct involvement beyond "measure," a deepened experience of embodiment. The perception of the unique leads to embodied consciousness rooted in immeasurables of depth and metaphor.

Immeasurability

"Mindfulness" is something we do (mind minds) without a tangible root for the "*–ness*." An axiom of archetypal psychology is that mind is *fundamentally poetic* in nature: root-metaphors of imaginative possibility are "the poetic basis of mind"[7]: there is no ultimate, literal truth or final equation to codify—no last, definitive image or explanation of self or mind to be resolved. Qualitative consciousness is *metaphoric by nature*. This view is also found in the field of cognitive linguistics; Linguist George Lakoff and philosopher Mark Johnson in their essay, "Conceptual Metaphor in Everyday Language" write,

> Metaphor is for most people a device of the poetic imagination and the rhetorical flourish—a matter of extraordinary language rather than ordinary language ... We have found, on the contrary, that metaphor is pervasive in everyday life, not just in language but in thought and action. Our ordinary conceptual system in terms of which we both think and act, is fundamentally metaphorical in nature. (287)[8]

Nouns (as connotations of things) are so prevalent in language that we lose sight of the fact that they are symbolic figurations, "placeholders" for objects. As the symbol of a thing, any given noun may *artificially* concretize or "lock-in" an immeasurable. In this sense, "mind" only *seems* to be a thing—an object—but try hunting qualitative, subjective mind down and we get no further than metaphors of metaphors: a *poetics* of being.

Of course, mechanisms of perception can be described: in the act of seeing the lens of the eye focuses light upon the retina, nerve impulses travel along the optic nerve, brain-neuronal processing and awake-states are consequently involved in the act of seeing—and we now know that perception is cognitively predictive as well as perceptually receptive.[9] But why do we feel *what it is like* to see things? In consciousness studies, this sense of ourselves as subjective beings with agency is referred to as the "hard problem" of consciousness: a problem currently unanswerable by science.

Mind is immeasurable in this sense, though as a noun, "mind" seems to be a thing, an object. How about an apple? An apple may not seem symbolic—yet the word, arriving in differing minds, in differing cultures, in differing eras and languages, reveals a great diversity in belief and imagination as to exactly what an apple is for a person: *What it is like* to experience an apple. In my hometown, raw horsemeat is a delicacy. Foreign visitors are often not only disgusted but offended when spontaneously offered this expensive dish. Signs arrive with signifiers. We might agree that there is *basashi* (raw horsemeat) on our plates—but our *poetics* (the feelings, concepts, beliefs, images, stories, and metaphors associated to an object) differ greatly—*what it is like* to experience even the appearance of *basashi*—may be greatly upset! So what is in a noun? It depends how far down the rabbit hole of subjective consciousness *qualia* you wish to go:[10]

> It is often possible to take up a point of view other than one's own, so the comprehension of [ ] facts is not limited to one's own case. There is a sense in which phenomenological facts are perfectly objective: one person can know or say of another what the quality of the other's experience is. They are subjective, however, in the sense that even this objective ascription of experience is possible only for someone sufficiently similar to the object of ascription to be able to adopt his point of view—to understand the ascription in the first-person as well as in the third, so to speak. The more different from oneself the other experiencer is, the less success one can expect with this enterprise.... A Martian scientist with no understanding of visual perception could understand the rainbow, or lightning, or clouds as physical phenomena, though he would never be able to understand the human concepts of rainbow, lightning, or cloud, or the place these things occupy in our phenomenal world....
>
> [In consequence] it *appears* unlikely that we will get closer to the real nature of human experience by leaving behind the particularity of our human point of view and striving for a description in terms accessible to beings that could not imagine what it was like to be us. If the subjective character of experience is fully comprehensible only from one point of view, then any shift

to greater objectivity—that is, less attachment to a specific viewpoint—does not take us nearer to the real nature of the phenomenon: it takes us farther away from it.... Most of the neo-behaviorism of recent philosophical psychology results from the effort to substitute an objective concept of mind for the real thing, in order to have nothing left over which cannot be reduced.... Does it [not] make sense, in other words, to ask what my experiences are *really* like, as opposed to how they appear to me? (Nagel, "What is it like to be a Bat?," 1974)

Hypothetically accepting that mind is fundamentally poetic/metaphorical in nature, to the extent that our interest is "to ask what my experiences are *really* like, as opposed to how they appear to me," the implication is that I may choose to reveal aspects of my awareness of the feeling of being alive—myself here, consciously—through choice of metaphor: I am a river. What is its source? Given that "river" and "source" are metaphors, the second metaphor depends on the first and deepens, that is, impels a further journey within the imaginative landscape. Metaphors deepen as they propagate, revealing landscapes and story as they *link-back* (the root meaning of *religio*) toward origins, sources and wellsprings.

In creating psychic landscapes and worlds of meaning, this deepening journey through metaphor defines the term *mythopoetic*. A useful term, in that we often create mythopoetic landscapes and narratives that carry idiosyncratic, subjective truths of *how it is* to know ourselves and the world. Mythopoetics is non-intersubjective (private, interior) in its arising.

The hypothesis that mind is metaphoric and poetic in nature does not obviate scientific knowledge of physical systems of brain and body, but it does allow for the valuing of further dimensions of knowing.

Uniquely feeling ourselves to be is an *immeasurable* matter.[11] A question that will be examined later is that in exploring the poetics of consciousness, to what extent can we expand toward its mystery—the *immeasurables of mind*, intangibles—and so *create some distance* between meaning and unknowing?

Out-of-the-box imagination allows for unconstrained speculation. A changed mind, does it remain yours, or do you adapt to *it*? The literary critic Harold Bloom advanced a Hamletian proposition concerning the subjectivity of modern consciousness: we think ourselves into new forms of subjective selves in a fictive spinning-out of speculation upon speculation (metaphor upon metaphor), applying imaginative logics.[12] This potency of thought has been defined in cognitive studies as conceptual blending:

> According to this theory, elements and relationships from diverse templates of thought are conceptually "blended" in a subconscious process which is assumed to be ubiquitous to everyday thought and language.... Conceptual blending is a fundamental instrument of the everyday mind, used in our basic construal of all our realities, from the social to the scientific.[13]

As a poetics of being (as poetic beings), we are the poems our stories become.

Sunny-side Up in Space

In a routine act of judgment, the simple choice of "sunny-side up or over-easy" for breakfast may lead to a well of knowing that reaches into the depths of soul for the taste of life incarnate, or be passed by unnoticed as a mere incidental, depending on one's sense of poetry and philosophy. Any perceptual surface has the potential to become metaphorically deep if we choose to contemplate it, 'seeing through' mythopoetically.

Since we are the only animals who have evolved an advanced cooking technology and modified eggs for the purpose of tasting nuances, does this evolutionary fact analogously argue for language diversification into thousands of tongues? Humanity has sought diversity and nuance in cuisine, the arts and fashion: the "cosmetics" of our humanistic cosmos. We also have created (through genetic breeding) pets, farm animals and gardens. Uniqueness implies plenitudes of diversity, along with immeasurability.

Dating the earliest human art, scholars have determined that "half a million years ago, on the banks of a calm river, someone scored a deep zigzag into a clam shell."[14] Though the origins of language remain unknown, it's thought that communicative ability made a leap in step with the arising of symbolic, image-making consciousness. Since that time, humanity has greatly diversified the "cosmetics" of its cultures. Concerning language, new lexical terms and collocations continuously arise, and foreign tongues cross-fertilize.

In considering humanity's operating manual—mind contemplating figuration, metaphor and symbol—may poetry extending from preliterate times offer a uniquely memorable form of "languaging"? May literatures based in bardic oral-traditions guide us in some way?

In the *Iliad*, Helen, "the most beautiful woman in the world" was born of a divine egg, from a clutch of two. In this way, ordinary activities, even a daily breakfast-egg recipe may follow a journey from a routine act into deeper mythopoetic aspects of soul which undergird culture, history and myth.

If the intention here is to attend, the goal is to *notice*: to "orient towards" in awareness—to examine how space is created out of metaphoric, poetic acts of imagination. Rather than answers, varieties of spaces are revealed, to participate in and describe. Mythopoetic activities of imagination can be considered a greatly expanded conception of the dream. We dream quite a lot—evidence suggests two-thirds of our lives are spent in imagination, dream and fictional worlds—including a third or more of each waking day.[15]

A science-fiction term for those who choose to live in outer-space environments rather than on the terra firma gravity of planets, is "spacers." Re-framed psychologically: as beings of *thoughtspace* we are placed within a potentially infinite, unknown cosmos. We create not only the stories of who we are and how worlds of imagination become; in a deeper origination—more invisibly, covertly, self-secretly—we create novel *spaces* of mind.

Lacking dimension or expanse, imaginal landscapes and narratives cannot themselves arise. This is the ground of *thoughtcraft*, cognate with a spacecraft, as a *vehicle*.

Soul

Stories, dreams, imaginations happen some*where*, and we psychologically exist within these spaces, as much as they do within us. James Hillman, drawing on Jung, addresses *place* as an aspect of soul:

> Man exists in the midst of psyche; it is not the other way around. Therefore, soul is not confined by man, and there is much of psyche that extends beyond the nature of man. (*Re-visioning Psychology*, 1975)

Hillman, a founder of archetypal psychology (a radicalization of depth psychology, instituted in the early 1970s) indicates that innerness has an inherently mythopoetic dimension that isn't just focused *in*—is not only experienced as *literally* inside us:

> "Interiority is a metaphor for the soul's *nonvisible and nonliteral inherence.*" This interiority is found everywhere, in animate and inanimate things. Hillman extraverts our sense of interiority, so that it becomes a property of the world. (Tacey, 2009, 152)

There are plenty of unknowns in "nonvisible and nonliteral inherence." Seen just below, interiority is related to soul as "a perspective rather than a substance." Hillman's use of soul is largely synonymous with imaginative possibility:

> This book is about soul-making. It is an attempt at a psychology of soul, an essay in re-visioning psychology from the point of view of soul.... By soul, I mean, first of all, a perspective rather than a substance, a viewpoint toward

things rather than a thing itself. This perspective is reflective; it mediates events and makes differences between ourselves and everything that happens.... the word refers to that unknown component which *makes meaning possible* [and] *turns events into experiences*.... Soul refers to the deepening of events into [personal] experiences ... By "soul" I mean the *imaginative possibility* in our natures, the experiencing through reflective speculation, dream, image, and fantasy—*that mode which recognizes all realities as primarily symbolic or metaphorical*. (*Re-visioning Psychology*, xv–xvi, emphasis added)

Soul is immeasurable ("a perspective rather than a substance"), intangible ("a viewpoint toward things rather than a thing itself"), and unknown ("that unknown component"). Yet both psychologically ("the imaginative possibility in our natures"), and functionally ("that mode which recognizes all realities as primarily symbolic or metaphorical"), exacting. These ideas can be restated more romantically: The heart of a poem is immeasurable, intangible and unknown; deep within the soul of our intimate, *private* imaginative natures arises something instrumentally beautiful, exquisite and exacting, which moves us.

To lack or devalue soul is to consider soul "confined by"—contained and controlled "by man." For if "man exists in the midst of psyche," then that which "extends beyond the nature of man" is perceived through "reflective speculation" via "dream, image, and fantasy." Psyche *encompasses* the literal, as *ecos* (natural habitat) and *oikos* (home).

There exists a parity of value among the spaces and architectures of thought, a radical equality, in that images, symbols, stories, and metaphors *metamorphose*: continuously transform into and through one another in a process-flow of co-dependent origination. And we deepen in experience, in attending to these *faces* of images.

Typically, ready habits freight imaginative play with extractive meaning, and this ends psyche's story—when it's decided all *this* really means is *that*—what is aborted is a further journey, a deeper attendance—a deepening of soul. In his lectures, Hillman often insists: *stick with the story!* This perspective is an encouragement to practice modes of poetic process as routes to feeling: a means of reviving ourselves and the world through soulful explorations of *thoughtspace*.

Space is the Place

Speaking of space is easy enough; we routinely use language metaphorically to convert time and object-states into spatial referents. Regarding state change, consider this sentence: "The streetlight changes [goes] from red to green." The *spatial* prepositions *from* [somewhere] and *to* [somewhere] are used to convert the object *states* (red-light state/green-light state) into spatial referents (red *goes* to green). Steven Pinker explores this topic further in *The Stuff of Thought* (2007), and in a 2010 talk, commenting on how time is likewise frequently converted into space, remarks

> In many ways, time in language is conceived of as a dimension of space. And happenings are considered like matter—as a kind of "time-stuff" that can be located or extruded along a timeline. We see this in the many spatial metaphors for time in our language, such as "the deadline is coming" or "we are approaching the deadline." We see it in the errors that children make, such as "Can I have any reading behind the dinner"—meaning "after the dinner."

There are two linguistic concepts I'd like to discuss in connection with *thoughtspace* as a ground of imagination. For metaphoric thinking to arise and develop into landscape and story, a sense of dimension—space (in a word)—is required: imaginal spaces in which images (and ideas, sensations) are natively emplaced. Thoughtspace—a subjective-imaginative space—may have little to do with literal three-dimensional space, or contiguous Newtonian space.

There is much linguistic debate concerning how thought arises and enters language. The debate is framed by the "Language of Thought Hypothesis" (LOTH). "In its most basic form, the theory states that thought, like language, has syntax" (*Wiki*). Do we think *in* language? This would imply that different language-speakers experience fundamentally different realities, due to differences of grammar, lexis and syntax—the position of linguistic relativism:

> The principle of linguistic relativity holds that the structure of a language affects its speakers' world view or cognition. Popularly known as the Sapir-Whorf hypothesis, or Whorfianism, the principle is often defined to include two versions. The strong version says that language *determines* thought, and that linguistic categories limit and determine cognitive categories, whereas the weak version says that linguistic categories and usage only *influence* thought and decisions....
>
> Lakoff [ ] argued that language is often used metaphorically and that languages use different cultural metaphors that reveal something about how speakers of that language think. For example, English employs conceptual metaphors likening time with money, so that time can be saved and spent and invested, whereas other languages do not talk about time in that way. ("Linguistic relativity," *Wiki*)

In the 2016 movie, *Arrival*, based on the 1998 novella *Story of Your Life* by Ted Chiang, is an evocative example of the Sapir-Whorf hypothesis, positing a circular language-form employed by extraterrestrials experiencing time past/present/future as co-existent. As the human protagonist gains fluency in the language, she too begins to experience her life within a circularity of time.

But there is a contravening perspective: that we do *not* think in language—at least language as we commonly conceive it. Universalist linguists deny linguistic relativity:

> Many followers of the universalist school of thought still oppose linguistic relativity. For example, Pinker argues in *The Language Instinct* [1994] that thought is independent of language, that language is itself meaningless in any fundamental way to human thought, and that human beings do not even think in "natural" language, i.e. any language that we actually communicate in;

rather, we think in a meta-language, preceding any natural language, called "mentalese." Pinker attacks what he calls "Whorf's radical position," declaring, "the more you examine Whorf's arguments, the less sense they make." (*ibid*)

In the egg of LOTH, it may be impossible to completely separate the yolk of mentalese (as mysterious "language-like" structures) from the white of linguistic relativity. It's also worth noting in passing that "LOTH is almost completely silent about consciousness and the problem of *qualia*."[16] Linguistic hypotheses concerning the language of thought may lead us closer to the wellsprings of poetic process, but as of yet they are unable to enlighten. That said, when depth psychology speaks to image and metaphor, importantly, the definition is not equal to *sentences* or *common language*. Some philosophers of thought (as lingustic relativists) state that a thought must be communicable, by definition; therefore all thoughts must embody propositions, and can ultimately be expressed in (common) language. But these hypotheses delimit the nature of thought to *typological* ideas of reality: versions of syntax and semantic structures.

While it's not my remit to offer a LOTH theory, witnessing the importance of the unique—both to creativity and in inculcating psychological depth of soul—for poets in particular, there are all manner of creative images and notions which take a great effort to "language" into the common tongue—so my bias leans towards forms of mentalese, with the caveat that poetic, idiosyncratic use of language can work on us from the outside in, reframing time and space *through poetic usage* of the common tongue.

Another element concerning "qualia" (e.g. the experience of the *redness* of red) in consciousness has to do with states of consciousness. How might a sudden or evolving insight relate to peak experiences of consciousness (in Maslow's terms), and to altered states—from the hypnagogic to the use of psychoactive substances used in visionary practices, likely since the dawn of symbolic art? With these considerations in mind, and lacking further evidence, it may be enough to say that both *how* and *what* we imagine powerfully affects our beliefs, values and sense of reality.

Some version of mentalese accordingly values the primacy of thought over normative language-constructions, and this notion allows for two propositions relevant to poetic imagination: 1) humbleness—we are faced with the mystery of how thought arises and becomes language; and 2) disambiguation—the uniqueness of images can be treated as *poiesis*—the play of metaphoric mind—which may or may not communicate intelligible, extractable meaning, but which always *displays* itself. Perhaps *we* are the extraterrestrials, experiencing *Arrival* every day as we "language" imagination—relativizing the universal, in ways yet to be scientifically discerned.

In Mandelbaum's 1995 translation of *The Metamorphoses*, Ovid offers a poetic origin-story that may be likened to the ground of *thoughtspace*, and is chosen here as a means to extend the concept of mentalese mythopoetically, through the use of metaphoric, poetic images woven into landscape and narrative story:

> Before the seas and lands began to be,
> before the sky had mantled every thing,
> then all of nature's face was featureless —
> what men call chaos: undigested mass
> of crude, confused, and scrumbled elements,
> a heap of seeds that clashed, of things mismatched.
> ...
> in the surrounding air,
> earth's weight had yet to find its balanced state;
> ...
> For though the sea and land and air were there,
> the land could not be walked upon, the sea
> could not be swum, the air was without splendor;
> no thing maintained its shape; . . .

in one same body cold and hot would battle;
the damp contend with the dry, things hard
with soft, and weighty things with weightless parts. (3)

Ovid does not begin with the void of non-being or emptiness. Rather, space is described in terms similar to modern chaos theory: "scrumbled elements ... [in which] no thing maintained its shape"— ascertained as a confusion or incomprehension; this space represents the "apparent randomness of chaotic complex systems."[17] As a fertile void, a world in potentium, "there are underlying patterns, constant feedback loops, repetition, self-similarity ... sensitive dependence on initial conditions" (*ibid*). It would take the hand of a divine artist (whom Ovid portrays anonymously as "whichever god") to arrange such "confused, and scrumbled ... things mismatched"[18]—as he articulates in the following stanzas:

A god ... separated sky
and earth, and earth and waves, and ... defined
pure air and thicker air. Unraveling
these things from their blind heap, assigning each
its place—distinct—linked them all in peace.
Fire, the weightless force of heaven's dome,
Shot up; it occupied the highest zone.
Just under fire, the light air found its home.
The earth, more dense, attracted elements
More gross; its own mass made it sink below.
And flowing water filled the final space;
It held the solid world in its embrace.
... whichever god it was—arrayed
That swarm, aligned, designed, allotted, made
Each part into a portion of a whole
...
The world's artificer

>Did not allow the winds to rule the air
>unchecked, set free to riot everywhere.
>. . .

Among many routes of interpretation, one strand of *Metamorphoses* reveals the hand of the creator as an artificer, likened to an artist who possesses the ability to transform "what men call chaos: undigested mass" via *alchemical skill*: re-arranging and transmuting substance into "pattern" and geomantic place. Synonymously, the poet orders psychic material, in forms of insight and revelation, as Gary Snyder points out, through discovering "the grain of things."

According to Ovid's creation-myth, in the beginning was psychic substance, as "undigested [chaotic] mass." But if chaos is here *opposed* to order, this oppositional duality breaks down as within *apparent* chaos, *order arises through craft* via the catalyst of active, soulful discovery, implemented by the hand of divine artistry. Does creation begin with meaning, with chaos, or do these antipodal terms become moot, at a certain psychological depth? Snyder addresses poet-as-artificer in "Unnatural Writing":

> So I will argue that consciousness, mind, imagination, and language are fundamentally wild. "Wild" as in wild ecosystems—richly interconnected, interdependent, and incredibly complex. Diverse, ancient, and full of information. At root the real question is how we understand the concepts of order, freedom, and chaos. Is art an imposition of order on chaotic nature, or is art (also read "language") a matter of discovering the grain of things, of uncovering the measured chaos that structures the natural world? Observation, reflection, and practice show artistic process to be the latter. (1996, 168)

Snyder asks a pertinent question in his use of "imposition," revealing a polarity: does the artist impose order on chaos, or through artistic process discover a "way," a flow of things? That is, nature may not express order in the way we conceive it from a human perspective—yet via art-process, Snyder indicates that mind can become less constrained by dualities, typologies, through "discovering the grain of things." This view seems a modern reframing of ideas presented in *Metamorphoses*.

"The grain" is crucial here, in that imaginative process concerns craft. Touch: the grain of wood is felt/sensed by the craftsperson—this melding of interiority (which can be sensed as much 'out there' in the world as 'in here,' within) approaches animism—as the craft-object exemplifies its own interiority, which is "read": entered into, following an intuitive sense of its "livingness" (soul) as felt-nature. There are numerous examples of artists speaking to these practices, worldwide.[19] So, I am thinking away from theory, as theory cannot be divorced from psychic display (substance), sensation and feeling: practices of embodied contemplation *and* alterations of habitual consciousness.

To close this muse, I propose that all art is an imposition of order to an extent, yet as art involves craft, a yielding and flowing with matter via transgressive, metamorphic alchemies, as well. Ovid begins his poem,

> My soul would sing of metamorphoses.
> But since, o gods, you were the source of these
> bodies becoming other bodies, breathe
> your breath into my book of changes: may
> the song I sing be seamless as its way
> weaves from the world's beginning to our day.

The "crude, confused, and scrumbled elements, a heap of seeds that clashed, of things mismatched"—represent the *potential* beginnings of emergent design-architectures in poetic imagination. A 'chaos of creation' implies "grain" as pattern, rhythm and structure—not necessarily anthropocentric in nature. This is the ground of thoughtspace: psychically, substantial possibility, a fertile void. Meaning here, not "void" as an emptiness or nothingness, but as seen in Ovid, an imminent, potent, fulminating, virtual-unknowingness out of which creation may inexplicably burgeon—from any locale—through (divine, sacred, artistic) actions of consciousness.

"My soul would sing of metamorphoses": the ground of thoughtspace both predicates and interpenetrates psyche's imaginal forms as *res extensa* (material substance): an "all-accommodating space," allowing for psychic fertility. In this view, space *as such* is regarded as an aspect of psycho-poetic landscape, given that space is *presence*—even if egoic or dream-self awareness is absent (to lose oneself, to be lost in space). As *foreground*, the perception of space, in which thoughts may come and go (or not arise for periods of time) is rare in contemporary life—though methods of cognitively exploring the ground of thoughtspace are found in contemplative practices, such as "formless" meditation (e.g. shamata-vipassana techniques).

Alchemical transgression (elaborated later)—"bodies becoming other bodies"—is a metaphor for the flux and flow, the "conceptual blending" of soulfully unconstrained creative imagination. Etymologically, soul or psyche is "breath," *Seele* in Jung's German, meaning a movement of air, wind—*spiritus* as inspiration (confusingly for English-translation, in *Seele*, psyche, soul and mind are not separated out). Concerning the loss of a mythopoetics of soul, in 1929 Jung commented that in modernity,

> ... the Gods have become diseases [*dis-eases*].... Zeus no longer rules Olympus but rather the solar plexus, and produces curious specimens [that] disorder the brains of politicians and journalists who unwittingly let loose psychic epidemics on the world. (*Commentary on The Secret of the Golden Flower*)

Perhaps belief is too readily manipulated when the *demos*, the "common inhabitants of a place"—as a collection of individual consciousnesses—lack interiority, lack a depth of imagination, a depth of soul.

3. "Immeasurable Intangible Unknown," 2017

Instead of answers perhaps there will be new questions.

The Specious Present: The Poetry-line & Haiku

The "specious present" is a location in time, experienced as a *space* of time. The term was introduced by E. R. Clay and developed by William James (1890), to denote a time-interval of about three seconds, "the short duration of which we are *immediately and incessantly* sensible."[20] Pinker adds:

> [The specious present] corresponds to our general sense of newness ... The duration of a deliberate action, like a handshake; of a quick decision.... It corresponds to the decay of unrehearsed short-term memory; the duration of a line of poetry, in all the world's genres of poetry. It's the duration of a musical motif, such as the opening notes of Beethoven's 5th symphony, which you don't hear as a note followed by another note followed by another note, but rather the first notes cohere as a gestalt. (2010)

The specious present is also, roughly, the time it takes to read a haiku.

Time also *stretches backwards* indefinitely (note the spatial metaphor). "Anything that happened from three seconds ago, stretching backwards to the big bang is treated equivalently in language—which is why Groucho Marx can say 'I've had a wonderful evening. But this wasn't it'" (*ibid*). As far as locating time-tense spatially in thought, another sense of time operates from about three seconds from now into the infinite future. "Three seconds from now, until the heat-death of the universe is given the same time-stamp when it comes to tense" (*ibid*). For example, *Tomorrow I will go*, and *In 5 billion years the sun will end its life* are equivalent future spaces which we create with *will+go* and *will+end*. Nothing actually *goes* or *ends* (these verbals are again spatial metaphors).

A *space* for the future is evoked in mind as a special variety of metaphor: this is one of a multitude of dimensions of *thoughtspace*.

Another example Pinker gives: "I'm going to start the end of my talk." We imagine a talk as a line, but literally, "the start of the end" is paradoxical, as there is no start to an end (only an end); yet we visualize in spatial metaphor a small segment of time just before the end. We imagine a chunk of space (as a kind of 'time-*substance*') just prior to the end as the "start of the end," because we reference time as space. Pinker comments:

> Why is the language of time so crazy? Why does it carve up time in such idiosyncratic ways?... The present is just another word for our consciousness—for what we are aware of at any given moment of wakefulness.... The past is that stretch of time which is potentially knowable, factual and unchangeable.... The future is that time which is unknowable, which is hypothetical, and which is potentially willable. (*ibid*)

Our language is rife with routine metaphors, spatial metaphors in particular, which potentially bring soul into language. These reflect consciousness and impel the way reality is imagined. When closely examined, language has little to do with the literal except in the consensual sense that we agree on what a phrase like "I will start the end of..." actually means. The words are not poetic, *yet our minds are*. We take the meaning as literal, because, as "languaged" beings, we consensually perform similar metaphorical conversions of space with time:

> All large-scale human cooperation is ultimately based on our belief in imagined orders. These are sets of rules that, despite existing only in our imagination, we believe to be as real and inviolable as gravity. "If you sacrifice ten bulls to the sky god, the rain will come; if you honour your parents, you will go to heaven; and if you don't believe what I am telling you – you'll go to hell."... People find it difficult to understand the idea of "imagined orders" because they assume that there are only two types of realities: objective realities and subjective realities. In objective reality, things exist independently of our beliefs and feelings. Gravity, for example, is an objective reality. It existed long before Newton, and it affects people who don't believe in it just as much as it affects those who do. Subjective reality, in contrast, depends on my personal beliefs and feelings....

Most people presume that reality is either objective or subjective, and that there is no third option. Hence once they satisfy themselves that something isn't just their own subjective feeling, they jump to the conclusion it must be objective.... However, there is a third level of reality: the intersubjective level. Intersubjective entities depend on communication among many humans rather than on the beliefs and feelings of individual humans. Many of the most important agents in history are intersubjective. Money, for example, has no objective value. You cannot eat, drink or wear a dollar bill. (Harari, *Homo Deus*, 168)

In habitual, mutual imaginative-understanding, we agree on what a given phrasal-metaphor signifies. We are so inured to our poetics of intersubjective knowing that we are not ordinarily aware of the metaphorical waters in which we swim. Metaphors clarify metaphors, ad infinitum, as the foregoing analogy (swimming in metaphorical waters) divines.

Through a variety of devices, poetry breaks or disrupts consensual habits of language, producing potent effects on consciousness concerning how we (re)imagine the world, and thus *who* we are. This often occurs in a given work through highlighting linguistic gaps between metaphor, what is taken as literal, and the manner in which language figuration (overtly "literary" metaphor) is applied.[21]

Between Meaning and Unknowing

In the penultimate paragraph of *Immeasurability* is written:

Uniquely feeling ourselves to be is an *immeasurable* matter.... In exploring the poetics of consciousness, to what extent can we expand towards its mystery—the *immeasurables of mind*, intangibles, and so *create some distance between meaning and unknowing?*

Instead of assuming that we know what "mind" is, as a thought-experiment it may be possible to separate ourselves from typical assumptions and preconceived notions. The phrase used to concretize this idea is *"create some distance."* This is an illustration of the space of mind (as metaphor). Somewhere, somehow—if for a brief moment or two—in reading any text, comprehension first involves creating abstract, hypothetical spaces of mind. In this example of the thought-construction process, four terms are parsed:

Distance
Between
Meaning
Unknowing

Space is created between the two abstract ideas: *meaning +/- unknowing*[22] in that there is *distance between* them. As "thought-fish" swimming brilliantly, we self-generate imaginal spaces, nearly instantaneously. There is a *meaning* space and an *unknowing* space—which together may be contained within some undefined (infinite) imaginal space. We can likewise experience the notion of *"between"*: this space *separates* meaning and unknowing. This *between space*—however it is sensed—has its own unique texture; as a "third" space, it is neither "meaning" nor "unknowing." It's a *relational* space offering its own specific nuances and textures, apart from the polar duality of the two abstract nouns (meaning/unknowing), positing a logical polarity.

So, *"between"* is a third, separate quality, yet is also connective: the phrase "[to] create some distance *between* meaning and unknowing" indicates there is a way of experiencing an alternate world in mind which is *neither* meaning *nor* unknowing. *"Between"* is a relational conduit in feeling-sense: it is both separating (spatially) and threading (interpenetrating). In "unpacking" the semantics—and especially *sensations* of thoughtspace—this example demonstrates both the craft and the artifice involved in how we "image" (imagine) even the simplest sentences.

To spend time in the contemplation of thoughtspace is 'feeling the space of thought.' Feeling *is* the space of thought. Imaginal space is textured by sensation. Any sentence conveys a quality of feeling, which includes the feeling-tone of "objective," dispassionate, as one familiar variety.

Phenomenologically, thoughtcraft astounds. This is a human ability more routine than cracking eggs: even the simplest sentences evoke complex spaces of thought. *Sunny-side up or over-easy?* evokes architectures of thought, including sensations, images and metaphors of cooking, and the sense of taste.

Here is another example:

Daphne meets Sam.

This is an exercise in envisioning nouns as persons. How do you "think" about this sentence? Take a few moments, noticing what is constructed in mind, in thoughtspace. Where do these two people appear in mind, how far apart, how short or tall? What is their state of dress or undress? Are they amorphous waifs, solid as trees? What does "person" *feel* like, in mind? Does this couple wave, move off, re-appear? Note the sense of space within mind. We must all vary in our imagining, yet we each generate varieties of spaces in which "Daphne meets Sam" takes place.

Next, consider the verb *meets* in Daphne meets Sam. What is the sensation-space of present tense? If the verb-tense is changed from meet to *met* (present to past):

Daphne met Sam.

What happens within your thoughtspace? Have these figures become more distant? Again, we have two nouns. This time, they are concrete objects (persons) rather than abstract philosophical concepts (meaning/unknowing). Yet they too partake of the poetic in thought, as mutable, metaphorical figurations. Importantly, they are not essentially different in kind to the abstract nouns *meaning* and *unknowing*. Just as *Daphne* and *Sam* can meet in mind, *meaning* and *unknowing* can likewise meet.

Whether our cognitive logic relates to abstract and paradoxical objects and their relations (the creation of "distance" between meaning and unknowing is literally paradoxical), or concrete objects possessing routine relations (Daphne and Sam)—both types of nouns are *equally* thinkable, as are their relational 'connectives' (between, meet, met).

Thoughtspace is existentially egalitarian because thought is continually metamorphic. Ranging from the most concrete to most abstract of nouns and phrases, we spawn imaginary alternative worlds with near instantaneity—worlds possessing immediacy. These are not usually simple worlds, but highly complex, multi-dimensionally interactive ephemeral worlds that quickly become extinct, except as tracings of past-thought vapor;[23] breadcrumbs we may return to. Thinking often happens with great rapidity: thoughts follow, return, jump, abort, dissolve, fade, morph: "bodies becoming other bodies" breathe new breath (soul) into life.

Whether as a writer of poems, prose or fiction, the nature of thought is wedded to how we "sentence" and "paragraph" possible alternative worlds, shared between reader and writer. As a community, we are mutually reliant on consensual, intersubjective familiarities—generally accepted rules and guidelines regarding a staggeringly complex metaphorical psychology—yet we also partake *privately* of an unconstrained mythopoetics of imaginative spaces.

Architectures to Inspire Dwelling

Like elegant 'spacefish' needing no particular literal atmosphere or environment, we can swim in any imagined dimension, create gravity, anti-gravity, attraction, collision, extinction; evade, blend, and erase worlds, physical laws and relations, at whim. From the simplest of notions, complex swum spaces and highly nuanced feeling-tones of spaces are self-generated. These can be termed *spatial thermoclines*. This coinage relates to how floridly nuanced and passionately creative the space of mind is, and consequently how spatial design relates to conceptual architectures of thought (illustrated by the "qualities," in Chapter 6).

"Architectures" as an attribute of thought can be applied constructively to indicate three main strata or states of thought-construction:

1. *Design-emergent intention*: the way thoughts and images conspire to construct notions. And in a further stage:
2. Architectures as *constructions* of landscapes, worlds. And in a deeper sense:
3. Architectures as *animate places* and spaces which inspire *dwelling*.

These ideas will later be applied pragmatically to explore how haiku evoke inhabitation as experiences of sanctuary.

Properties of Thoughtspace

To open the psychological space between meaning and unknowing is one means to begin articulating a personal poetics. These ideas of process lead to psychologically rich, if somewhat intangible concepts. To concretize this topic, the following six notions are postulated in regard to psycho-poetic landscapes of thought (here in outline form—the last two notions have been drawn from succeeding chapters):

Six Notions Concerning the Psycho-poetic Landscape of Thought

Thoughtspace is 1) spatial—*there is a sense of breadth and distance.*
- As beings of "thoughtspace" we are placed within a potentially infinite, unknown cosmos. We create not only the stories of who we are and how worlds of imagination become; in a deeper origination—more invisibly, covertly, self secretly—we create *spaces* of mind.

  Lacking dimension or expanse, the landscapes and narratives cannot themselves arise. This is the ground of *thoughtcraft*, cognate with a spacecraft, as a *vehicle*. (*Sunny-side Up in Space*)

Soul 2) deepens—*this relates to feeling, attendance and story.*
- Soul is immeasurable ("a perspective rather than a substance"), intangible ("a viewpoint toward things rather than a thing itself"), and unknown ("that unknown component"). Yet both psychologically ("the imaginative possibility in our natures"), and functionally ("that mode which recognizes all realities as primarily symbolic or metaphorical"), exacting. (*Soul*)

3) Abiding—*via* contemplation.
- As "thoughtfish" swimming brilliantly, we create self-generated imaginal spaces, nearly instantaneously. There is a *meaning* space and an *unknowing* space—which together may be contained within some undefined (infinite) imaginal space.

To spend time in the contemplation of thoughtspace is 'feeling the space of thought.' Feeling *is* the space of thought. (*Between Meaning and Unknowing*)

4) <u>**Volitional (philopoetic) formations**</u>[24] *of thought-enactment arise as a locus of human value.*
- The world for moments becomes holistic in perception—untypeable into any schema, category, set of qualities, properties, gender or genre, impossible to divide dialectically into fact versus fiction. In such moments, what has hitherto been least tangible arises as matchless fulfillment of reality. (*The Perception of the Unique*)

5) <u>**Poetic-philosophic ideas**</u> **are born.** *The term philopoetics is a coinage to indicate the native arising of poetic-philosophic ideas.*
- As poems that alter and expand perceptions are examined, we experience evidence of **philopoetic volition**. Combining the words "philosophy" and "poetic," a zone of the true or real is evoked which need be neither strictly rational nor irrational, scientific nor nonsensical. (*Philopoetic Volition, Chap. 2*)

6) **The <u>"third" space</u> of mind** *through which consciousness revisions both world and self.*
- *This between space*—however it is sensed—has its own unique texture: as a "third" space, it is neither "meaning" nor "unknowing." It is a *relational* space offering its own specific nuances and textures … A mysterious space "between living and dreaming" … the "intelligence of the heart" is expressed "by means of images which are a third possibility between mind and world" (*cf.* Hillman, 1992). A psychology of sanctuary represents one way of formally regarding this "third thing"—conceptual architectures of the poem provide *ways in* to visibility and feeling. (*Between Meaning and Unknowing & Remystification*)

Returning to an idea expressed earlier this chapter—how far can we expand towards the mystery of consciousness, and so create some distance between meaning and unknowing—based on the foregoing discussion, the space (*distance*) between meaning and unknowing, as *thoughtspace*, can be ascribed seven properties (the last two elaborated in later chapters):

Seven Properties of Thoughtspace

1) **Perception.** *No one but you can perceive it; imagination is private.*

    In creating psychic landscapes and worlds of meaning, a deepening journey through metaphor defines the term mythopoetic. A useful term, in that we often create mythopoetic landscapes and narratives which carry idiosyncratic, subjective truths of how it is to know ourselves, and the world. Mythopoetics is non-intersubjective (private, interior) in its arising. (*Immeasurability*)

2) **Shared communication via nomenclatures.** *We consensually share similitudes of thoughtspace as we know enough of how minds mind (intersubjectively) to agree on what we're talking about.*

    We are so familiarized to our poetics of intersubjective knowing that we aren't aware of the metaphorical waters in which we swim. Metaphors clarify metaphors, ad infinitum. Through a variety of devices, poetry breaks or disrupts consensual habits of language, producing potent effects regarding how we (re)imagine the world, and thus *who* we are. This often occurs in a given work through highlighting linguistic gaps between metaphor, what is taken as literal, and the manner in which language figuration (overtly "literary" metaphor) is applied. (*The Specious Present*)

3) **Conditional ephemerality.** *Thoughtspaces are conditional, provisional, and ephemeral felt-spaces.*

Thoughtspace is existentially egalitarian.... We spawn imaginary alternative worlds with near instantaneity—imaginary worlds possessing immediacy. These are not usually simple worlds, but highly complex, multi-dimensionally interactive, ephemeral worlds that quickly become extinct except as tracings of past-thought vapor; breadcrumbs we may return to. Thinking often happens with great rapidity; thoughts follow, return, jump, abort, dissolve, fade, morph: "bodies becoming other bodies" breathe new breath (soul) into life. (*Between Meaning and Unknowing*)

4) **Fictional.** *Creative throughtspace is fictive, a 'chaos of creation.'*

Dream-food and survival food are not confused. So, why create fictions in thoughtspace? I would suggest it is in order to design, and not merely as incidental sketch: design is wedded to intention.

The "crude, confused, and scrumbled elements, a heap of seeds that clashed, of things mismatched"—represent the *potential* beginnings of emergent design-architectures in poetic imagination. A 'chaos of creation' implies "grain" as pattern, rhythm and structure. (*Space is the Place*)

5) **Design-intention.** *Varieties of space are imagined in which our design-intention self-creates impossible (as well as possible) fictive worlds which are uniquely idiosyncratic.*

By "architectures" of thought is meant, most basically: 1) design-emergent intention: the way thoughts and images conspire to construct notions; and in a further stage, 2) architectures as constructions of landscapes, worlds; and in a deeper sense, 3) architectures as animate places and spaces which inspire dwelling. (*Architectures to Inspire Dwelling*)

6) **Explorative desire.** *We enter.*

We extrapolate, construct and reconstruct ongoing spaces of thought. Lacking this process, we cannot really think. That is, we would not have the ability to imagine—to apply abstraction upon abstraction fictively (in conceptual blendings) in order to orient ourselves in *thoughtspace* throughout the expanse.

Metaphor and meaning would remain rational sciences in "stiff and stubborn, man-locked set," lacking a desire for imaginal inhabitation—these are generally indescribable qualitative experiences, each individually unique. While it may be possible to analyze how language creates poetic architecture and design (conceptual, imagistic, juxtapositional, etc.), it's impossible to determine the landscapes a reader inhabits—in what manner one dwells. Inhabitation is a private (evocative, even ecstatic) *matter*. (*The Shape of Jazz, Secrecy*)

7) **Hypothetical humanity.** *This is a "third": place or zone of knowing, neither fictional nor non-fictional.*

What lies between realism and imagination, between living and dreaming, is a particular form of sanctuary; a space of *poiesis*. It seems most fragile and nuanced, insignificant and ephemeral—yet it calls or we call, is seeking deeper, more enriching, increasingly multiple, multifarious dimensions of knowing in psyche. (*Haiku, an Ethics of Freedom: Quality 32. Distance*)

Through such ongoing processes as "self-creating, self-generating, design-intentions," personal theories of mind evolve. If there were no *thoughtspace*, no means to find pathways through this space, no first-creation through which thought could blossom in design-intention and orientation, it would be impossible to "language"—to speak or perceive, beyond the brute literal. This notion of relational awareness as "theory of mind"[25] applies first to ourselves; then another.

II. Philopoetic Volition

4. "Spatial Thermoclines," 2017

Sense may only be found in the inseparable weave between image, rhythm and story.

II. Philopoetic Volition

It is impossible to predict how a poem arises—and to what extent a given text is poetic is debatable. We can however agree that there are poems that as they are read and contemplated alter and expand perceptions. These experiences are evidence of *philopoetic volition*. Combining the words "philosophy" and "poetic," a zone of the true or real is evoked which need be neither strictly rational nor irrational, scientific nor nonsensical. *Thoughtspace* is imbued with a sense of poetry in part because each of the polar opposites just mentioned may be present as a conceptual blend of thought, in any given instant. Templates of thought (mathematical, mythological, anthropological, etc.) are inexhaustible; philopoetics is inclusive of all templates, models, modes, and perspectives that may be imagined. The design-architectures of philopoetics are as universal as poetry itself.

The term "philosophy" usually implies a series of rational, constructive thoughts that follow a logical structure with agreed-upon rules and lexical definitions, as a foundation for mutual understanding. However, poetry (excepting the overtly philosophical poem) isn't generally considered to impart philosophy with the art. I would assert the opposite, that every poem *inherently* demonstrates philopoetic volition. The story of poetic thought is always personally philosophic—it's just that the philosophy isn't necessarily restricted to any specific non-poetic, logical order. Every poem constructs a world in mind—writer-to-reader-mind—via language. The space of thought in which the poem lives is architectural, and can be felt as a structured, epistemic knowing—even if the meaning isn't possible to nail down—as sense may only be found in the inseparable weave between image, rhythm and story.

Although poetic philosophy isn't often extractable as separable, discrete, definitive meaning, we are deepened, moved, enriched in dimension, and at times sensibility, via poetic evocation. This is evidentially, philosophy. Even if poetic philosophy does not extend its limit to rational universals or abstract law, its potency of proof is inseparable from the intimacy of the personal (or collaborative-author) voice. *Philopoetics* is natively a perception of the unique. It's this third world of value that has long been culturally absent, or denied.

Regarding philopoetics, a sense of psychic space is evoked both as breadth ("in the midst of") and depth ("psyche that extends beyond").[26] From this soul-egg, notions of dwelling and sanctuary arise, and it becomes possible to advance an ethics of freedom and resistance in contemporary poetics.

Volition: Enactments of Personal Philosophy

Before returning to language and space, a few words on Simone Weil. Her notebooks and letters are autobiographical, and were not originally meant for publication. Discovered within is her adamantine honesty. Weil's writing is often piercingly intimate—rare within published philosophical contemplations. Relevant to this discussion, Weil's ambition represents an unceasing (and at times desperate) attempt to challenge and evolve her personal poetic philosophy. In her appreciation of Weil, Susan Sontag writes:

> We read writers of such scathing originality for their personal authority, for the example of their seriousness, for their manifest willingness to sacrifice themselves for their truths, and—only piecemeal—for their "views."
>
> ... In the respect we pay to such lives, we acknowledge the presence of mystery in the world—and mystery is just what the secure possession of the truth, an objective truth, denies.... [Simone Weil] is rightly regarded as one of the most uncompromising and troubling witnesses to the modern travail of the spirit. (1963)

Poetry and literature uniquely inform Weil's thought. Stephen Plant (Cambridge University) mentions Weil's lasting influence:

> [She] has influenced ... literary philosophers, or perhaps philosophical writers. People like Murdoch, Eliot, Camus—people for whom the world of philosophy is something you want to carry out as it were, as part of the conversation that is literature. And because of her interest in literature and the way she integrated thinking about literature with philosophy, she has a particular attraction for [such] writers ... (2014; *cf. Endnote 2*)

Philopoetic volition embodies a social dimension: poets "for whom the world of philosophy is something you want to carry out." Czeslaw Milosz in his 1980 Nobel lecture remarks, "Simone Weil, to whose writings I am profoundly indebted, says: 'Distance is the soul of beauty.'... Only through a distance, in space or in time, does reality undergo purification."

Just as notable poetry is unique, its artistry is inseparable from personal philosophy—our evolving philosophical thoughts metaporphosing subliminally in sustained, contemplative effort. Snyder (1980) refers to such peregrinations as "the real work." In Japan, pioneering haiku poet-critic Kaneko Tohta discusses philopoetics, employing the term *shisō*, the development of one's personal philosophy as *living ideology*:

> *Shisō* is not, strictly speaking, philosophy or theory as such. *Shisō* can be considered a [personal] "philosophical organization," in Japanese.... meaning conceptualized thought organized as a philosophy.... A person who has not absorbed and integrated an ideology into their daily life *cannot be trusted*. I cannot trust a person who lacks a *living ideology*. That's why I don't have any faith in terms such as "communism," "socialism" and the like. Especially words that have an "*-ism*" attached to them.... [Kobayashi Issa] was able to put his thinking into action "through the body." This is his real *shisō*. You could never affix an "*-ism*" to what he represented. If you tried, what " ism" would be applicable? On this topic, as you know, Issa advocated *arabonpu* in his later career, didn't he. Issa was *arappoibonpu*: "a wild, ordinary man." (Gilbert et al, 2011)

For Kaneko, the development of a living personal philosophy (*shisō*; philopoetic volition) is fundamental to a poet achieving a stance: a position, based on freedom of thought, he says, from which is achieved the ability to relevantly critique society.

Milosz expands on his contemplation of Weil's "distance," in articulating his own philopoetic stance:

> Reality calls for a name, for words, but it is unbearable and if it is touched, if it draws very close, the poet's mouth cannot even utter a complaint of Job: all art proves to be nothing compared with action. Yet, to embrace reality in such a manner that it is preserved in all its old tangle of good and evil, of despair and hope, is possible only thanks to a distance, only by soaring *above it* …
>
> A few minutes ago I expressed my longing for the end of a contradiction which opposes the poet's need of distance to his feeling of solidarity with his fellow men. And yet, if we take a flight above the Earth as a metaphor of the poet's vocation, it is not difficult to notice that a kind of contradiction is implied, even in those epochs when the poet is relatively free from the snares of History. For how to be *above* and simultaneously to see the Earth in every detail? And yet, in a precarious balance of opposites, a certain equilibrium can be achieved thanks to a distance introduced by the flow of time. "To see" means not only to have before one's eyes. It may mean also to preserve in memory.
>
> "To see and to describe" may also mean to reconstruct in imagination. A distance achieved, thanks to the mystery of time, must not change events, landscapes, human figures into a tangle of shadows growing paler and paler. On the contrary, it can show them in full light, so that every event, every date becomes expressive and persists as an eternal reminder of human depravity and human greatness. Those who are alive receive a mandate from those who are silent forever. (Nobel Lecture, 1980)

Although Weil's ostensible concern in her later writings is theological, one of her thematic observations illumines the notion that poems as enactments of personal philosophy embody a creative language which draws us out—in distance upon distance—from experiences of formatively-volitional activations of thoughtspace, to writing on the page, to interactions between the writer-reader through novel forms of language. "Distance is the soul of beauty" implores: how vast is the heart, how limitless is our space of thought, how deep the soul of attendance from which we might speak? Milosz develops Weil's "distance"—leading him to "reconstruct in imagination" (echoing Weil's, "We reconstruct for ourselves the order of the world in an image," *cf.* Appendix 3)—and adds an ethical demand, and indicates a danger: that the work not "change events, landscapes, human figures into a tangle of shadows growing paler and paler."

A subtle erosion of presences continually impends: the past retreats, ever paler. Who will serve as Mnemosyne, anamnesis? The poet does more than memorialize; reconstructing memory through novel (dishabituated) uses of language creates fresh philopoetic enactments that may offer us sanctuary *as anamnesis*. The space of fresh thought is a refuge from forgetting.

Through cycles of history, the poetic news is not always smiles. Eras of poetic diminution have frequently occurred. In certain eras in Japan for example, the haiku (earlier *hokku*) form devolved into a hackneyed, formulaic poem, composed by professionals for given occasions—a marriage, a death—paid for by a family member at great expense. Such eras represent a loss of poiesis—cycles of institutionalized, formulaic literature (as occurs in all cultures), are evidence of cultural tragedy. For any culture that loses the soul of its poetry, history becomes "a tangle of shadows growing paler and paler"—seen in the recent arrival of fake news and alternative facts.

Remembrance and Distance

Milosz is also concerned with the poet's duty to remembrance; when he says "it [the artwork] can show them in full light," he indicates an *agon*—between the poem (and world), and the necessity of the poet's distance—as a space, apart.[27] In his Nobel lecture is articulated "a precarious balance of opposites" for the poet, between necessary involvement in action (history) and the necessity of distance from it. In that one's aim or desire is to find language that "persists as an eternal reminder of human depravity and human greatness," Milosz, reminding, brings to soul a nobility of purpose, concerning poetic activity. On the part of those who can no longer speak for us, we "receive a mandate from those who are silent forever." In this sense, remembrance seems an inherent aspect of creation.

> The oldest of the old follows behind
> us in our thinking, and yet it
> comes to meet us.
>
> That is why thinking holds to the
> coming of what has been, and
> is remembrance.

This philopoetic notion of Heidegger (2001) is lent support by the nascent field of neurophenomenology—the neuroscientific study of consciousness. A recent paper substantiates a common phenomenon:

> Memories or novel simulations [spontaneous thoughts] are often said to "come to us"—a phrase reflecting the common subjective experience of mental content arising in a bottom-up fashion and capturing our attention reflexively in the process. The neural antecedents identified ... are consistent with this subjective experience.... [S]pontaneous thought in the present study closely parallels the pattern of brain-activation consistently associated with mind-wandering and spontaneous thought in prior work... (Ellamil, 2016)

Spontaneous thoughts are often felt subjectively to "come to us" from a distance, one which involves, to quote Heidegger, "The oldest of the old [which] comes to meet us"—"thinking holds to the coming of what has been, and is [sensed/felt as] remembrance," via the blending-together (conceptual blending) of diverse scenarios of metaphor and analogy.[28]

Distance is the line of sunset at the ocean's horizon, earth from moon, a trace of pattern in the energy-range of the Higgs boson, the feeling of a lover's heartbeat. What calls out to be remembered, reconstructed? Whatever we choose to narrate as story becomes identity. What we nourish through creative, philopoetic volition persists for us to inhabit and so bring to life again.

III. The Shape of Jazz to Come

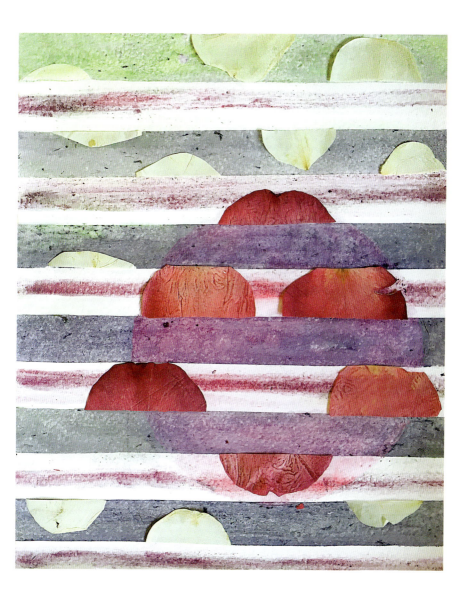

5. "Roses for Ornette," 2017

We entrain our brains when in dialogue with others, neuroscience has found: both rhythmically and via location, similar styles of brain-activation are exhibited.

III. The Shape of Jazz to Come

A Memoir

The Shape of Jazz to Come is the title of a jazz album recorded by Ornette Coleman with his quartet and was said from the outset to revolutionize jazz. On the 1959 cover image Coleman confidently holds his sax, providing a classic look from Atlantic Records. The album title was one I continually *misread* as "The Shape of Things to Come." It felt futuristic—especially after hearing the music. This one-line title may have been my first unknowing experience of aesthetic arrest in relation to poetry. Can a single line of text not ostensibly meant as a poem create a poetics of imagination as puissant as the reading of any poem?

I put the album on our aging Harman-Kardon tube amp, connected to a pair of KLH 5 bookshelf acoustic-suspension speakers—our family then lived in a rented, converted carriage house whose living-room ceiling was some two-stories high. Though the hi-fi was modest, having once been a small stable, the sound from the two-way system with 10" woofers created a naturally reverberant small-hall space.

Instantly, I heard the sound of the future echoed in its torturous cries, beseechings and wails, life and death in profound mystery—confusions, irresolutions and new harmonic forms. Though I never entirely grasped the meaning of the title, the album and its sonic architecture remained framed by its title text. What is the shape of the future, the shape of things to come? Until that album, even as a speculative-fiction buff, I'd never *felt* its *shapes*.

In imagination, the music created textures complexly felt and emotionally strong and tender, nuanced—as if voiced, almost human—how humanly vocal an alto sax and cornet (played by Don Cherry) duet can be. "Drummer Shelly Manne said that when Coleman play[s], 'he sounds like a person crying … or a person laughing.'"[29] Writing about this experience, decades of music listening later, I muse that some understanding was absorbed concerning poetry. By which I mean psychic possibility.

Possibilities of imagination have to do with the complexities of form, feeling, texture, shape—*architectures* that in their movement and swim are often impossible to describe or illustrate.

This *raw* expressiveness was like an ever-evolving Koan, which stimulated a question: How is *this* the shape of things to come? And, what does it mean, "shape"? Then also: "I'm listening to its actuality, its real demonstration through the the music," every time I drop the needle.

Inhabitation

Of the various topics this memoir brings to mind, two are striking: first, the need for secrecies, of privacy; and second, how certain architectures of poetry may become inhabitation. These seem two necessities in the formation of philosophic and philopoetic *sanctuary*. A utile, pragmatic aspect of thinking relates to communication—the sharing of discourse and ideas. We entrain our brains when in dialogue with others, neuroscience has found: both rhythmically and in activation sites, parallel modes of brain-activation are exhibited. In secret, I was in communication through the music, listening—open, and learning. By which I mean *impelled* to conceive and dwell in new worlds of ideas, images and feelings—with no answers given, just words from an album title a wayside guide.

What can be expected from poetry? is the wrong question. At best, we are lucky to encounter poeisis and put ourselves in "harm's way" in a sense. *The Shape of Jazz to Come* is a challenging listen. It doesn't partake of the romantic or sublime, the music isn't programmatic or very danceable. It's often beautiful and painful in the same instant of time. In other words, this music doesn't fit into any ready literary or aesthetic slot—unless the entire work, and my story is diminished: "He was just listening to jazz." Reduce the experience to a label and it's end of story.

I had no great realizations consequent to this music. Likewise at some deep level I was changed. Pulled by something like an undertow—an artistic passion and vision on the part of these artists. I'm describing an experience of dwelling, of poetic inhabitation, and what I mean is fairly simple: there are psychic and psychological building blocks (as presented in Chapter 1), but then there comes a twist. The realms now under purview extend into the social and political.

Imagination begins with space, followed by orientation, and then design—this is *thoughtspace* (e.g. "seven properties of thoughtspace"). Some might call this daydreaming, or mind wandering (or listening to jazz!)—phenomena of ephemera, let's say; asides to life. I'd agree, with a caveat—these asides have value, only its hard to put a finger on them. The social problem of poetry in a nutshell is that its use and value are not easily described; I can't explain the significance of this particular LP in my life. Yet this writing could not exist otherwise.

Intentional-design in thoughtspace is represented in writing and the arts via language-communication. But whether shared socially or not, design-intentions are *performed internally* all the time via explorative desire—from deciding on a breakfast egg-dish to lifelong contemplations. Nonetheless, it seems a rarer thing to *dwell, to inhabit,* when in some manner life is lived beyond oneself, and the world circulates, is illumined, returning to us from a great distance—remembrance—bringing with it the soul of beauty.

In Review: And Why Haiku?

Pausing to review, design-intention may develop as architecture and inspire inhabitation. Haiku (and short poems) employ minimal language, yet are potently architectural, world-creating. As philopoetically volitional worlds are created with near instantaneity, I am impelled towards inhabitation, and exploratively *enter* these architectural spaces in mind.

Why should a bare minimum of words evoke complex architectures of thought? World-building from extreme brevity isn't limited to haiku, or even "literature" (e.g an album-title); certain diamondlike compressions of language exemplify potent mysteries of consciousness—depending upon reader interest and attunement.

Inhabitation, the feeling of livingness in philopoetic moments, relates to aesthetic arrest—the startled pause of inspiration (kinesthetic and metaphoric), accompanied by a momentary intake of breath. Like white light through a prism each poem brings novel nuances of hues and refractions, varieties of inhabitation, experiences of enriching-presence. Not everyone likes jazz, and of those who do, many won't warm to *The Shape of Jazz to Come*. In a like sense, haiku aren't especially evocative for some readers, and for others only a certain style will magnetize.

As Wallace Stevens wrote, in moments of poetic imagination we are choosing to live in a "supreme fiction": a fiction which you know to be fiction, yet choose to willfully believe:

> Yet I am the necessary angel of earth,
> Since, in my sight, you see the earth again,
> Cleared of its stiff and stubborn, man-locked set."[30]

We want more from the world than to merely *live* in it.

Secrecy

Metaphor and meaning would remain rational sciences in "stiff and stubborn, man-locked set" lacking the desire for imaginal inhabitation—these are generally indescribably unique, qualitative experiences. While it may be possible to analyze how language creates poetic architecture and design (conceptual, imagistic, juxtapositional, etc.), it's impossible to determine the landscapes a reader inhabits—in what manner one dwells. Inhabitation is a private (evocative, even ecstatic) *matter.*

> There is no better means of intensifying the treasured feeling of individuality than the possession of a secret ... It is important to have a secret, a premonition of things unknown.... [One] must sense that [one] lives in a world which in some respects is mysterious; that things happen and can be experienced which remain inexplicable; that not everything which happens can be anticipated. The unexpected and the incredible belong in this world. Only then is life whole. (Jung, 1961)

This form of privacy is socially valuable as an attribute of personal authenticity. Privacy is crucial to deepening the life of inhabitation in imagination. Whether or not we become more knowledgeable poetically as individuals cannot be said, but the practice (and skill) of creating and inhabiting multiple imaginative worlds presently seems to carry little social or educational value.

Consumerist culture devalues imaginal space as non-productive, wasted time; and increasingly, online distractions result in interrupted journeys and psychic erasure. Dimension, nuance and novelty are absenting themselves from public discourse. In this sense too, the practice of poetry represents an act of resistance.

IV. Privacy Matters

6. "Imagination is Unclaimed," 2017

The act of poetic thought and composition is an inherently private act.

The Panopticon

From Bambi to Banksy, the stereotypical naiveté of a Disney fawn to anonymous displays of city graffiti art, images percolate, permutate and permeate, altering paradigms of thought. Privacy concerns our ability (and decision) to seek uninterrupted time, and the subliminal fears of isolation and loneliness that surround this issue. Two points of departure arise—State surveillance and social media as these are germane to poetry and an ethics of freedom.

As privacy becomes devalued[31] in contemporary life, so does freedom of thought—*thoughtspace* disappears as well—the public and private spheres are linked. Glenn Greenwald in *No Place to Hide* (2014), argues that regarding privacy and freedom, issues of State-sponsored mass surveillance need to be urgently addressed. The kernel of his thesis is exerpted from his TED talk, "Why Privacy Matters":

> [M]ass surveillance [including government and corporate agencies that collect and analyze internet, email, cellphone, street, and store video] creates a prison in the mind that is a much more subtle though much more effective means of fostering compliance with social norms or with social orthodoxy, much more effective than brute force could ever be....
>
> A society in which people can be monitored at all times is a society that breeds conformity and obedience and submission, which is why every tyrant, the most overt to the most subtle, craves that system.
>
> Conversely, even more importantly, *it is a realm of privacy, the ability to go somewhere where we can think and reason and interact and speak without the judgmental eyes of others being cast upon us, in which creativity and exploration and dissent exclusively reside*, and that is the reason why, when we allow a society to exist in which we're subject to constant monitoring, we allow the essence of human freedom to be severely crippled. (2014; emphasis added)

Acts of poetic thought and composition are inherently *private* acts. Will we fight for this value? Though Greenwald's evidence detailing social control through surveillance cannot be recounted in full, in discussing the panopticon—a one-way viewing tower designed for monitoring prisoners—he remarks that social-science studies have repeatedly shown that in the presence of *possible* surveillance, we subconsciously adapt our behavior, especially our thoughts: self-censoring, based on a subliminal knowing that we *might* be being watched. For thoughtspaces as inner, private spaces to persist, *physical spaces* (external environments) in which we can be assured of privacy are a necessity.

Another theme Greenwald addresses relates to privacy and dissent:

> The other really destructive and, I think, even more insidious lesson that comes from accepting this mindset [that mass surveillance isn't problematic] is there's an implicit bargain: If you're willing to render yourself sufficiently harmless, sufficiently unthreatening to those who wield political power, then and only then can you be free of the dangers of surveillance. It's only those who are dissidents, who challenge power, who have something to worry about.... You may be a person who, right now, doesn't want to engage in that behavior, but at some point in the future you might. Even if you're somebody who decides that you never want to, the fact that there are other people who are willing to and able to resist and be adversarial to those in power—dissidents and journalists and activists and a whole range of others—is something that brings us all collective good that we should want to preserve. Equally critical is that the measure of how free a society is ... [is] how it treats its dissidents and those who resist orthodoxy.
>
> But the most important reason is that a system of mass surveillance suppresses our own freedom in all sorts of ways. It renders off-limits all kinds of behavioral choices without our even knowing that it's happened. The renowned socialist activist Rosa Luxemburg once said, "He who does not move does not notice his chains." (*ibid*)

All authentic poetry is loosely speaking, dissent, in that new forms of language and thought and the novel worlds created thereby are its lifeblood. Poetry intrinsically breaks with conventional thought in language, image, story, and often content—not exempting the "traditionalist" poem. In considering the role of freedom,

> We haven't thought about the idea of freedom enough. It needs to be internalized as an inner freedom from "demand" itself: the kind of freedom that comes when you're free from those compulsions to have and to own and to be someone....
>
> Remember that in the early days of the feminist movement, they refused to have a leader; different women would just stand up and speak. The early feminists were very careful to not put what was spontaneously arising back in the old bottle. So I think it's a matter of being free-wheeling, and trusting that the emerging cosmos will come out on its own, and shape itself as it comes. That means living in a certain open space—and that's freedom. (Hillman, 2011)[32]

Imagination is *unclaimed*, when "internalized as an inner freedom": privacy matters. One defining landmark of sanctuary is "living in a certain open space." Those places and spaces that allow thoughtspace to be free are inherently absent of surveillance.

Time Slips Away

Another social issue affecting the poetic space of imagination concerns distraction. Within a global society of exponentially increasing mass surveillance, our days are also increasingly composed of moments that become minutes of distraction; breakdowns or the disappearance of focused modes of attention. Distraction obviates aesthetic creativity. Below, a few 2015 US statistics on text messaging (*PEW Research*):[33]

- The average Millennial exchanges about 67 text messages/day (4-7 per waking hour).
- The average adult spends 23 hours/week texting.
- Text messages have a 98% "open" rate (20% for email).

- On average, it takes 90 seconds to respond to a text message (90 minutes for email).
- Over 6 billion text messages are sent in the US daily.

Solutions to the problem of increased distraction caused by the mind-sucking "attention economy" of social media platforms are being sought through nascent ethical-technology design movements. Meanwhile, distraction trends continue to climb. Design ethicist Tristan Harris offers his personal experience:

> These days, it feels like little bits of my time kind of slip away from me, and when that happens, it feels like parts of my life are slipping away ... I check things ... I have to click it right now. But I'm not just going to click "See photo," what I'm actually going to do is spend the next 20 minutes ... the worst part is that I know this is what's going to happen, and even knowing that's what's going to happen doesn't stop me from doing it again the next time.... [M]y phone is a slot machine. Every time I check my phone, I'm playing the slot machine to see, what am I going to get? What am I going to get? Every time I check my email, I'm playing the slot machine, saying, "What am I going to get?"...
>
> You're either on, and you're connected and distracted all the time, or you're off, but then you're wondering, am I missing something important? In other words, you're either distracted or you have fear of missing out. Right? [E]very time we interrupt each other, it takes us about 23 minutes, on average, to refocus our attention. We actually cycle through two different projects before we come back to the original thing we were doing. [This] actually *trains bad habits*. The more interruptions we get externally, it's conditioning and training us to interrupt ourselves. We actually self-interrupt every three-and-a-half minutes. (2014)

George Washington Carver writes, "Start where you are, with what you have." Haiku and short poetry, requiring minimal reading time, excel in catching attention. So, might distraction be co-opted to open the space of the day? *Rattle*, a poetry magazine with a subscriber-base of around 8,000 is working to re-orient attention on Facebook.[34] Poems from the magazine are selected from its archives and posted with themes often coinciding with current events.

Clicking on a few phrases above a photo (an attractive, visual link), a new page opens. Prefaced by a brief editor's introduction, each poem is also followed by a brief author statement. This fore-and-aft framing creates a psychologically transitive space—a non-distractive context within the generically distractive social framework—much the way a curtain opens and closes at the beginning and end of a play. Distraction is put on pause just before entering, to just after leaving the poem presentation. In this way, through the short poem, it may be possible to become "distracted by distraction" into creative thoughtspace. As editorial attention has been given to the primacy of the relationship between poem and reader, *Rattle* is an example of online poetry activism.

Concerning distraction as a "leasing" of our perception, Marshall McLuhan darkly envisioned:

> Once we have surrendered our senses and nervous systems to the private manipulation of those who would try to benefit by taking a lease on our eyes and ears and nerves, we don't really have any rights left. Leasing our eyes and ears and nerves to commercial interests is like handing over the common speech to a private corporation, or like giving the earth's atmosphere to a company as a monopoly. (*Understanding Media*, 1964)

McLuhan was pessimistic concerning the erasure of private space and the co-opting of "our senses and nervous systems" by institutions, within online social networks. As our brave new world accelerates into paradigms of increased distraction, accompanied by the erosion of privacy, forms of sanctuary represent modes of resistance, recovery, healing, contemplation—and compensation. A single poem or reading of haiku may not seem to amount to much—yet for some moments imaginal space opens out and becomes inhabitation, from poet to poetic mind.

Does the poem hint at something that is wished for: a deepening of consciousness, of soul, of life, to which we are only rarely able to give voice? To the extent that "attention is the rarest and purest form of generosity," this question pertains to sanctuary—especially as the digital attention-economy (and its data-gathering surveillance) overtakes public space and discourse. But there yet exist possibilities of community, if we're willing to drop the needle.

V. Sanctuary

7. "Theatre of Dwelling," 2016

In the poem we may dwell, yet inhabitations are provisional; one cannot house the unhousable.

V. SANCTUARY

> Between living and dreaming
> there is a third thing.
> Guess it.
> — Antonio Machado (1983)

The relationship of sanctuary with architectural, constructed spaces of the sacred plumbs the depths of human history. Mircea Eliade[35] contends that sacred space (and its taboos) are proto-human. Sanctuary historically partakes of *sanctity*, as notion of place. Over the centuries "sanctuary" has come to represent places of physical haven and safety. The Abrahamic religions each offer patterns of precincts (architectures) defining and bounding the sacred. For example, in Christian tradition, the church (or a part within) has long been considered a sanctuary allowing for at least limited stays of secular punishment. In the Qur'an (9:6) is the counsel, "If one among those [who are without knowledge of God] asks you for protection and assistance, grant it to him ... escort him to where he can be secure." And within Hebraic tradition, the Temple being a sanctuary of God, gaining access to the Temple gate was to gain access to the gate of sanctuary—six Levitical towns of refuge were established wherein one could claim the right of asylum.

Even in exile, on the road as it were, it is possible to create sanctuary:

> And let them make me a sanctuary; that I may dwell among them. According to all that I shew thee, [construct it] *after* the pattern of the tabernacle, and the pattern of all the instruments thereof, even so shall ye make *it*.... Who serve unto the example and shadow of heavenly things ... that thou make all things according to the pattern shewed to thee in the mount. (*Exodus* 28-9; *Hebrews* 8:5, KJV)

The "shadow of heavenly things" indicates mimesis, rather than imitation: an artwork or *crafting* of presentation that evokes, "mimes"—brings into being the "heavenly" or sacred. Importantly, here presentation and ritual performance to an extent subsume representation. This concept is found in the Greek temple, as in temple shrines and their precincts around the world.[36] In Indian and East Asian traditions (i.e. pantheist traditions), the precincts of the sacred are local, animistic and natural. A *deva* or *kami* as a personified local deity both *is*—and *is of*—that place: fountainhead, tree, or knoll. Sanctuary as bounded space becomes sacred or holy as an animate *inhabitation* of sacred space, and of divinity.

Theatre of the Sacred

Regarding sanctuary in relation to poetic dwelling, historical transitions have occurred in which sacred space and sanctity, evolving from religious into contemporary, secular contexts have been reframed. In the early-modern era, Hölderlin's passage, "Full of merit, yet poetically man dwells on this Earth" inspired Heidegger's phenomenological idea, the "primordial poeticizing" of being as an aspect of the holy:

> It is only because language as such is the primordial poetizing that poesy, which uses language as its medium, enjoys a primacy among other forms of art .... [P]oetic images are imaginings in a distinctive sense: not mere fancies and illusions but imaginings that are visible inclusions of the alien in the sight of the familiar....
>
> In bringing the Word to be, [poetry] places the thing in the dimension of greatest reality, where past and present and future meet, to transcend this man or that, this time or that—the dimension of the pure act of illumination itself, which in its total reality transcends the thing, the man, the epoch to become what is lasting—for that is what is "Holy." (Heidegger 2001, "...Poetically Man Dwells...")[37]

There is a vast sense of distance implicit in "imaginings that are visible inclusions of the alien in the sight of the familiar." "Imaginings" being roughly equivalent to creative mind. Taking a more psychological approach, Gaston Bachelard, whose works on poetic imagination are of unique value, writes:

> On the side of the dreamer, constituting the dreamer, we must then recognize a power of poetization which can well be designated as a psychological poetics; it is the poetics of the psyche where all the psychic forces fall into harmony. (*The Poetics of Reverie*, 1969)

Here, to "fall into harmony" is evocative of a precinct, a psychic space of sanctuary. In both Heidegger and Bachelard, frameworks pertaining to "the word of God," the "divine" (with their implicit sense of commandment) are transmuted; retained is a link to a primordial sense of sacred construction "in bringing the Word to be ... the pure act of illumination itself ... [which] transcends the thing, the man, the epoch." This idea is echoed by Bachelard's "all the psychic forces fall into harmony." Depth of soul is invoked as a dimension of the sacred. For these authors, in dwelling (i.e. "poeticizing") is retained a sense of awe.

From altar, to the book and stage—from divine presence to democratic *polis*—the lineage of the sacred as literary tradition persists in the practice and production of contemporary poems and plays. The poem creates an architecture: story becomes stage, as a *theatre* of dwelling. The poem creates its own center, a "linking back" (*religio*) to origins of presence as mimesis of the divine. The shift from oral-tradition poetry to plays appearing on the ancient Greek stage is outlined by Dudley Young,[38] who links indigenous group-shamanic, ecstatic practices to later bardic oral-traditions (Hesiod and Homer), and hence to the first western literatures of dramatic poetry. The sanctified space of the Greek theatre belongs to the unhousable God Dionysus:

> Housing the sacred? Very difficult when Dionysus comes on stage.... His insistence on occupying the most difficult territory, the border country that separates and confuses cosmos and chaos, sanity and madness, love and ha-

tred.... The one thing he most certainly does not do is "abide in his room" ... the sacred cannot be housed [and] perhaps the human cannot be either, in which case the idea of tragedy is not far off.

He is the dramaturge ... the indestructible spirit of life itself (*zoē*), and he issues a mask to each of the contestants [actors], whereby they represent the ... two times of himself, the waxing and the waning. Thus in the foreground, the lethal play of life against life (*bios* versus *bios*), and in the background the indestructible *zoē*, which both gathers and scatters the coming and going of individual existence and promises the reconciliation of the *yin* with *yang*. In this way ... we should understand the double masks of Dionysus ... a motif that reaches its conclusion in the two masks that preside over the drama that emerged in the Great Dionysia [theatre],[39] one mask for comedy and one for tragedy. (*Origins of the Sacred*, 1991)

In the poem we may dwell, yet inhabitations are provisional: one cannot house the unhousable—the Dionysian cannot be 'managed.' This ancient sensibility is echoed in Snyder's contention that "mind is fundamentally wild"—that is, mind is at root unmanageable, free: an unmanaged, "unhousable" wilds, as *zoē*. Snyder hints at forms of order in the phenomenology of consciousness which are perceived as chaotic, yet enfolded within are "wild ecosystems—richly interconnected, interdependent, and incredibly complex ... diverse, ancient, and full of information," suggesting that we not label incomprehensibility/disorder as "chaos"—particularly in opposition to "civilization."

Snyder's unique contribution is to regard the phenomenology of "wild mind" synthetically, as "the grain of things," a conception resonant with Hillman's (2015) definition of soul as "that which deepens"; both authors achieve a stance regarding *being* as an *activity*, psyche as poeticizing (metamorphically) autonomously, at (metaphoric) depth. Snyder and Hillman see the fundamental nature of mind as a mystery, yet also suggest 'eco-sense': Hillman (from Jung) discusses the holism of psyche as *Anima Mundi,* the world soul (indefinable if not intangible in its nature); Snyder employs the term "interconnectedness," implying that wildness too is indefinable by nature: that is, by culture or language. It's worth noting that both authors argue against a predilection to anthropocentrism, evidenced in much humanistic philosophizing. Hillman, drawing on mindfulness practices developed by Jung, and Snyder (a Zen-Buddhist practitioner), both suggest a variety of anarchic means for attending to the depth of psyche—the unhousable, Dionysian wildness of mind—as *practices*, rather than managment. In nurturing the soul-egg of creativity, imagination is not to be constrained or corralled through acts of ego-centered will. Continued contemplative practice develops greater awareness, knowledge, and skill *in* the practice.

Key to such practices are ways of opening to and allowing passion, emotion: "There is no change from darkness to light or from inertia to movement without emotion ... emotion is the moment when steel meets flint and a spark is struck forth, for emotion is the chief source of consciousness" (Jung, 1939).

In contrast to management or control, mindfulness—as phenomenological craft—*invites, even invokes, passionate involvement.* Theatrical potency in poetic language is an aspect of *religio*: a linking back to primordial notions of non-duality between chaos and cosmos—this third thing, at a distance. How to define this distance? Perhaps as a process of psychological deepening—as depth itself implies distance (in Hillman); or, of discovering and intuiting "the grain of things" in wild mind (Snyder's idea).

This discussion began with notions of poeticizing as the "holy." Connotations regarding mind, being, and poeticizing, on the part of Heidegger, Hillman and Snyder are in accord with Antonio Machado's "third thing between living and dreaming," which lies at the heart of the poem.

Though the authors presented here arrive from different perspectives, they each articulate a means of "housing the unhousable." In divine notions of sanctuaries are spaces (once) inhabited by sacred presences: timeless precincts of divine origins. As will be discussed in *Beyond the Salon*, this "third" thing is related to desire, emotion—a loving arising in the heart: the "intelligence of the heart."

Machado in his epigraph, "between living and dreaming" indicates that "poetically man dwells"—that we dwell mythopoetically. Architectures of poetry link us back through theatres of story—this is thoughtspace as journey, and something more, a journey towards authenticity.

Sanctuary, Temenos and Risk

> *Inferior and average talent remains for the most part safe and faultless because it avoids risk and does not aim at the heights.* — Longinus (2012)

One aspect of sanctuary concerns protection, another is risk, the dangers and rewards of exploring "something that is unknown or that has an unknown outcome ... knowledge about risk is knowledge about lack of knowledge."[40] The notion of *temenos,* a term from Jung's lexicon,[41] provides a relevant ground from which psychological risk can be explored within protected space:

> A Greek word meaning a *sacred, protected space*; psychologically, descriptive of both a personal container and the *sense of privacy* [in] *relationship*. Jung believed that the need to establish or preserve a *temenos* is often indicated by drawings or dream images.... The symbol of the mandala has exactly this meaning of a holy place, a *temenos, to protect the centre*.... It *is a means of protecting the centre of the personality from being drawn out and from being influenced from outside*. [emphasis added]
>
> One does not become enlightened by imagining figures of light, but by making the darkness conscious ... there is no coming to consciousness without pain. The debt we owe to the play of imagination is incalculable. It is therefore short-sighted to treat fantasy, on account of its risky or unacceptable nature, as a thing of little worth. (Jung)[42]

V. SANCTUARY

Temenos is a *place* in space: the establishment of a ritual architecture—a mandalic precinct as sacred ground in which to work. As Jung discusses, we may propitiously find our authentic selves within this protected space. Landscapes of sanctuary can present themselves in a multitude of forms, which may be why haiku (and the short poem) act on consciousness with immediacy: they provide ephemeral, spontaneous scenes arising in the specious present, as *places of temenos*. To enter and explore a *temenos* requires attendance upon psyche; "making the darkness conscious" is an attendance to mystery, a deepening of psychological *distance* between meaning and unknowing.

A *temenos* may arise anywhere:

> The multiplicity, or even the infinity, of centers of the world raises no difficulty.... For it is not a matter of geometrical space but of an existential and sacred space that has an entirely different structure, that admits of an infinite number of breaks and hence is capable of an infinite number of communications with the transcendent. (Eliade, 1959)

Eliade's "transcendent," taken psychologically, indicates a deepening of soul. Thomas Moore describes an "everyday" *temenos*:

> When we choose a seat or standing area on a bus or train, when we arrange space in an office or workplace, when we decide where to put a garden, or chairs on a porch, where to sit on the riverbank to have lunch, where to play with the children—all of these decisions have to do with *temenos*, marking out a space appropriate for a certain spirit that breathes life into our activity.[43]

Temenos is that space of distance in which a "third thing" may arise. A world or landscape of depth and dimension which is mythopoetic, neither fact nor fiction, that remains hypothetical—and in which a poet's failure is likewise possible—yet also where new explorations portend. *Temenos* is a protected space of privacy wherein dimensions of self-knowing are given permission to be. As with any birth, rawness and vulnerability exist, hence the need for protection; illumination being an internal experience of private imagination, with kinship to aesthetic arrest.

This is the crucial turn, toward soul, regarding attendance:

From: "This poem (author) is illumined."

To: "Something akin to an experience of illumination occurs psychically (to me) regarding this poem."

This "turn" of psychological orientation is a shift away from a poetics of externals, and toward the possibility of shared private interiorities—conversations involving risk and exposure (which is why they are so rare). Historical models can serve as guides to soulful articulations; ideas of the Muse in relation to inspiration present interiority as process, with linkage to *temenos* as a sanctuary of contemplation, a topic Denise Levertov discusses in "Some Notes on Organic Form" (1965):

> To contemplate comes from *"templum*, temple, a place, a space for observation, marked out by the augur." It means, not simply to observe, to regard, but to do these things in the presence of a god. And to meditate is "to keep the mind in a state of contemplation"; its synonym is "to muse," and to muse comes from a word meaning "to stand with open mouth"—not so comical if we think of "inspiration"—to breathe in.
>
> So—as the poet stands open-mouthed in the temple of life, contemplating his experience, there come to him the first words of the poem: the words which are to be his way in to the poem, if there is to be a poem. The pressure of demand and the meditation on its elements culminate in a moment of vision, of crystallization, in which some inkling of the correspondence between those elements occurs; and it occurs in words. If he forces a beginning before this point, it won't work.

In the poetic process, attention is placed on the phenomenology of self throughout moments of an illumined (numinous) sense of presence. And in such contemplations, a "keeping of the mind" occurs within the precincts of *temenos*.

A *temenos* is a zone of the arising of the sacred, a protected space of sanctuary—precincts within which habitual identifications of self and language may be risked.

The space of *temenos* allows for confusion *and* clarity, Dionysian wildness within stillness. *Temenos* may portend a process of psychological discovery in which "all the psychic forces fall into harmony," as Bachelard writes, or as Levertov (in discussing inspiration's muse) remarks: "a place, a space for observation, marked out ... The meditation on [the poem's] elements culminate[s] in a moment of vision, of crystallization, in which some inkling of the correspondence between those elements occurs," autonomously. Vision, the poetics of imagination as a correspondence of elements, occurs serendipitously, autonomous to egoic will.

The crafting of the poem as *dwelling* is a hallmark of the unhousable western god of theatre. New language is animate, alive, risking edges and crossing borderlines. There are no "safe" poems or "pretty" haiku. Authenticity requires more of us.

Beyond the Salon

> *You can go home again so long as you understand that home is a place where you have never been.*
>
> *The idea is like grass. It craves light, likes crowds, thrives on crossbreeding, grows better for being stepped on.*
>
> — Ursula K. Le Guin (1974)

The 'intelligence of the heart' relates to self-authenticity, to ways we may desire to imagine—and re-imagine—*self* and *world* more deeply and essentially. With reference to "the desert of modernity" (see *The Perception of the Unique*, above), authenticity of the heart may only become possible within alternative societies, as the imagination of the heart is held in exile, "captive, where 'the thought of the heart' has become adulterated in our contemporary heart diseases: sentimentality of personalism, brutalism of efficiency, aggrandizement of power, and simple religious effusionisms" (Hillman, 1992, 4). Speaking to the thought of the heart, "intelligence" of the heart may seem off-putting—however the notion seems relevant: indicative of a *lacuna* in social value—

> The power of the heart is what is specifically designated by the word *himma*, a word whose content is perhaps best suggested by the word *enthymesis*, which signifies the act of meditating, conceiving, imagining, projecting, ardently desiring—in other words, of having (something) present in the *thymos*, which is vital force, soul, heart, intention, thought, desire. (Corbin, 1977, 224)

> [W]e are bereft in our culture of an adequate psychology and philosophy of the heart, and therefore also of the imagination. Our hearts cannot apprehend that they are imaginatively thinking hearts, because we have for so

long been told that the mind thinks and the heart feels and that imagination leads us astray from both. Even when the heart is allowed its reasons, they are those of faith or feeling, for we have forgotten that philosophy itself—the most complex and profound demonstration of thought—is not "wisdom" or "truth" in an abstract sense of "*sophic*." Rather, philosophy begins in a *philos* [loving] arising in the heart of our blood, together with the lion, the wound, and the rose. If we would recover the imaginal we must first recover its organ, the heart, and its kind of philosophy. (Hillman, *ibid*, 6)

Poetic imagination relates to authenticity as a matter of heart, a seeking for essential truths in life. Authenticity does not require a self as a "known"; we may remain unknown to ourselves—in the Heart Sutra are the phrases: "There is ... no eye, no ear, no nose, no tongue, no body, no mind ... no ignorance, no end of ignorance up to no old age and death, no end of old age and death ..."[44] Each paradoxical image or idea impels a 'seeing-through' of conceptual figuration; clinging to concepts as *merely* literal creates functional ignorance, a loss of the intelligence of the heart. When concepts are literalized at the expense of mythopoetic play, imagination is constrained.

The literalizing (ego) function of consciousness is not itself a problem, but an unconscious attachment (unexamined acceptance) of self and world as *merely* literal loses the lion—trades the play of poetic imagination for factive and fictive certainties:

> Philosophy enunciates the world in the images of words. It must arise in the heart in order to mediate the world truly, since, as Corbin says, it is that subtle organ which perceives the correspondences between the subtleties of consciousness and the levels of being. This intelligence takes place by means of *images which are a third possibility between mind and world*. Each image coordinates within itself qualities of consciousness and qualities of world, speaking in one and the same image of the interpenetration of consciousness and world, *but always and only as image* which is primary to what it coordinates. This *imaginational intelligence*

resides in the heart: "intelligence of the heart" connotes a simultaneous knowing and loving by means of imagining. (Hillman, *ibid*. 7; emphasis added)

Drawing on Buddhist thought, one of Atisha's Lojong Slogans (mind training, awakening empathy and compassion for the benefit of sentient beings) reads, "One should regard all dharmas [phenomena] as dreams." To regard all phenomena as dreams means to treat these neither as mere fantasy nor merely literal fact—to become more consciously aware of a third, mythopoetic reality.

Anarchic Sanctuaries, Collaborative Worlds

Constructions of anarchic sanctuaries arise in forms unique to its membership and are ephemeral—an anarchic sanctuary evolves and disintegrates, its members re-integrating with the larger world. How do we define these modest alternative societies, flying under existing cultural and media radars? What is their value to poetic imagination, with reference to authenticity?

To explore this topic, a group of poets has responded to six questions provided in written-interview format. The transcripts are edited for brevity with pseudonyms used to protect anonymity.

Q1. What for you is an anarchic sanctuary?

Q2. Would you provide some examples?

Mr. M Haller[45] *@40, Able, Oregon.*

For me, the words "anarchic sanctuary" conjure a very specific sense of community that I've participated in directly and observed from a distance, both online and in the real world. In reality, I don't think true anarchy is possible except as a liminal state between two existing structural orders. Nature, or at least human nature, abhors a vacuum, so there will always be an organizing principle or set of rules that develops, given enough time. What I take from the term "anarchic" in this context is not so much a lack of rules or set of social customs, but an environment or community that rejects mainstream morality or social conventions and involves a sense of transgressing, transcending or otherwise escaping what constitutes normal, sanctioned behavior in society at large, often through a mediated interface and a sense of fantastic, imaginary or creative play.

Sanctuary is of course the operative word here, and it is only through the safety and trust engendered by generally private, semi-private or virtual safe spaces that allow members of the anarchic sanctuary to strip away their normal inhibitions on behavior. Online, or in virtual space this is achieved through anonymity or the adoption of an avatar or persona.

The anarchic sanctuary is a place where masquerade is expected, where attitudes and identities can be made up at will and discarded just as easily. People define who they want to be in act of performative self-definition, and may completely re-envision themselves between sessions or even have multiple identities or roles within the group that they use alternately. If regular society tells the individual who they are and what is expected, in the anarchic sanctuary individuals decide what they will be and what their role is to be and any rules or constraints put in place are through mutual agreement rather than authoritarian coercion.

Livejournal was an early blogging platform that I was involved in during the aughts. Many journals were private and people really shared some intimate details of their lives, to the point that their friends on *LJ* knew more than some of their friends and family in real life. It was a confessional, cathartic outlet and the people you were sharing with were usually strangers from different cities or even foreign nations. I think the anonymity and distance gave room for a loosening of inhibitions that led to a kind of shared intimacy that created very strong personal connections. The circle of people I gravitated to were all aspiring writers. I still stay in contact with people I consider good, close friends from *Livejournal* that I've never even met in person due to the distances between us. I think it might even ruin some of the magic to meet in person.

We bared our souls and explored philosophy, supported each other's development as writers and human beings. That's an anarchic sanctuary. People still do this through a variety of outlets and it seems like the trend in younger people is moving more toward visual media like Snapchat or Youtube vlogging. Younger generations seem to have less concern about privacy, as they have shared so much of their lives online for so long.

I think message boards also have that anarchy to them, and the more strictly anonymous they are the more anarchic they can get, to the point that no one poster has an identity, it's more a single hive mind.

Mz. A Djuna @50, Rouses Point, New York.

flame-lit park
inexpressible possibilities
a Kennedy-jawed girl, running still

Anarchic to me means undefined, unprescribed, unbound, unplugged. It also means wild, as in Thoreau's definition of self-willed. It implies a profound faith, or trust, in the intelligence of the "field," and all the parts (technologies, persons, tools, etc.) that contribute life-force and information to the ever-evolving field.

Virtual community: Facebook and email, of course. Google docs. Forums. Improvisational theatre and jazz.

Mr. H Teki @60, Kapiti Coast, New Zealand.

Both anarchy and sanctuary are often interpreted as negative responses to attempts at control by outside forces. My life experience has imbued both words with positive and creative overtones. Anarchism as political philosophy: Anarchism advocates stateless societies based on voluntary associations with origins in the teachings of Taoists Laozi and Zhuangzi, Greeks Diogenes the Cynic and Zeno, in the teachings of Jesus Christ and as styled into a modern theory by Pierre-Joseph Proudhon and Leo Tolstoy.

Anarchism as community: "The faithful all lived together and owned everything in common; they sold their goods and possessions and shared out the proceeds among themselves according to what each one needed. They went as a body to the Temple every day but met in their houses for the breaking of bread; they shared their food gladly and generously; they praised God and were looked up to by everyone" (*Acts* 2:44-46).

Sanctuary as a place set aside for creative freedom: Land set aside for wild plants or animals to breed and live. Sanctuary as Holy of Holies (at the heart of the Temple): "When you pray, go to your private room and, when you have shut your door, pray to your Father who is in that secret place, and your Father who sees all that is done in secret will reward you" (*Matt.* 6:6).

This would make an anarchic sanctuary a consensus-driven free association of people where the needs of each individual and of the community for creative and transformative freedom are in unforced accord. The empowerment to participate fully and voluntarily in such community is the reward that is received from time spent in one's private room.

In the later 60s and early 70s, many of us became active participants of a ferment of artistic creativity, menial labour, art galleries, fringe films, poetry readings, alternative art and poetry journals, theatre, scratch orchestra, anti-war and Maori rights protests and hitchhiking around the country when the mood took us. I skirted the edges of the mob mindset that was fueled by and was satisfied by drugs, sex and rock 'n' roll.

X. Colonel Um *@60, Western Connecticut.*

Inspired by fantasies of café society in Paris, our collaboratively created anarchic sanctuary existed as a social milieu without organization beyond its two founders. Our only goal was to maintain necessities of disorder. (Those seeking control need gentle reminders.) There was vociferous speechifying, outrageous flirting, intense intellectual discussion and mindful drinking. As a co-founder of The Plant, an arts cooperative and as a Colonel I often dressed in low-cut garments—along with my partner in crime, General Din, we quite unintentionally magnitized isolated artistic folk from various environs of our violent and pathetic city. They flocked to the disused space we'd discovered.

For a few years, The Plant was an evolving flower of fluidic desires. To create a workshop, "shouting down" was the method. Pound on the table—stand on a chair, and speak up! The workshops that evolved (these became rife) were always held outside the hallowed ground-dirt barroom floor of our aimless fellowship. The Plant was an ecosystem, a complex, organic flow of social interaction. As young Americans, we indulged our fantasy of wine-drinking European intellectual café lives as seedbeds of secret revolution. There's nothing virtual to touch it these days, though there soon may be. We were inspired by books, especially Samuel Delany's *Dhalgren*, and were largely apolitical; there was no "Plant-*ism*." It wasn't for everyone, though most who arrived stayed. Our city was composed of aging factories, a chemical storage dump and a freight yard.

Q3. How would entering a virtual social world contrast with reading speculative fiction?

MHal: A good book makes the protagonist come alive within the reader, there is a flowering inside of a new consciousness and an unfolding of a new inner world. With video games, you choose or make your avatar and you enter a world that is more external and mediated, more concrete and thus less imaginative, so it's less a possession by or fusion with a foreign, well developed personality through imagination and more an immersion into a new, external world by proxy, wearing the avatar as a mask and adopting a role.

And I think the mask is a common theme in the anarchic sanctuary. The Eleusinian Mysteries, secret societies, celebrations of carnivale or a masquerade, the burlesque or cabaret, these cultural products of the past functioned as anarchic sanctuaries, and they all have some element of losing one's proscribed identity from the outer world and assuming a new one of esoteric ritual significance, or of one's own invention. The current renaissance in Burlesque and rising popularity of cosplay show how interested in the anarchic sanctuary this current generation is. There is a con for all kinds of groups and styles, from steampunk, to comic-con to furries, and they're all anarchic sanctuaries for these people to share a sense of imaginative play.

A lot of video games ultimately derive from Dungeons and Dragons—traditional role-playing games—so they too have a real world equivalent and basis which is loosely literary and sci-fi/fantasy derived. And nowadays people even go to the extreme of live-action role playing with elements of acting and costuming. This is really elaborate, imaginative play. So how did we get from people rolling dice around a table to virtual worlds and grown adults running around dressed as elves and hitting each other with blunted swords?

People have always had exceptions to normal behavior; whether in Saturnalian spectacles or private fetish clubs, some people always want more, a little more freedom than normal society allows and have always sought it out in safe spaces underground, or set periods of increased freedom. But for a long time, mainstream society maintained strict hegemony and alternative behavior was severely policed. The grey flannel dissidents of the 50's are pretty tame in terms of deviance compared to the hippies of the late 60's, who in turn are pretty tame compared to the club kids of the 90's who are pretty tame compared to contemporary Satanists or fetish clubs. Even looking back as recently as the 80s, comparing mainstream views on homosexuality, trans-identity, Atheism and recreational drug use, there has been a seismic shift in social mores and the acceptance of behaviors that used to be forced into private sanctuaries and viciously attacked by normative society. So what happened in a generation?

I think people are spending more and more of their lives in virtual spaces. In my youth, the avatars were primitive and we weren't plugged into a network, but we played video games and fell into these artificial worlds and explored them for hours and hours. I think the growth of cosplay, steampunk fashion, the really elaborate and fantastical comic book, video game and animation-inspired styles that I see more and more of are all just kids extending the kind of freedom they experience online into the real world, and it drives older people nuts, which I suppose is kind of the point of any youthful rebellion. I see this in the non-binary gender movement too. A lot of older people don't get the non-binary thing. They're stuck in the physical world, in an older, mainstream culture.

These kids are saying, you can't tell me who I am, I will define that and I can be whatever I want. They've come to expect that as the norm because they spend most of their lives in a non-physical or augmented reality. As biological implants, cybernetics and truly immersive virtual reality loom larger on the horizon, the future looks pretty wild.

HTek. To enter a virtual social world is to enter an egalitarian society. The playing field is leveled. Each person participating in various online fora is free to express his or her thoughts, wisdom, insights on an equal footing with someone who may be a CEO, a Nobel laureate, a spiritual leader, an impoverished student, a labourer, a single young mother, a geriatric, even an athlete. One's social, economic, political or academic status does not necessarily exclude anyone from full and active interaction with other participants.

ADju: Well, in virtual realities, you are a character in the plot. You change the plot and you influence the other characters.

ColUm: Yes, certain works of fiction are generators of anarchic sanctuaries because characters are multiple and we are, too. But it's the rare read that deeply challenges the status quo, inspiring a penchant for psychic autonomy. I mentioned *Dhalgren* as an important literary inspiration for The Plant, so would like to quote an extract from William Gibson's 1996 Foreword, "The Recombinant City." He gets it.

> Samuel Delany's *Dhalgren* is a prose-city, a labyrinth, a vast construct the reader learns to enter by any one of a multiplicity of doors. Once established in memory, it comes to have the feel of a climate, a season. It turns there, on the mind's horizon, exerting its own peculiar gravity, a tidal force urging the reader's re-entry. It is a literary singularity. It is a work of sustained conceptual daring, executed by the most remarkable prose stylist to have emerged from the culture of American science fiction.
>
> To enter *Dhalgren* is to be progressively stripped of various certainties, many of these having to do with unspoken, often unrecognized, aspects of the reader's cultural contract with the author. There is a transgressive element at work here, a deliberate refusal to deliver certain "rewards" the reader may consider to be a reader's right. If this is a quest, the reader protests, then we must at least learn the object of that quest. If this is a mystery, we must at least be told the nature of the puzzle. And *Dhalgren* does not answer....
>
> I place *Dhalgren* in this history:
>
> No one under age thirty-five today [1995] can remember the singularity that overtook America in the nineteen-sixties, and the generation that experienced it most directly seems largely to have opted for amnesia and denial.
>
> But something did happen: a city came to be, in America. (And I imagine I use America here as shorthand for something else; perhaps for the industrialized nations of the American Century.) This city had no specific locale, and its internal geography was mainly fluid. Its inhabitants nonetheless knew, at any given instant, whether they were in the city or in America. The city was largely invisible to America. If America was about "home" and "work" the city was about neither, and that made the city very difficult for America to see. There may have been those who wished to enter that city, having glimpsed it in the distance, but who found themselves baffled, and turned back. Many others, myself included, rounded a corner one day and

found it spread before them, a territory of inexpressible possibilities, a place remembered from no dream at all.... America and the city seeping into one another, until there is no America and there is no city, only something born from their intermingling....

When I think of *Dhalgren,* I remember this:

A night in DuPont Circle, Washington, D.C., amid conditions of civil riot, when someone, as the police arrived with their staves and plastic shields, tossed a Molotov cocktail up into the shallow stone bowl of the Admiral's memorial goblet. The District's lesser monuments were often in decay, and the Circle's tall fountain had stood dry for however many summers, and I suppose trash had accumulated there, mostly paper, crumpled Dixie cups tossed up by children making baskets in imaginary hoops.

I did not hear the bottle shatter, only the explosive intake of gasoline igniting, flames throwing black shadows against the concrete; our shadows, running. We were all running, and in the eyes of a Kennedy-jawed girl from the Virginia suburbs I would see something I had never seen before: a feral shiver, a bright wet shard of ancient light called Panic, where dread and ecstasy commingled utterly. And then the first canisters fell, trailing gas, and she was off, running, like a deer and in that moment as beautiful. I ran after her, and lost her, and sometimes I imagine she is running still ...

I was there as well, we all ran together, "rounded a corner one day and found it ... a territory of inexpressible possibilities.... America and the city seeping into one another ... something born from their intermingling." I too lived in the city until it became me.

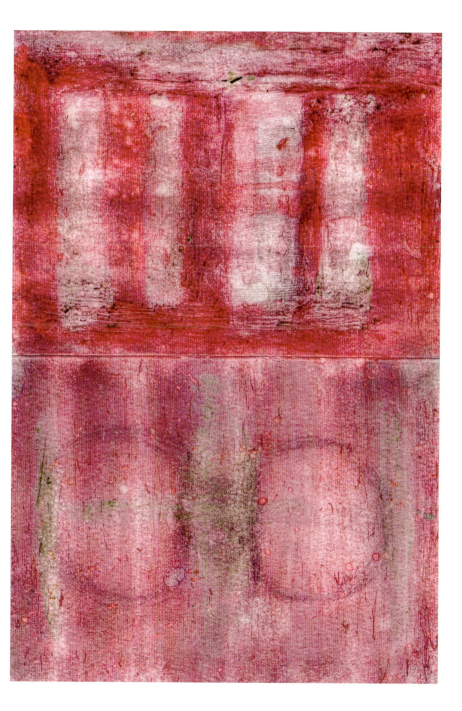

8. "Anarchic Sanctuary," 2017

Philosophy begins in a philos *arising in the heart of our blood, together with the lion, the wound, and the rose. If we would recover the imaginal we must first recover its organ, the heart, and its kind of philosophy.*

Q4. Experiencing group-creative social & virtual collaboration, what are some benefits and contrasts?

Mz. M @50, Distance, New Jersey.

Yes, I have personally experienced what you have referred to as *anarchic sanctuaries*, in forums where participants are free to pick up on resonant discursive/poetic threads and artistic themes and respond in an atmosphere of experimentation, with no specific agenda beyond the prospect of collaboration. I find that such virtual worlds have an advantage over in-person collaboration in that there tends to be less personal history between participants, and thus the creative work is more likely to be perceived and responded to without distortion or preconception.

Artistic inventions and intentions are afforded an island of sanctuary among a sensitive audience whose participants have hopefully grown to trust and value one another purely through the exchange of ideas, thus enjoying the liberation of 'seeing' each other more purely through the creative process itself. At its best, this opens a sacred space for transpersonal communication that is perhaps less about personality and a little more about soul.

It is worth noting that such forums can benefit from an atmosphere of play. This setting lessens the pressures of egoic performance, is liberating, even joyful, opening the way to creative source connection, where, to quote Martin Buber: "Play is the exultation of the possible."

Mr. Pablo H @30, Southern California.

At the end of high school, I got pulled into taking Argentine tango lessons by a friend. I got hooked. The world of social dancing was in many ways an anarchic sanctuary. I was 18, people encouraged me and I learned fast, I benefited from a lot of generosity and indulgence from the community, who were mostly in their early 30s to mid-50s and wanted to encourage younger people.

We drank wine and danced until 4-5 am. The Argentine Tango casts a spell. It's powerfully collaborative in the sense that the dance is composed of minute basic elements and is entirely improvised; it depends on very subtle and precise non-verbal communication between the partners. At a higher level, it's taken step by step, moment by moment, the lead and follow are connected so thoroughly that one's body awareness extends into the other, and partners move as one individual. It's a flow state that involves not just the couple, but the entire room, where there are often many couples packed into a small space, and of course there's the music. The energy is incredible.

And, because it has imported Argentinean culture and the people involved are a diverse group of people from all over the globe, it is a subculture with its own mores that fall slightly outside of normal American values.

Americans have huge personal space issues. They have giant cars, giant houses, give each other wide berth, shake hands aggressively and hug awkwardly. On the trains in Tokyo you're pressed body to body like sardines in a tin; on public transit in the US you get horrified looks if you accidentally brush your knee against somebody. In a *milonga* (tango event) you can walk in and ask someone to dance without a word, just eye contact and a nod called *el cabeceo* and then dance with a complete stranger, have this incredibly intimate, powerful and moving experience of collaborative, kinetic art and sublimated sensuality, and not even know the person's name or anything about them. Your bodies are pressed against each other, your foreheads are glued together and you can taste each other's sweat but it's also nearly anonymous and private. There's magic in that.

There's anarchic sanctuary in the warm embrace of an utter stranger. Of course, you get to know people over time and intimacies, friendships or romances evolve, but it's topsy-turvy and completely unlike anything I've experienced outside of the social-dance community. Once the neuroses and quirks of the dancers come out there's a lot of stuff that goes on in the *milonga* that stays in the *milonga*, so I definitely found an anarchic sanctuary with that community.

That's a very physical collaborative form of artistic, social play. But with writing, it's totally different. It's not sensual, it's intellectual. It's Apollonian vs. Dionysian. I write linked verse in the Japanese tradition, renku. That's something I can do via email with no physicality. It's also immensely satisfying. If anything, I prefer to write linked verse and then go back and take the good elements and publish those as independent haiku, or if the whole series is strong then publish that complete, rather than to try and write haiku on their own.

I don't really like to write haiku on their own, per se. In the American haiku movement people love to fetishize the "haiku moment," to get deep into this Zen conception of capturing an ephemeral moment. I like the original sense of *haikai* as a collaborative social act. The connection to the previous verse, the art of linking and the surprise of how your partner responds and transforms the imagery, it's improvisational and musical like jazz, it's a complex intellectual congress like Hesse's *Glass Bead Game*. It's a drier pleasure and is more intellectualized, but it is very rewarding, stimulating play.

I'm also on a lot of online poetry groups that share poetry and give feedback, though these tend to be a little reserved and less intimate than the truly anarchic spaces I've been involved with in the past. I think the fear of offending, whether in feedback or content, keeps them from being truly anarchic. I'm sure that more anarchic poetry boards exist, I just haven't sought them out.

In terms of opposing realities? I think neither the physical artistic space nor the digital one is "real." Tango is escapist, writing is escapist, and in general the *anarchic sanctuary is an escape from the limits of the banal* and the socially acceptable. Art is something outside of reality, for me anyway. There are a lot of reasons and motivations for people making art, and different things people get out of it. For some it's group identity formation, for others it's understanding the human condition. For me, I tend toward the ecstatic mode. Meaning, art is a means to reaching an exalted state, connecting with the Godhead. I'm not religious, I mean I don't believe in God in any traditional sense, but for me art has the potential to catapult you into altered states of consciousness and to transcend banal reality with sublime beauty.

ADju: For me, there is something more ... enlivening? to a field when one participates in physical proximity, just like watching a sunset or a mountain lion on a mountain is more enlivening than seeing a video of either. The field is infinitely enriched by "all of the messages coming through" (Rumi): sounds, smells, the direction of the wind, the sense of being in the center of that moving circle.

Virtuality just changes the art-making process so much. The sensuousness and immediacy are lost. I am lonely; perhaps I have an exaggerated sense of object-permanence. I want body chemistry and peripheral vision for touchstones and a shared ecology/stage for a sense of wholeness. VR may change this; maybe it will have some elements that make up for a sense of smell, for example, so there won't be a sense of "less than." These days, in the absence of nearby humans, I'd often rather turn to nonhuman collaborators for my anarchic sanctuary—and of course I do.

HTek: There is a hairy old observation about one section of the population that goes something like "get two or more NZers together and they'll form a committee to discuss the matter in hand." The implication is that any proposed group-creative activity of these people would get bogged down in committee—a sure-fire way to quench the communal creative spirit among motions, seconders, points of order etc., etc.

Among the few more interesting times of cool group-creative social collaboration that I have participated in was with a Scratch Orchestra at Auckland University in about 1970. Relevant and concurrent to this were the comings together of activists mobilising against NZ participation in the war in Vietnam,

Maori rights, official sporting support/contact with apartheid South Africa, and a nuclear-free NZ.

Generally, I tend to avoid group activities, as often I discern an underlying current at work that words like "group manipulation" and "mass hysteria" evoke. Thus I tend to avoid and question most mass activities. Virtual collaborations are more fruitful, as each person has the freedom to come and go anytime during the process to go back to somatic life, reflect on matters discussed, get refreshed etc., without having to endure time-wasting repetitions, quarrels, or egos. Such collaborations epitomise a revolving door policy of collaboration.

Q5. Is somatic physicality (being present in physical proximity) overrated as to social congress?

MHal: Yes and no. I believe that in the digital age more and more of people's identity and consciousness is invested in non-physical spaces such as social media, internet chat-rooms and the virtual worlds of computer games. Even television can be immersive enough for people to dissociate from their body for a time. But this immersion in the ether has some very real physiological drawbacks that can negatively affect the mind and interpersonal relationships. At the extreme end, the individual can become so immersed in another reality that they neglect their bodies to the point of death. For instance, there have been a number of cases where extreme video game "marathons" led to gamers dying of pulmonary embolisms or strokes caused by blood clots that occurred from sitting for so long. But even less severe than that, the lack of vitamin D, the lack of "green time," the dissociation from nature and social isolation resulting in completely ignoring physical reality can really be detrimental to one's mental health and lead to depression and social anxiety. Video game, smart phone and television addiction are very real problems for this generation, something presciently addressed by David Foster Wallace in *Infinite Jest*.

On the other end, digital narcissism, an addiction to shallow, petty social stroking in the form of up-votes, "likes" and all that, can lead to a poor sense of self-worth and a neurotic need for the constant approval of others. That's not socialization, that's solipsism. So those are the two traps at the extreme ends of virtual space, neither of which are conducive to healthy social interaction, and there's ample evidence that these problems are fairly common. But there are unhealthy forms of real world interaction too, so social dysfunction isn't unique to the digital world, it's just that the way it manifests is novel.

The Facebook "like," as with any social stroking, gives positive feedback and a little bit of dopamine. But does that satisfy a deeper longing for connection and intimacy? Maybe when you get that feeling of vulnerability and sharing intimate secrets there is some of it, but I think people still need physical affection to be truly satisfied. Until virtual interfaces can provide the tactile responses biological triggers for all the physiological needs of the human animal, we can't abandon the physical altogether.

I think contemporary consumer culture, the way it promotes instant gratification, the way it sells the idea that we should be happy all of the time, that things should be easy and fun, and the way people are pressured to show a pro-social, successful mask on social media like Facebook is a huge part of contemporary ennui. Most consumer goods and interactions are cheap and disposable and people bring that into their relationships because it's all they know. We could have the same technology with a different culture and have less of these problems. I think that beneficial digital environments with healthy cultures already exist to some extent in various anarchic sanctuaries, it's just that mainstream, commercial technology can be more of a hindrance than help in this regard.

Q6. How do you imagine the future, in relation to a positive sociality which values anarchic forms of sanctuary?

ADju: I think there must always be a sense of integrity of the players, including the environment, for it to work. Integrity as in wholeness. Also as in skillfulness, or development, or discrimination; you have to be a skilled musician in order to improvise with others.

So, supposing the elements all have some sense of integrity ... hmmm ... even a White Supremacist has integrity. So in order to be pro-social, you'd have to have some wisdom, too, or at least some contingents in the field with wisdom enough to absorb or eject the anti-social contingents. It can't just be all *Lord of the Flies* or a Roman orgy that subjugates the lower classes.

A live scenario would be a kind of "drop-in" rave, like churches used to be drop-in. A creative chill-space in nature, e.g. the amphitheater at Red Rocks; with musical instruments; painting spaces; meditation vortices; excellent, web-rated childcare; poetry written on the wall to inspire.

So what would it look like? Well, I imagine taking my VR camera into a field of wildflowers and my friends taking their VR cameras into fields of wildflowers, and out there, beyond right and wrong, we could dance or chat or trade stories. That's a VR scenario. I also imagine, in that VR scenario, speaking through or as wildflowers to each other... in this way, one can bring in the wildness of wilderness and all those messages into a VR collaboration. The result could be a kind of chorus of millions.

HTek: It would be of the nature of what I have witnessed and experienced with monks in Trappist monasteries.

PabH: I'm not a very optimistic person. I think we're always only a generation away from utter savagery. I think *Lord of the Flies* is pretty spot on for painting essential human nature and I think that the dystopian novels of William Gibson are a foreboding of evils that may come from the rise of multinational corporations that have more power than any national government. At the same time, online sanctuaries are bringing people from around the world together and we can find friends who share similar interests easier and more quickly than ever before, so even as power consolidates into the corporate oligarchies of many of the world's leading economies, and nativist right wing ideologies close off borders at the national level, making mobility harder, people are finding freedom and connecting with each other. Fringe groups are able to find solidarity and organize to fight for their rights through digital sanctuaries.

I think digital natives are trying to bring the freedom of anarchic sanctuaries out of the internet and into the real world. Advocacy through social media is becoming a force for genuine social change and making mobilization easier. People in marginalized groups can find that they're not alone and create local groups with less danger than before. But I think that with every victory we gain in bringing some element of freedom and alternative lifestyle into the mainstream, we face the danger of reactionary blowback.

The Weimar Republic was full of anarchic sanctuaries that created some of the 20th century's most radical and revolutionary art, then within a decade or two those artists were being labeled degenerates, having their art destroyed and in many cases being put to death or being forced to flee Germany. So I think we have to recognize how fragile any success we have will be. Marriage equality stands for now, but we can't pretend there isn't still intense homophobia or that LGBTQ people are safe when our Vice President believes we can torture people out of their gayness with conversion therapy.

There's a human rights crisis in Chechnya right now that sounds like the beginnings of a holocaust; families are murdering their gay sons or brothers, the state is creating detention centers and torturing homosexuals before putting them to death or forcing their families to do so. This supposedly is backlash against gays coming out and trying to have pride parades and bring their lifestyle into the mainstream. That's terrifying, and I don't think it's out of line to worry about what could happen here in the US.

To be ridiculously Utopian, I think, would be to hope that within a generation or two, digital natives will have brought more freedom of self-expression and inclusiveness of the alternative lifestyles we already find underground in virtual anarchic sanctuaries. And to the extent this reality enters the mainstream, compassion and openness will triumph over fear and bigotry. It would be nice if society itself were an anarchic sanctuary. I think in certain neighborhoods in certain cities, small arts enclaves and minority communities already strive for this, but progress is fragile and hard won.

Any movement toward a more peaceful, equitable and free society will have to address the violent, tribalistic and predatory tendencies in humanity. The far left is trying to make things safe for the oppressed with safe spaces and call out culture, but in their eagerness to accomplish this, they are flirting with authoritarianism in the way they attack their critics and police the language and behavior of others. So how can we create a safe society that is also free? It's a catch-22. (*Personal communications*, May-June, 2017)

Where We Have Never Been

The capacity to create intentionally-collaborative anarchic sanctuaries involves social mechanisms allied with speculative fiction to re-define relationships between participants. Crucially, anarchic sanctuaries reframe consensual social reality, standards and delimitations of thought prevalent in normative culture and unconsciously accepted intersubjectively as truth. Yuval Harari addresses the issue of intersubjective fictions in *Homo Deus*:

> Fiction isn't bad. It is vital. Without commonly accepted [intersubjective] stories about things like money, states or corporations, no complex human society can function. We can't play football unless everyone believes in the same made-up rules, and we can't enjoy the benefits of markets and courts

without similar make believe stories. But the stories are just tools. They should not become our goals or our yardsticks. When we forget that they are mere fiction, we lose touch with reality. Then we begin entire wars "to make a lot of money for the corporation" or "to protect the national interest." Corporations, money and nations exist only in our imagination. We invented them to serve us; how come we find ourselves sacrificing our lives in their service? (2016, 206)

Concerning poetic imagination, within the precincts of soul, sanctuary is invisibly retained as a locus of "difference" which challenges the heart's diminishment, as

> Artistic inventions and intentions are afforded an island of sanctuary among a sensitive audience whose participants have hopefully grown to trust and value one another purely through the exchange of ideas, thus enjoying the liberation of 'seeing' each other more purely through the creative process itself. (M)

In valuing uniqueness and finding visibility in socially-alternative societies, one gains soul. In order to let lions roar, anarchic sanctuaries represent "island[s] of sanctuary," a much under-reported social phenomenon, one creative solution to "consensus mind."

This chapter began with an exploration of sanctuary as a precinct, allowing for explorations of the life of the soul—inhabitations contained within a *temenos* of the sacred or holy. The poem may itself become a precinct, a temporary means of "housing the unhousable," the fundamentally "wild" nature of mind. Depending on reader reception, the poem brings revelation (as Levertov discusses) as it brings to consciousness philosophical intentions arising through 'the intelligence of the heart.' The poem may also function as a lens through which we connect to mythopoetic space. Octavio Paz writes, "Poet and reader are two moments of a single reality" (1956).

Those who have spoken here bear witness to collaborative anarchic sanctuaries as communal precincts instrumental to the thought of the heart. Federico Lorca reinforces this positive sense of anarchy for the poet:

> The artist, and particularly the poet, is always an anarchist in the best sense of the word. He must heed only the call that arises within him from three strong voices: the voice of death, with all its foreboding, the voice of love and the voice of art. (1933)

This must be familiar to some, "the call that arises within." It's fair enough to consider the intelligence of the heart as a search for authenticity, one that sometimes requires solitude and solitary contemplation—yet we also desire *authentic community*. As sites of social interaction, anarchic sanctuaries support expressions and invocations of the unique by providing a *temenos*, a sense of sanctity in which novel forms of societal dwelling may be found as home.

"We bore our souls and explored philosophy, supported each other's development as writers and human beings. That's an anarchic sanctuary" (M Haller). "Anarchic to me means undefined, unprescribed, unbound, unplugged ... wild ... It implies a profound faith, or trust, in the intelligence of the 'field,' and all the parts that contribute life-force" (A Djuna).

"The Plant was an ecosystem, a complex, organic flow of social interaction. As young Americans we indulged our fantasy of wine-drinking European intellectual café lives as seedbeds of secret revolution" (ColUm). "A consensus-driven free association of people where the needs of each individual and of the community for creative and transformative freedom are in unforced accord. The empowerment to participate fully and voluntarily in such community is the reward ..." (H Teki).

"... At its best, this opens a sacred space for transpersonal communication that is perhaps less about personality and a little more about soul" (M).

VI. Haiku, an Ethics of Freedom

9. "Emily's Darlings," 2016

Contained is an appreciation of a broad range of haiku styles and the panoply of creativity evidenced by its authors.

> *Becoming what you are presupposes that you do not have the slightest idea <u>what</u> you are.*
>
> — Nietzsche (1888)

Remystification

The mystery of living is a craft of being. The mystery of being—where this *essai* began, as an exploration of the space of thought. For the sensitively-engaged reader, the space of thought as a form of aesthetic arrest applies to poetry, as Emily Dickinson describes in her illimitable style:

> If I read a book and it makes my whole body so cold no fire can ever warm me I know that is poetry. If I feel physically as if the top of my head were taken off, I know that is poetry. (Bloom, 1999)

Poems, readers (and consciousness) cannot be corralled via interpretation. The presentation of haiku to follow takes Susan Sontag's perspective in *Against Interpretation*; "the true task, Sontag argues, is not to ask what the work means, but to appreciate what it is; or, as she puts it, 'In place of a hermeneutics we need an erotics of art'" (1964);

> Sontag is strongly averse to what she considers to be contemporary interpretation, that is, an overabundance of importance placed upon the content or meaning of an artwork rather than being keenly alert to the sensuous aspects of a given work and developing a descriptive vocabulary for how it appears. (2009)[46]

There is a distinction to be made between analysis and interpretation. In the following exegesis, "sensuous aspects" of the works are associated with "qualities," as appreciations. In "The Heresy of Paraphrase," Cleanth Brooks reinforces the notion that poetry, being "an experience rather than any mere statement about experience or any mere abstraction from experience," cannot properly be interpreted; meaning is largely intuited. Nonetheless, while a poem's savor—its completeness as experience—cannot be extracted, ideas can be posed and analyzed regarding the poem's effect on consciousness; analysis "against interpretation," so to speak.

Excellent haiku enhance the mysterious space between living and dreaming. As an illustrative appreciation, the present analysis represents one reader's journey. In desiring the mystery of consciousness to be honored via the poem, 'intelligence of the heart' is expressed "by means of images which are a third possibility between mind and world." A psychology of sanctuary represents one way of formally regarding this *third thing*: conceptual architectures of the poem provide *ways in* to visibility and feeling—this "third thing" about which Machado teasingly writes, "Guess it."

Concerning groupings of haiku into 36 "qualities," two aspects of "the third" should be mentioned. The first is generic: mythopoetic authenticity is implicit in each of the poems selected. However there is a more specific aspect of "the third"—as a term used to denote the seventh property of thoughtspace; selections of haiku in this Property exemplify phenomenological aspects of mythopoetic dwelling. (*cf.* Appendix 1, *Verbose Description*, "The 'Third'").

Analysis: Conceptual Architectures of Thoughtspace

A brief outline of "36 qualities," drawn from the "Seven Properties of Thoughtspace" (Chapter 1), is found in Table 1, below. Also see "Appendix I. *Seven Properties of Thoughtspace & 36 Qualities, Verbose Description,*" presenting crystallizations of each "quality," based on an analysis of themes spawned from contemplations of each thoughtspace property (in the preceeding chapters of this book). To arrive at 216 selections—6 haiku for each of 36 qualities—around 10,000 haiku in English have been perused.

Table 1

Outline: 36 Qualities of Thoughtspace Derived from 7 Properties

Seven Properties of Thoughtspace
   1) Perception {**SPACE**};
   2) Shared communication {**LANGUAGE**};
   3) Conditional, provisional ephemerality {**THOUGHTSPACE**};
   4) Fictional {**METAPHORICS**};
   5) Design-intention {**ARCHITECTURES**};
   6) Explorative desire {**SOUL**};
   7) Hypothetical humanity {**THE "THIRD"**}.

1) SPACE. (Perception):
   1. Minimal creation (space of mind). **2.** Novel worlds. **3.** Immeasurability. **4.** Unknown unknowns.

2) LANGUAGE. (Terminologies & Shared Communication):
   5. *Concreta* vs *abstracta*. **6.** Conceptual blending. **7.** Neologism (unusuality). **8.** Possible worlds. **9.** Inferred narratives. **10.** "Staging" theatres of story.

3) THOUGHTSPACE. (Conditional Ephemerality):
   11. Philopoetic volition (& enactment). **12.** Practice of Invention. **13.** Spatial thermoclines.

4) METAPHORICS. (Fictional; "To be as"; Reality Deformation):
   14. Fantasy imagery. **15.** Paradox (of time, space, logic). **16.** Alternativity. **17.** Idiosyncrasy (fallacy). **18.** Crafting of presentation. **19.** Mimesis.

5) ARCHITECTURES. (Design-Intention):

    20. Design-architectures. 21. World-building, construction. 22. *Temenos*. 23. Precincts (of sanctuary). 24. Construction (sacred construction). 25. Notions of anarchic sanctuary.

6) SOUL. (Depth as Process):

    26. Soul (as a core value). 27. Remembrance and Distance. 28. Grit, guts. 29. Desire, passion. 30. Emotion. 31. With Risk.

7) THE "THIRD." (Hypothetical Humanity):

    32. Distance. 33. Forms of resistance. 34. Inhabitation (dwelling). 35. Place. 36. Consciousness—revisions of world and self.

Example-haiku have been sourced from several recent anthologies and an international archive—publication sources and acronyms used are found in the endnotes.[47] Contained is an appreciation of a broad range of haiku styles—the panoply of creativity evidenced by its authors. As the mode of investigation is that of personal taste, no claim can be made regarding universality; haiku have been selected in accord with Dickinson's dictum.

Also, any haiku may righfully be viewed from multiple perspectives—each inherently possesses multiple qualities. With this in mind, the goal of the following analysis is not to label any particular poem or grouping by a single quality, especially to the exclusion of others. Placements within a taxonomic structure illustrate how a particular quality works within a specific grouping of poems, as a means of bringing greater visibility to each "quality" through emphasis or exemplification (rather than definition).

Regarding technique, the use of disjunction (lexical, semantic, etc.), creates degrees of "disfluency" (termed "reader resistance" in *The Disjunctive Dragonfly*, Gilbert, 2013): excellent haiku resist easy reader-interpretation regarding meaning. Appendix II provides a discussion of strong versus weak disjunction, which lends specificity to the notion of disfluency.[48] In Adam Alter's 2013 explanation:

> [Disfluency] lead[s] you to think more deeply [in] that it forms a cognitive roadblock, and then you think more deeply, and you work through the information more comprehensively. But the other thing it does is it allows you to depart more from reality, from the reality you're at now.[49]

Disjunction, a defining technique of haiku, separates haiku from epithet, affirmation, or naïve, imagistic "pictures" of static scenes. Due to their brevity, haiku are non-narrative (or barely so). Disjunction deepens us psychically by creating *lacunae*, which can be considered "wounds" between words: syntax and grammar are deformed, abused, broken or fragmented (*katakoto*, in Japanese), and in this sense "harmed"—recalling Mallarmé's aphorism that the role of the poet is "to purify the words of the tribe" via "a violence to language"—an idea indicative of the violence of natural forces rather than aggression, here explicated by Octavio Paz:

> Poetic creation begins as a violence to language. The first act in this operation is the uprooting of words. The poet wrests them from their habitual connections and occupations: separated from the formless world of speech, words become unique, as if they had just been born. The second act is the return of the word: the poem becomes an object of participation. Two opposing forces inhabit the poem: one of elevation or uprooting, which pulls the words from the language; the other of gravity, which makes it return. (1956, 28)

As an appreciation of the potency of haiku, critical perspectives presented here do not dwell on technique (how the writer applies disjunction, a particular style of metaphor, etc.), but rather on philopoetic effects indicating architectural designs of thought observed within a *temenos*—presences and contemplations of dwelling and inhabitation "as if they had just been born"; intuitively derived qualities and properties of poetic imagination.

1) SPACE (Perception)

> Any perceptual surface has the potential to become metaphorically deep if we choose to contemplate it, 'seeing through' mythopoetically (*Sunny-side Up in Space*).

1. Minimal Creation

What might be a "minimal" haiku, from the perspective of the creation of space and depth? "Minimal" indicates an extreme brevity of word- and/or syllable count. There is debate as to genre-limits—the outré example of "minimal" is the one-word haiku, exemplified by "tundra" (Cor van den Heuval, 1963, *HIE*). This single word is placed in the middle of a blank, white page. But lacking this specific layout the disjunctive effect is lost. A visual ku, "tundra" requires a specific layout for effect. As a range-limit of minimalism, "tundra" is an excellent example. Several other single-word minimal-visual haiku have recently been published.

While the single-word haiku is noteworthy as a genre limit, the focus here is on haiku which do not require a specific visual layout:

pig and i spring rain

spring wind –
I   too
am   dust

just please how to forgive spring rain

(Marlene Mountain, *HIE* 1979; Patricia Donegan, *HIE* 1998; Michelle Tennison, *H14*)[50]

These three haiku span 35 years of US haiku history. Minimal-to-maximal: objects plain, without ornament. The context and scenario of life is left to the reader; one the reader must autonomously compose. Creation is a cosmos out of dust, or of two nearby animals (one human), or, of forgiveness from rain.

The objects. *Concreta*: "pig" (not "a pig" or "the pig": these, being determined, lack surprise). "pig+I"; "I+dust"; "just+please"— particles of instantiation within a specious present, the syntax of subject blends into dyadic rhythmic-pairs, creating figuration. The "altogetherness" of the collocational presentation of these pairs exists as a moment: a location or locale, in thoughtspace. In Donegan: from, I+dust to Idust to du'I'st ("I" merges with dust); in Tennison, the plea in "just please how to forgive," a beseeching of internal, reflective speech—all are commentaries on unknown situations, distant from the reader. The distance of poetry, yet with intimacy and immediacy of feeling, as emotions are engaged.

So, unexpected: "just please"—as with "pig," as with "dust." These three environments: of rain, time and wind, arise instantaneously from the ground of thoughtspace. Human dramas of life and death are emplaced within objective (wider) contexts, poetic precincts. This sense of philopoetic volition is something the reader creates from these three environments of spring—an entire philopoetic world cohering in 4–7 syllables.

When applied to minimal haiku, "concision" may be inadequate: perhaps *atomistic* is the better term. Here are several atomistic haiku, drawn from *Disjunctive Dragonfly*:

silence
like it

isms with our clothes on

> anchor
>
> i
>
> tic

(Jack Galmitz, *DD* 2013; Paul Pfleuger, Jr., *DD* 2013; Philip Rowland, *DD* 2009)[51]

2. Novel Worlds

A philosophical-poetics utilizing new forms of language and thought spawns novel worlds of mind. These compositions reveal how imaginative modes that break with conventional thought—in language, image or story—not only surprise, but may inspire revolutions in how a "world" is defined, or comes into existence.

> MY LIFE BEHIND GLASS
>   so lonely, the little verbs
>
>   a blue coffin one nail escapes the solar system
>
> from somewhere else youre a prairie skyline

(Sabine Miller *H16*; Peter Yovu *H14*; John Martone *DD* 2012)

Miller's "my life" is unusual in the way the first line in the couplet is headlined; it may be viewed as an epitaph or (prison) sentence, or signboard explaining an animal (as in a zoo); what is the creature behind that glass? Vulnerable, tender volitions of language, here personified—there is also heart and rhythmic music in "so lonely, the little." Novel worlds challenge rules of physical reality—by eliding "impossible" architectures of philopoetics, a certain profundity is achieved. In Yovu, is the resurrectional ascent of the impossible: a coffin nail flies outward towards the cosmos—why only "one nail"? This image posits a philopoetic idea. Martone's obscure lead-in, "from somewhere else" is a purposeful instantiation of self (identity) as an intangible—also note the semantic disfluency of "youre."

The first three haiku above play with violent semantic and epistemic shifts, which throw us out of habitual consciousness. Next presented are novel worlds based on *measureable* nouns:

first frost I give a beggar nothing

im-mi-grant . . .
the way English tastes
on my tongue

first light
not enough words
for green

(Anna Maris *LHA* 2015; Chen-ou Liu *LHA* 2013; Susan Constable *LHA* 2006)[52]

Maris's haiku is composed of *concreta*—concretely objective, "measureable" nouns and noun phrases (*cf.* Endnote 11). Yet here as well, a novel world appears in which the reader too becomes someone whose heart appears hardened cold as frost. "First frost" is also a traditional season-word; does the overt admission of altruism undone reveal a guilty secret? Liu's haiku is likewise concrete in style, eloquently posing a synaesthetic, cultural otherness (presenting disfluency literally) in his first-line utterance. Constable's "first light" has similarity with Miller's novel use of language, above—though rather than personifying the objectively intangible ("verbs"), it is the *world* for which the *word* itself (language itself) is not enough—this then, is a novel world.

3. Immeasurability

The art of infinity—if only we could simply feel it, without aid from imagery. Immeasurability emblematizes the potency of haiku regarding methods that impel or pose infinities, intangible abstractions as sheltering skies, sanctuaries beyond *literal* borders or boundaries. Whether overt or inferred, the sense of *immeasurability* embodies a philopoetic questioning in how the reader "answers" or assembles the implied immeasurables of vision within life (via the poem).

how
on earth
on earth

        between wound and weapon the milky way

            bomb nor embody to take blue sky

  more signs
  bout the next town
  —
clouds stretching out of existence

            running forever
            spring after
            tragedy

beyond
stars beyond
    star

(John Martone *H16*; Lee Gurga *H15*; Mark Harris *H14*; Gary Hotham *DD* 2011; Richard Gilbert *LHA* 2012; L. A. Davidson, *HIE* 1972)[53]

For Martone's "how," *how* or what *is* the "how"—this is infinity as a tangible intangibility. What might lie *between* wound and weapon *in* the milky way, in Gurga? What comes before or after "bomb nor embody" as philopoetic concept, in Harris? How tangible or intangible (real or fantastic) is the space provisionally described in the tailing-off finality of Hotham's "out of existence"? In Gilbert, the immeasurables of "forever" and "tragedy" offer the reader little of the literal, except suffering, which extends (immeasurably) "forever." In Davidson, is retained a sense of immeasurable romance: cosmos as a "beyond" encompassing a paradoxical semantics as plural merges with singular: "stars/star."

4. Unknown Unknowns

If immeasurables are infinitudes, *unknown unknowns* appear more forensic. The poem is "looking through" the real into an unknown space—venturing forth; exploring and giving expression: presenting exactitudes to indeterminacy. For something to actually be unknown *as* an unknown, we must possess enough knowledge to know that this state of unknowing exists. In the right hands, the haiku form can exemplify this notion.

this side of the equinox this side

if glass breaks easily a bird

out of place just in time

dense fog . . .
I dream walk
my sense of I

plum blossoms
    a specimen of my dream
sent to the lab

        swallow flight
        looking out the window
        long after

(Eve Luckring *H16*; John Stevenson *H15*; Jim Kacian *LHA* 2011; Kala Ramesh *LHA* 2009; Fay Aoyagi, *H21* 2009; Jim Kacian *DD* 2006)[54]

In each of these haiku is a force of insistence, emanating from the precise design-space created by the poem. Consider the "equinox" of Lucking's palindromic in "this side … this side" ("this" can also flip into a "that"); there are hints also of the history of seasonal cycles in the Earth's planetary orbit. Stevenson poses an "if-"—is there (as the poem seems to insist) a "-then" clause to complete the cause-and-effect proposition? The *unknown unknown* in this haiku is poised as a fulcrum—the reader joins that "unknown" space between glass and bird; but to which phrase does "easily" apply ("breaks easily" or "easily a bird")? Here, "easily" acts as a relational and semantic fulcrum between "known" and "unknowns." Kacian's playful minimal-ku poses two familiar idioms ("out of place/just in time") against each other, an *agon* creating a near-perfect obliquity of meaning.

    The double-dream within-a-dreamscape in Ramesh focuses on the mystery of interiority, the unknown quality of self. The choice of environment as "dense fog" creates an exacting, mirror-like parallelism between internal and external worlds. In "plum blossoms," Aoyagi (as in a number of her haiku) exhibits playfully ironic humor, with her memorable line: "a specimen of my dream"—a dream being examined forensically. Wry, the poem is also a philo-poetic culture-critique. Last, a second haiku from Kacian which plays with the unknowability of time and perception: the adverbial "long after" creates an *unknown space* of time between seeing and the memory of having seen.

10. "Rose in Time," 2016

*The poem is "looking through" the real into an unknown space—
venturing forth; exploring and giving expression:
presenting exactitudes to indeterminacy.*

2) *LANGUAGE (Terminologies & Shared Communication)*

The uniqueness of images can be treated as poiesis—the play of metaphoric mind—which may or may not communicate intelligible, extractable meaning but always *displays* itself. Perhaps *we* are the extraterrestrials, experiencing *Arrival* every day as we "language" imagination—relativizing the universal (*Space is the Place*).

This area of consideration draws on a poetic lineage which includes language experiments throughout the modernist era—notable examples can be seen in the experiments of E. E. Cummings, Oulipo and Language poets. Novel aspects of language use are implemented within haiku schema—conceptually, syntactically and semantically—to implement or induce philopoetic enactments. These often include themes treating social issues, consciousness and identity.

5. Concreta vs Abstracta

Here, *concreta* are regarded as measurable things. Qualities of phenomenal objects, such as the shapeliness of shape, or color-sense of color, define themselves as "of a kind," "elements within a range of," "a difference among a spectrum of," among (measurably) comparable others, like or unlike; thus, "likened to." *Measure* here is seen as a means of discovering and observing the tangible underlying the intangible:

> Measurement, believe it or not, is a widely misunderstood concept. It's often mistaken for a process that produces an exact number. If you are told that something cannot be measured because there is no way to put an exact number on it, then you know that the problem is a misunderstanding of the measurement concept. The way scientists see it, measurement is the reduction of uncertainty about a quantity through observation. ("Everything Is Measurable," *cf. Endnote 11*)

Each of these haiku utilize the measurability and tangibility of *concreta* which in turn impel intangible (immeasurable) *abstracta*.

blue throated bird's sky voice

                            testing
                            elasticity
                            robins

hiding in everything plain sight

                     a word that takes time defoliation

mosquito wings —
the colour of evening
so thin

                Lily:
                    out of the water . . .
                    out of itself.

(Joseph Salvatore Aversano *H16*; Barbara Snow *H15*; Don Wentworth *H14*; Johannes S. H. Bjerg, *DD* 2012; Ajaya Mahala *LHA* 2016; Nicholas Virgilio *HIE* 1963.)[55]

In Aversano, "blue throated bird's sky" is composed of familiar (usual) nouns and adjectives, which produce a sensual, tangible composition—until "sky voice," which offers a song less tangible in character. Snow's minimal-ku may place robins on a high tension wire, or a branchlet, or pulling worms out of the ground: each word ("testing" [continuous-present verb] + "elasticity" & "robins" [nouns]) argues for measurability, yet the total effect creates delightful unusuality—a fairly intangible faith that robins do test elasticity; there's a sly anthropomorphism in Snow's word-choice here. Wentworth uses semantic and syntactic indeterminacy to create a highly abstract, paradoxical, philopoetic observation concerning human perception, and notions of existence with "hiding in ... plain sight." In a sharp cultural critique, Bjerg converts time into speech, implying ecological destruction ("defoliation") as a social issue with unclear, long-term consequences. The semantic elision (vis, "the time it takes" and "defoliation") creates a pause (gap) between causes and potential effects. Mahala plays with the application of "thin" as a quality—is this meant as the thickness of wings, a color hue, a feeling tone, a psychological state? *Abstracta* are indicated in the subtle yet precarious imbalance of design-spaces in meaning: the literal images (mosquito wings, evening, color) interact with multiply overlaid, abstract concepts of "thinness."

One of the signature works in the English-language haiku pantheon, Virgilio's "Lily" haiku eloquently transforms between concrete tangibility and intangibility, as worlds of literal form transmute (in the third line) into the philopoetic enactment of 'being in itself'—concrete ("out of the water") and abstract ("out of itself") combine, impelling a reversal or paradoxical relationship of signs. "Out of itself" is as much saying 'out of language' or 'out of [arising from/being of] consciousness' (i.e. self nature, identity) itself.

> 'Mindfulness' is something we do (mind minds) without a tangible root for the "*–ness*." An axiom of archetypal psychology is that mind is fundamentally poetic in nature: root metaphors of imaginative possibility are 'the poetic basis of mind' (*Immeasurability*).

6. Conceptual Blending

From the 1990's, the term *conceptual blending* has evolved through the linguistic works of Gilles Fauconnier and Mark Turner, and is refined in their book, *The Way We Think* (2008). While not a comprehensive theory of creativity, the authors posit that "Conceptual blending is a fundamental instrument of the everyday mind, used in our basic construal of all our realities, from the social to the scientific" (Turner)."[56] In thoughtspace, diverse concepts, themselves originating from diverse conceptual frames, are continually being blended in mind—an activity akin to associational or loosely-associational thinking. In this haiku grouping, the basal conceptual frames (whether given as collocational or phrasal parts of the haiku) are not necessarily notable or unusual, yet the "blends" are:

winter orange an unborn at the end of a scalpel

   against the wind the slightest witness

the way rain starts a morning myth

   dandelion: dos & dont's

ants begin to look like an idea

   war zone . . .
   a mouse giving birth,
   to stars

(Don Baird *H16*; Markeith Chavous *H16*; Robert Epstein *H15*; Aditya Bahl *H14*; Scott Metz *DD* 2009; Dick Whyte *LHA* 2012.)[57]

Baird's haiku contains four conceptual blends: "[a] winter orange," "[being] unborn," "at the end," "a scalpel"—the eliding or fusion of these images—their conceptual *blends*, create a language-oriented haiku, expressing a philopoetic idea. While it's easy enough to extract interpretive meanings from this haiku (e.g. relating to the garden, scientific experiment, surgery, abortion), the critical focus here pertains to the potency and use of "blends" as creative conceptions constructing multiple novel-architectures of poetic imagination.

In Chavous are three blends: "against the wind," "the slightest" and "witness"—they seem to cohere into a figure, hovering between worlds of fact and fiction, mythopoetically. In Epstein are four blends: "the way," "rain," "starts," "a morning myth"—each is rooted in easily-grasped image schema, yet conceptually blended, the haiku suggests mythopoesis in the manner of its coherence. In Bahl are the blends, "dandelion" + "dos & dont's"—the colon also represents a semantic blend, defining a dependent relation between the dandelion (image) and rules (dos & dont's) one assumedly follows.

In Metz, a traditional fragment/phrase haiku is subverted by a semantically radical blend: "ants" + "begin" + "to look like" + "an idea"—and rather playfully, "begin" can be attached (semantically) to the first fragment ("ants") or last part of the haiku. In Whyte's poem of war are four blends: macrocosm (as "stars") is posed against a vulnerable mammal "giving birth," in the midst an all too earthly microcosm of war—each image is a conceptual stretch from the previous, creating a multilayered and strongly emotional communication.

7. Neologism (Unusuality)

In *The Disjunctive Dragonfly*, "neologism" was described as one of the 24 techniques of disjunction in haiku—here, the idea of neologism (coinage) is broadened to include the linguistic concept of unusuality: words, collocations or phrases that are highly-infrequent in usage—within a particular context (e.g. literary genre). The examples below activate poetic imagination through irruptive nomenclature.

c

you're just

light's　　　　　　　　starfish in the mathematical Bahamas

by-
product

flash mob daffodils

flown the audible
amnesia
　　fields

as an and you and you and you alone in the sea

even, if, because
plum blossoms
in the courtyard

(John Martone *H15*; Mike Andrelczyk *H14*; Alan S. Bridges *H14*; Barrow Wheary *H14*; Richard Gilbert *HIE* 2011; Miriam Sagan *DD* 2011.)[58]

In Martone, the mathematical constant "*c*" (the speed of light), as a single line of poetry absented from a mathematical equation is highly unusual, a near-coinage, indicating philopoetic volition. Each of these haiku act similarly to create volition through neologism: "mathematical Bahamas" in Andrelczyk; "flash mob daffodils" (as a neologistic phrasal-collocation) in Bridges; "audible amnesia" in Wheary; in the last two haiku are seen neologistic phrasal collocations: "as an and you and you and you" in Gilbert, and "even, if, because," in

Sagan. Such language play is often light-hearted as well as explorative, conjuring novel worlds through semantic unusuality.

8. Possible Worlds

In literary study, *possible-worlds* theory describes how we visualize in imagination—the theory has usually been applied to possible-worlds in prose fiction: "A literary universe is granted autonomy in much the same way as the actual universe ... possible-world theory is also used within narratology to divide a specific text into its constituent worlds, possible and actual" (*Wiki*). Conceptually, a possible world assumes its own autonomy as a reality, epistemologically equivalent to an actual (literal) world. In haiku, a possible world is potently felt as *actual*—it's this sudden actuality of a propositional possible-world that numinously deepens feeling. The possible does not supplant the actual—yet the actual itself partially dissolves to meet the possible—this "halfway" space is known as *twilight consciousness* in depth psychology. A commonplace example would be the sense of confusion that occurs seeing unclear objects at dusk, or the alterity of thoughts occurring in hypnagogic states between wake and sleep.

The poem moves us into indeterminate (*metaxic*) psychic realms in which divergent, even paradoxical worlds and notions of reality can co-exist simultaneously (at dusk, the rope is a snake is a rope). This experience confers psychological richness, nuance and subtlety. A unique pleasure in the text arises by holding in mind simultaneously multiple, divergent world-views and frameworks of truth.

at the window end of winter night

          night
          the side of earth the noun
          is on

          decisively parting her parentheses

tunnel graffiti my brain is such a soft surface

          the river
          the river makes
          of the moon

    as a window to
    a   window of
    as father seen

(Joseph Salvatore Aversano *H15*; Gary Hotham *H14*; Jeffrey Winke *H14*; Tyrone McDonald *HIE* 2011; Jim Kacian *HIE* 1997; Scott Metz *DD* 2013.)[59]

In "at the window end," Aversano invites an imagination of an end as a spatial "window end"—a possible world in which the author's narrative story seems fictive/impossible, yet when interpreted as a 'night at winter's end,' reasonable enough. A more fantastical possible-world is posed in Hotham's "the side of earth the noun is on." In this world, nouns are languaged forms harbored in an animate night—advancing a philopoetic idea. Winke tickles the fancy of symbolic representation in (possibly) "parting her," parenthetically. McDonald advances the notion of a possible world in which his entire single-line statement is singular and true—the fiction here relies on the *be-* verb "is"—haiku humor challenges the reader to expand imaginative space into a possible world in which psychic sight espies a visible or exposed brain as a mirroring of "graffiti"; a graffitied cityscape projected within a tunnel. Kacian's possible world resides in the creation of metaphoric fusion: the river and moon together create a third, inferred (imaginal) image: "the river the river makes"—this metaphorical river, as a possible-world, deepens psychic reality. In Metz, multiple psychological perspectives and temporal senses of fractured thoughts, images and feelings concerning "father" collide, yet due to the broken phrasing do not quite cohere; this creates multiple possibilities of possible worlds: what is and is not "seen" of father, in this haiku?

9. Inferred Narratives

In Mark Turner's *The Literary Mind* is expressed the idea that at a subliminal level we function in the world via *image-schema*. These are deeply subliminal mini-stories. For example, in drinking coffee there are several small stories, such as: "pick up spoon," "place in cup," "rotate spoon," "stir liquid." These unite thought and motor action, and are forms of narratology (story), though on a minute scale. In Turner's view, any such thought/action is intrinsically *story*. Taking this idea into the realm of haiku, a reliance on an underlayment of minimal-narrative story—regarding ourselves as cognitive actors in the world—is evidenced in the way that when linked together, via (disjunctive) haiku concision, minimal image-schema can impel the arising of large-scale narrative worlds.

father dark on the frozen lake I follow

waging war when you had to be there

so greenly history puts forth thorns

> morning fog ...
> when my embryo had gills

Silent Night
drifting in from the neighbors –
I relearn Chinese

> Passover eve -
> all the thoughts I won't
> bring to the table

(Matthew Caretti *H16*; John Soules *H15*; Eve Luckring *H14*; Tyrone McDonald *H14*; Chen-ou Liu *LHA* 2011; Roman Lyakhovetsky *LHA* 2014.)[60]

In Caretti, there is an inferred narrative "why?" or "what for?" or "what has already happened?," "what will next occur, as story?" in relation to a dark father, a frozen lake, and "I follow." In Soules, there is a gap, a sense of *incomplete* story that urges narrative query, posed by the phrase "when you had to be there": a contextual scenario is inferred, and through such inference the reader creates novel worlds. In Lucking's haiku, what does it mean for history, if imaged as an animate, growing lifeform which "puts forth thorns"? A narrative story (green, blooming and prickly) is hinted at, which the reader embellishes, filling in context, for the haiku to cohere. McDonald proposes the outrageous, yet biologically accurate "when my embryo had gills," recalling Haeckel's 19th century catchphrase, "ontogeny recapitulates phylogeny," leading to possibilities of narrative inference. In Liu, "I relearn Chinese" offers a backstory related to immigration/emigration in a narratively-inferential context. Similarly, in Lyakhovetsky, a specific cultural encounter is indicated by "Passover eve"; the reader is called on to inferentially fill in "the thoughts I won't bring" (say out loud) in this specific social situation—and the reasons why.

In each of these examples, a novel imagistic sequence is revealed, burgeoning from minimal phrasal-expressions indicative of image-schema, through which larger narrative stories bloom.

10. Staging — Theatres of Story

Unlike inferred narrative, the story here is given—each haiku offers a glimpse, snapshot, or compositional frame of a story, as if already staged. "Story" plays a prominent role in how *thoughtspace* evolves through these haiku worlds, and the story is here foregrounded; though as with most haiku, context is largely absent and left to reader imagination. We enter the story as foreground yet must *construct a world* (or enframe a world) for the story to cohere. In consequence, imagination becomes a form of inner theatre.

> further into
> the same war
> white breath on the window

> blue sailors the strange eyes of a daughter

> midnight mockingbird Allen Ginsberg
> in my bed

In Pretti the story is given: an ongoing war and wintry breath on the window foregrounds the scene. In Suresh, the "eyes of a daughter" are foregrounded among "blue sailors"; though the story is less certain—this *mise-en-scène* offers a sense of staging. Similarly, in a most playful and lightly mocking haiku by Wilson, Beat poet Allen Ginsberg makes a sudden, irruptive appearance "in my bed." In this *mise-en-scène*, whom mocks whom in "midnight mockingbird" rhythm?

>   sun on the horizon
>   who first
>   picked up a stone
>
>
>   body bag
>   not asking
>   not telling
>
>
>   whom one falls for on the skylight hard rain

(Sharon Pretti *H16*; Aashika Suresh *H16*; Kath Abela Wilson *H14*; Paul Miller *H21* 2009; Jerry Kilbride *HIE* 2003; Philip Rowland *DD* 2012).[61]

The theatre of story becomes ancient in Miller, imagining the first human almost mythically as the "who"—standing on a *horizon-line dawn* of conscious-awareness of time, picking "up a stone"; the conceptual blends create a foregrounded drama. With biting sarcasm, Killbride references the now defunct "Don't ask, don't tell" policy of the American military in his potent image of an anonymous body bag—one out of thousands returning from a foreign theatre of war—mainstream media was censored from showing these returning dead. The foreground is lit with political deceit, avoidance of brutal truths and catastrophe. And in Rowland, as the rain lands hard, an aural storm is foregrounded, focusing the author's contemplation on love and its raw, forceful power.

11. "Contiguous Spaces," 2017

*A possible world assumes its own autonomy
as a reality, epistemologically equivalent
in substance to any actual (literal) world.*

3) *THOUGHTSPACE (Conditional Ephemerality)*

Concerning the subjectivity of modern consciousness: we think ourselves into new forms of subjective selves in a fictive spinning-out of speculation upon speculation (metaphor upon metaphor), applying imaginative logics (*Immeasurability*). For metaphoric thinking to arise and develop into landscape and story, a sense of dimension—space (in a word)—is required: imaginal spaces in which images (and ideas, sensations) are natively emplaced. Thoughtspace—a subjective-imaginative space—may have little to do with literal three-dimensional space, or contiguous Newtonian space (*Space is the Place*).

11. Philopoetic Volition

Discussed in Chapter 2, *philopoetic volition* posits enactments of poetic-philosophic ideas (visions), that provide artistic and societal value:

Every poem constructs a world in mind—writer-to-reader-mind—via language. The space of thought in which the poem lives is architectural, and can be felt as a knowing—even if the meaning isn't possible to nail down. Sense may only be found in the inseparable weave between image, rhythm and story (*Philopoetic Volition*).

In these selections, an emphasis is placed on compositionally unique styles of imaginative knowing meant to offer support for novel avenues of poetic inquiry in relation to social value. Imagine where some of the haiku below might best be read: in a public square, subway spaces, a lit billboard in New York's Times Square, projected on the Sydney Opera House, inside the ISS. In the past, visual artists have claimed public space as usurpations of consumer space—the billboard space of product, political-pitch "Vote For Me" ads, etc. Charles Bernstein in his literary criticism urges poets to take their works off the page and address public space:

> Against the Romantic idea of poems as transport, I prefer to imagine poems as spatializations and interiorizations—blueprints of a world I live near to, but have yet to occupy fully. Building impossible spaces in which to roam, unhinged from the contingent necessities of durability ...
>
> I believe that artists and intellectuals have a commitment to try to make their work and the work they support available in public spaces, not in the watered down forms that only capitulate to the mediocracy, but in forms that challenge, confront, exhilarate, provoke, disturb, question, flail, and even fail. (1999)[62]

Philopoetic volition is consequent to an interior authenticity that as an expansion of *thoughtspace* nourishes through what is absent: "blueprints of a world I live near to, but have yet to occupy fully. Building impossible spaces in which to roam." The reader autonomously determines the nature of philopoetic volition intended. Each of the haiku below are volitional: each *is* the enactment. Philopoetic enactment in its comprehensive sense includes any human activity or vision, any blueprint of a world—there is no delimitation in terms of productive form.

An example can be seen in MacVane's haiku, set within brackets. I first saw this work on a journal page and took it for a misprint. The disjunctive aspect is strong, as the poem *empties out* a space—the reader is instructed to place "your crucifixion image"—the haiku acts as placeholder for consensus-based, intersubjective theological notions. (The *fiction* reflects the "truth" of consensual fiction). This haiku takes a stance both intimate and formal, regarding the haiku genre:

[your crucifixion image goes here]

Philopoetic volition is a potent element in Stillman's "leaves turning to half truths," both as the end of life (as) fall season, and symbolic of a loss of ideals, disappointments leading to philosophy.[63] Lanoue's "spring dawn" posits a non-/trans gender identity as an origin-point of conscious awareness, prior to habitual determinations:

> leaves turning to half-truths

spring dawn
I put on
my gender

The following haiku play with "betweeness" in the space of thought. Newton's haiku introduces a relationship between chaos theory, impossibility and clowns, a highly idiosyncratic philopoetics; Swede finds a different sense of "between" in an exposition of playfully absurdist *metaxic* twilight consciousness, in "between what I think and what is" + pink "lawn flamingo"; Lather presents a Socratically philopoetic balancing-act on either side of a horizon-line poised on the fulcrum of "and" (rather than "or") at the poem's center: "why and why not"—the merged question of *cause* becomes paradoxical, leading deeper into the roots of philopoetic inquiry.

> impossible clowns introducing the theory of chaos

between what
I think and what is
lawn flamingo

horizon
why and
why not

(Joy MacVane *H16*; Jeffrey Stillman *H15*; David Lanoue *H14*; Peter Newton *H14*; George Swede *H14*; Rajiv Lather, *HIE* 2003.)[64]

12. Practice of Invention

Any excellent poem is inventive. The poems in this section highlight variations in inventiveness—whether as play, revisionings, insights, innovations, or other novel explorations of haiku concept and form. The entirety of haiku presented in this book might be placed here, as all are indicative of creative haiku practice.

hold your glass against the syllable rain

"Do you want me?"
she whispers, and turns
to leaves

old
black
book
whisper

a love letter to
the butterfly gods with
strategic misspellings

where the lines end and the absence begins an architecture or so

> my fingerprints
> on the dragonfly
> in amber

(Cherie Hunter Day *H16*; David McCann *H15*; Paul Pfleuger, Jr. *H15*; Chris Gordon *LHA* 2011; Chris Gordon *DD* 2002; Jim Kacian *DD* 2003.)[65]

Invention as a *practice* implies that haiku may inspire our own inventiveness. Each example here reveals a unique aspect of inventive creativity. Day's conceptual mergence of "glass against the syllable"; McCann's "she ... turns to leaves" (not turns *and* leaves) likewise plays (if differently) upon a word (does "she" also 'turn to leave'?); the list-form lines of Pfleuger's poem shift perception from concrete form to memory and the intangible "whisper" of an old book—two syllables ("whisper") pose a dialectic to the single-syllable/single-word lines, prior. Chris Gordon's selections play with mischance ("strategic misspellings") and fantastical allusion (e.g. "the butterfly gods")—and in his second haiku, from "where the lines end" begins a series of iterative paradoxes: "as lines end," "absence begins," "begins an architecture," and the grammatically irruptive, paradoxical non-ending of "or so" creates and erases space in thought at the same time. Language is used to suggest and erase forms, yet there is design-intention: paradox becomes itself an architecture.

The detailed discussion of Kacian's haiku, presented in *The Disjunctive Dragonfly,* is summarized here. Semantic expectations are overturned as the subject ("my fingerprints") needs or seeks a verb and an object. The second line ("on the dragonfly") seems a bizarre place for fingerprints, while in the third line presents a substantial object ("in amber"). Semantically then, "fingerprints ... in amber" may be what is first cognized as a subject-object pair. This is the implicit semantic expectation. But how can a fingerprint be in amber, which is a kind of rock? Does the poet really mean inside, within? We expect that fingerprints, which can only exist in relation to surfaces, be on and not in them. So, the fingerprints (as subject) carry definitive existence, yet semantic expectations are overturned as the relational object (in amber) is in doubt. This is contemporary haiku pun; misadventure in reading as the specious present interweaves with geologic time—the image of a prehistoric dragonfly fossilized in translucent amber gradually coheres, along with the poem's architecture.

13. Spatial Thermoclines

Regarding *thoughtspace*, the qualitative emphasis here is on nuance of thought, feeling and landscape—and a melding; a volitional metamorphosis of such notions. The sensibility of thermoclines pertains to spatial *ambiance* (a sense of ambient atmospheres): delicacy of feeling, a resonance which lifts away from gravity; buoyancies, a softening in receptive tone. Hesitancy, gentleness, sadness, longing—distance and intimacies—these are given sensual expression.

Inside my laughter a stone looks at the sky.

                                blossoming pear . . .
                                a dream slips
                                from its chrysalis

moon beggar hesitant

                monologue
                of the deep sea fish
                misty stars

autumn mist oak leaves left to rust

Just enough of rain
To bring the smell of silk
From umbrellas

(Rob Cook *H15*; Rebecca Drouilhet *H15*; Alegria Imperial *H14*; Fay Aoyagi *HIE* 2002; Marlene Mountain, *H21* 2003; Richard Wright *HIE* c. 1960.)[66]

Resonance concerns in part what we are left with. As well, there is a vibratory 'struck bell' sense of expanding space and landscape as the poem is re-read. In these examples, emotional nuances continually shift in resonance. Each shift presents a change in philopoetic 'vibration' (felt-sense of meaning). A mystery inside a mystery, in Cook: how is it that inside laughter a stone "looks"? This postulation poses an emotional dialectic, a "stone" within is usually something hard, emotionally rigid, or painful—and yet that stone "looks at the sky." In these irresolvable phrases, emotions shift and elide. In Drouilhet, from the fruit a dream "slips" (creative verb-use here) from a chrysalis—born as a butterfly or moth, something winged, soft, and sweet. Imperial's "moon beggar hesitant" elides with darker tones of night and poverty—why hesitant? This haiku is likewise irresolvable as to meaning, yet evinces a depth of nuanced feeling. Aoyagi's use of "monologue" implies both personal and mythic speech, as though a "deep sea fish" speaks—the poem seems a mini-mytheme reflecting a dreamlike felt-environment, exemplified by "misty stars." Mountain contrasts nature (autumn oak leaves) with *technos*, the culture of the machine ("left to rust") in a playful reversal that deepens, as cultural commentary. Finally, in Wright, a most-nuanced haiku, which begins its emotional journey with "just enough"—a sensual poem in which the lightest touch of rain yields scent on silk, evoking the colors of Parisian umbrellas, perhaps on a street not far from his home, near the time of composition.

12. "Thoughtcraft," 2016

*Stories, dreams, imaginations happen some*where.
*And, we psychologically exist within these spaces,
as much as they within us.*

4) METAPHORICS *(Deformational fictions; 'to be as')*

Metaphors deepen as they propagate, revealing landscapes and story (*Immeasurability*). The "shadow of heavenly things" indicates mimesis, rather than imitation: an artwork or *crafting* of presentation that evokes, "mimes"—brings into being (*Sanctuary*).

Creative *thoughtspace* is plainly fictive. Why create fictions in thought-space? I would suggest it is in order to design—and not merely as incidental sketch, as design is wedded to intention. So, not to "think the impossible," but rather to *think into further possibility*—one means of doing so is by allowing "impossibles" to exist as substantially as the possible. That is, to grant the wild a less well-managed space, in mind.

The practice of metaphorics in haiku turns some aficionados off. Reading the negative critiques, particularly odious are those who attack authorial intention—authors have been labeled "arrogant," "selfish," "elitist," "snobs," etc. This vitriol has historical precedents. Consider for example those jazz musicians who moved away from popular styles to produce art projects outside popular taste. Ornette Coleman received a number of negative reviews when *The Shape of Jazz to Come* was first released—though it's now considered a landmark masterpiece. There are numerous examples to be had.

What is striking in the personal attacks is the sense of ownership of genre territory—accusations and author insults are often reactions to a perceived disloyalty to the form, lineage or spirit of whatever art-form is under purview.

In fact, unusuality in metaphorics will not suit every reader's taste, but the scope of haiku (and poetics in general) necessarily encompasses a diversity of experiments and styles of expression. My use of the term "metaphorics" (and *metaphoria*) draws on the linguistic concept of "cognitive metaphor":

> The most recent linguistic approach to literature is that of cognitive metaphor, which claims that metaphor is not a mode of language, but a mode of thought. Metaphors project structures from source domains of schematized bodily or enculturated experience into abstract target domains. We conceive the abstract idea of life in terms of our experiences of a journey, a year, or a day.... [So] Emily Dickinson's "Because I could not stop for Death" is a poem about the end of the human life span, not a trip in a carriage. This work is redefining the critical notion of imagery.... [C]ognitive metaphor has significant promise for some kind of rapprochement between linguistics and literary study. (*Linguistic Society of America*)[67]

One means of effecting consciousness change is through cognitive dissonance—and *metaphoria* are highly effective dissonators. Metaphoric styles in poetry deserve a separate study; while they cannot be comprehensively discussed here, in the "qualities" below, six metaphoric styles are presented.

14. Fantasy Imagery

The reader may question whether these works actually contain metaphors at all. From a literary-historic standpoint, probably not. I. A. Richards in 1937 first described the two parts of a metaphor as the *tenor* and *vehicle*; the contemporary terms used are *ground* (the subject of the applied attributes) and *figure* (the second image, of borrowed attributes). I suggest that cognitively and psychologically, the concept of metaphor extends into the primary activity of qualitative consciousness: how we signify reality. There exists a semiotic schism or metaphoric "gap" between sign and signifier concerning words as symbols, in that commonplace metaphoric figurations are taken as literal (*cf.* the concept of time, discussed in *Space is the Place & The Specious Present*).

In this group of poems, cognitive dissonance is strong, yet at the same time suspension of disbelief is voided, so that fantasy becomes overt. Metaphoric dissonance creates a playful sense of depth—the world (or worlds) proposed seem 'fantastically tangible.'

turn the record over and start snowing

                     through eyes of rain leaf light

another bird dream probing the tenderness under a wing

meadow speaking the language she dreams in

                     salt wind ripples on an inner lake

    without child
        i find my wife inside
    an inedible mushroom

(Melissa Allen *H16*; Ann K. Schwader *H15*; Melissa Allen *H14*; Scott Metz *HIE* 2009; Cherie Hunter Day *HIE* 2010; Scott Metz *DD* 2011.)[68]

Because there is no "I" and no inside/outside environment given, the two actions relating to "turn" and "start" in Allen's haiku imply a fantastical merging of two actions. Of the many possible meanings might be, "You turn the record over and I start snowing"; a fantasy-sense of meteorology is indicative of dissonant *metaphoria*. Schwader's "eyes of rain" is an overt creation of fantastic *metaphoria*. The idea that "metaphors project structures from source domains of schematized bodily [ ] experience into abstract target domains" is presented in Allen's second poem: "... bird dream probing the tenderness ..."—bodily experience is the dream itself, and the abstract target-domain involves "tenderness" (under the wing, probed by a dream). In Metz, "she dreams" represents bodily experience, with dissonant *metaphoria* interpreted in various combinations due to syntactical play: "meadow speaking," "speaking her language," "the language she dreams in"; these metaphoric ideas exist simultaneously as design-intentions—architectures in thoughtspace creating multilayered realities. In Day, "salt wind ripples"—literally, waves, it might be thought, but the closing phrase "on an inner lake" evokes fantastic, dissonant *metaphoria*. And Metz again creates a complex, fantastical scene, which begins with the source domain "without child" to tell a metaphorically dissonant (and dysphoric) Alice in Wonderland story, with "inedible mushroom" adding an ironic touch.

15. Paradox

In these examples, *metaphoria* are highly paradoxical in their joining, as in: "wormhole/without a hole" in Galmitz; "out of nowhere isn't" by Mountain, and; "nothing matters how green" in Stevenson.

In another form of paradox, the consensual sense of space, time and/or story is severely deformed, as in "touch-move rule gently a little death" in Linke; "bat's ear ... rose ... star" in Luckring; and a more straightforward perceptually synaesthetic paradox, in "the sound of light" by Duc.

    touch-move rule
    gently
    a little death

                      a wormhole
                      without a hole

                                      inside a bat's ear
                                      a rose
                                      opens to a star

    carpentry
    the sound of light
    on the snow

out of nowhere isn't

nothing matters how green it gets

(Ramona Linke *H15*; Jack Galmitz *LHA* 2013; Eve Luckring *DD* 2011; Hélène Duc *LHA* 2012; Marlene Mountain *H21* 2007; John Stevenson *HIE* 2007.)[69]

16. Alternativity

Features denoting alternativity may contain one or more of these specific aspects: 1) cognitive estrangement, 2) paradox, 3) futurism, 4) time-space subversion, 5) speculative mythopoesis.[70] Each poem below employs cognitive estrangement to varying degrees. Alternativity is related to possible-worlds theory, found in the speculative-fiction studies of Darko Suvin. *Cognitive estrangement*, a term Suvin coined, implies an awareness on the part of the reader that the text does not present a world as familiarly known, but rather a cosmos whose alternative phenomena, through the displacement of empirical and materialist views, impels a reconsideration of habitual, scientifically-based perspectives. The following haiku present alternative possible-worlds that deform physical laws in various ways.

    white breath
    my shadow confesses
    a crime

        raw umber the hill's
        shorthand for want

            at seven we are replicants

pain fading the days back to wilderness

> forgotten for today by the one true god autumn mosquito

> the government of winter in her coal dyes

(Fay Aoyagi *H15*; Cherie Hunter Day *H15*; Helen Buckingham *H14*; Jim Kacian *HIE* 2007; Lee Gurga, *H21* 2003; Peter Yovu *DD* 2011.)[71]

Aoyagi's haiku includes white breath as a season of winter, wherein a "shadow" expresses agency in a space of darkness, "confesses" (as religious idea, experience of guilt?); a "crime"—a *noir-like* cinematic sensibility, the alternate-physics of a shadow confessing a crime offers an abundance of cognitive estrangement. Day personifies "hill" via the phrasal collocation "hill's shorthand for want," describing an internal question regarding a raw experience of life—color ("raw umber") becomes a placeholder for (the author/the hill's) emotion. Buckingham explores the science-fiction genre, evoking and conceptually blending androids or clones with the psychology of child development, offering a philopoetic proposition. Kacian confounds reader-orientation with alternativity, as pain (impossibly) 'fades days' "back to wilderness"—evocative of the wilds of mind, and loss of memory. Gurga's haiku presents alternative possibilities for time and omnipotence: how long is a day to a god; and what is the relationship between the autumn mosquito, and "the one true god"? Also, who or what is "forgotten"? Here, poetic imagination challenges religious belief, along with physical laws. And in Yovu's haiku, wordplay creates two simultaneous readings as 'cold eyes' or "coal dyes." "The government of winter" sets the stage for bitter experience within the nation-state—alternativity is everywhere indicated in this poem, as each phrase deforms persons, places or things by figuration, lexical or syntactic play.

17. Idiosyncrasy (Fallacy)

Idiosyncrasy retains the use of surprise, whether in an imagistic, linguistic or psychological sense, to create a poem which often delights through reversals of expectation regarding time and space. "Linguists (e.g. Ferdinand de Saussure) state that words are not only arbitrary, but also largely idiosyncratic signs" (*Wiki*). Idiosyncrasy here indicates "a property of words or phrases which cannot be derived by the rules of a language."[72]

photon for communication chrysanthemum for storage

blind evolution my eye

lettuce your grandmother's car

whale song
I become
an empty boat

this morning
it takes the iris to open
forever

The sweet smell
from an unknown tree
repulses the metropolis

(Fay Aoyagi *H16*; Christopher Patchel *H16*; Jim Westenhaver *H14*; Michelle Tennison *H15*; Michele Root-Bernstein *H14*; Kai Falkman *DD* 2004.)[73]

Idiosyncrasy as a dissonant *metaphorics* is here evidenced in phrasal and/or lexical relationships. For example in Aoyagi, the idiosyncratic relationship between a photon and chrysanthemum; in Patchel's "blind evolution" and his eye (I/opinion); in Westenhaver, the relationship between "lettuce" and your "grandmother's car"; in Tennison, regarding how "whale song" relates to the way one "become[s] an empty boat"; in Root-Bernstein, the temporal deformation of relations between the "forever" of "morning" and the opening of an iris; and in Falkman, the idiosyncrasy of how an unknown "sweet smell," from an unknown tree, repulses "the metropolis" (and poet).

18. Crafting of Presentation

A poem may be metaphorically crafted in a step-by-step process, much like numbers indicating steps in an instruction manual for assembling furniture, or a model. Haiku can act as models—as a *structured metaphorics*: in this case as forms of world-creation. As well, the idea of craft implies a flowing with "the grain of things": the precision, and care, taken to reveal an astounding form—the sanding smooth of surfaces until they glow.

only a drawing
of a labyrinth, only
the moon's pull

cosmos as cranium as cavern as temple as map as board game

drinking
a bowl of green tea
I stopped the war

Gettysburg
the hushed silence
of fallen snow

a long hard lie swells into perjury. spit or swallow?

> deep snow
> in a dream, I find
> her password in

(Mark Harris *H15*; Michael Nickels-Wisdom *H15*; Paul Reps *DD* 1959; Gregory Longenecker *LHA* 2012; Eve Luckring *DD* 2012; Mark Harris *HIE* 2011.)[74]

In Harris, note the symmetrical structure of two phrases separated by a midpoint comma, each beginning with the *relational* "only"—structural symmetry undergirds how the three main images (drawing, labyrinth, moon) craft the enfolded metaphorical presentation. Nickels-Wisdom uses "as" constructively, as a (metaphoric) connective, building six iterative metaphors which "forward-feed" in a serial manner, also reflecting back upon each other in imagistic feedback—again, strong symmetry is evident. In his well known "classic" haiku, Reps crafts a metaphorical world though inference, "drinking a bowl of green tea" relates to Japanese culture and Zen Buddhism specifically—these referential images are juxtaposed by the last line, "I stopped the war," which can be taken contemplatively, ironically, literally, or inferentially, at the same time.

In a more naturalistic haiku, Longenecker crafts a world with a single-word first line, "Gettysburg" possessing a potent historical resonance; referential complexity allows metaphoric worlds to build: the "hushed silence of fallen snow" therefore takes on multiple meanings beyond the literal/naturalistic. Luckring presents a mysterious subject, with several possibilities hinted at—intimate sexual relationship, and sociopolitically charged topics; the crafting of this haiku is unique, with a central period and final question-marked phrase, "spit or swallow?" causally referencing the leading phrase, "a long hard lie swells into perjury"—a raw haiku with an in-your-face kinesthetic question posed for author and reader, emanating a sexual atmosphere of psychological harm. The presentation is crafted through sharply cutting images and irruptive syntax. In Harris (a second appearance), the hanging-indent of "deep snow" becomes the entrance to the dreamer's dream, or the author's dream of the dreamer's dream (etc.), within his dream (or her's?) "I find her password in"; it's not easy to say what is literal or dream-self in this haiku—a strong sense of lucid dreaming is conveyed.

Each of these haiku reveal how a skillful crafting of *structured metaphorics* results in a creative poetics.

19. Mimesis ("Shadow of the Divine")

From as early as 500 BCE, theater became the first performative art of literature, and through this medium of expression the Greeks mimed the divine. Mimesis invites reenactments or reiterations of the sacred—origins recapitulated. The parenthetical "shadow of the divine" is meant to reflect on these Western origins, as in Ovid's creation-story of the principal elements of creation originating out of a "chaos: undigested mass of crude, confused, and scrumbled elements" (*cf. Metamorphoses*).

> Poetic originality does not spring from nothing, nor does the poet extract it from himself: it is the fruit of the encounter between that animated nature, possessing an existence of its own, and the poet's soul. (Paz, 1956, 143-44)

This is mimesis as an artwork or crafting in which presentation and ritual performance, to an extent, subsume representation.

mimesis

)sea,
  (dew

                      take it off, no
                      not the red dress the mask
                      that is the red dress

in the incandescence let me let me read me to you

                      silence   the heart   the heart   the heart

        she slips into
        the ocean the ocean
        slips into

                    one by one to the floor all of her shadows

(Sabine Miller *H15*; Donna Fleischer *H14*; Paul Pfleuger, Jr., *DD* 2011; Joseph Salvatore Aversano *LHA* 2013; Peter Yovu *HIE* 2009; George Swede *HIE* 1980.)[75]

In Miller's atomistic haiku, "mimesis" becomes a world, with "sea" and "dew" outside and inside reversed parentheses—does semantic dissonance (disfluency) here suggest how a world of being might be hidden from consciousness? Recalling Heidegger's assertion,

> The *world worlds*, and is more fully in being than the tangible and perceptible realm in which we believe ourselves to be at home. World is never an object that stands before us and can be seen. World is the ever-nonobjective to which we are subject ... (2001, 43)

From the paradoxically reversed parenthetical sea and dew—waters of micro- and macrocosmic life—a philopoetic notion occurs: a mimetic depth in which "the *world worlds*" as "the ever-nonobjective to which we are subject," is made more tangible (sensually felt) via the *unmasking* of being through poetic language. The broken syntax is irruptive, and crafted to evoke or indicate mimesis.

The "red dress" and its "mask" in Fleischer feels erotic, as *stripping* inferentially reveals what is normally hidden in being—image ("red dress") as metaphor is challenged as mask. So, to "take it off" is to unmask being; how might theatre and secrets impend, philopoetically? There is resonance here with a theatre of mimesis in the drama of the red dress as *mask*.

In Pfleuger, the "incandescence" which burns through *unmasks* cognitive dissonance in an intimate relationship, plying personal-pronoun identities of the dyadic "I" and "you" with the semantically dissonant phrases "let me let me" and "read me to you." What is revealed of two selves in being, within this incandescence?

In Aversano, the triune repetition of "the heart" beats trancelike through layers of language, *unmasking* mimesis. Yovu plays with multiple elisions of person, world and word, in pairs of mirrored repetitions (also trancelike) with "slips in ... slips in" and "the ocean ... the ocean" reflecting a mimetic sense of *metaphoria* which erotically *unmasks* form. Finally, in Swede is another form of revelation: the inference that the dropping of shadows as removal brings forth truth as an unmasking. Will the sanctity of Orphic light rescue his Persephone?

13. "Amnion," 2017

Sometimes out of conscious darkness, poetry illumines this journey or echoes it.

5) ARCHITECTURES *(Design-intention)*

By "architectures" of thought is meant, most basically: 1) design-emergent intention: the way thoughts and images conspire to construct notions; and in a further stage, 2) architectures as constructions of landscapes, worlds; and in a deeper sense, 3) architectures as animate places and spaces which inspire dwelling (*Architectures to Inspire Dwelling*).

20. Design-architecture

Design indicates necessities inherent in construction, including aesthetic, functional and sociopolitical considerations—both within the design itself and throughout the design process. In this "quality," poetic architecture is particularly evident. "A 'chaos of creation' implies 'grain' as pattern, rhythm and structure ... the potential beginnings of emergent design-architectures in poetic imagination" (*Space is the Place*).

a word
after a word
at war

the beach road the beach house the beach painting the rain afterwards

jasmine scent of the other woman is me

strawberry blonde reading thackeray with a daiquiri

spring wind
a cosplay girl
adjusts her wings

> a seed capsule bursts
> & there is
> a solar system

(Hansha Teki *H16*; Adan Breare *H15*; Roberta Beary *LHA* 2013; Carlos Colón *LHA* 2001; Carmen Sterba *LHA* 2011; John Martone *DD* 2012.)[76]

Beginning with "a word," Teki builds his poem word by word and line by line to create his "afterwards," designing an *agon* of language; Breare uses the definite noun "the" in quadruple repetition, in constructing a design-intention of story and place. In Beary, the unexpected architecture of erotic relationship ("jasmine scent") is sensually inferred via the intentional design-reversal of "other" and "me." In Colón's playful Calderian spinning-mobile rhythmicity of "strawberry blonde," his haiku offers a postmodern swim, constructing a somnambulant suburban scene reminiscent of Ashbery (excepting the rhyme, which is pure Carlos). In Sterba are the unexpected *adjustments* between reality and fantasy as a "cosplay girl" faces the wind—her "wings" crafting a poetic fantasy-play of fashion as intentional (existential) design. And in Martone, Eliade's *eternal* as an infinite cosmic return of life, time, and space are knit together by "& there is." Design-architecture burgeons in an instant as a seed capsule bursts into solaria.

21. World building, Construction

In devising this "quality," descriptions of world-building presented in Michele Root-Bernstein's book, *Inventing Imaginary Worlds* (2014) have served as inspiration, and her work suitably leads off here. A main element in haiku world-building concerns referentiality. Often, an image or word-collocation in the poem references historical events, a literary text, a scene portrayed in film, etc. Referentiality may propagate with additional iterations, as the first-reference populates itself. Following the threads of reference encapsulated in the poem provides a unique sense of *vertically deep* imaginal architecture.

mimsy borogoves words in the mouth of a snapdragon

                    still river
                    still pond
                    still winter

      Seldom   from that under-
         world   moon hooks   itself
        wind-fertilized   in birds

lunar landing shipwreck of my slave name

    manhole steam
    two men with briefcases
    from the other world

                the galactic aquarium shatters
                  our arms ending in starfish

(Michele Root-Bernstein *H16*; Don Miller *H15*; Rebecca Lilly *H14*; Tyrone McDonald *DD* 2012; Chuck Brickley *HIE* 2009; Peter Yovu *DD* 2010.)[77]

In Root-Bernstein, referentiality plays a significant role: "mimsy borogoves" is taken from the nonsense poem *Jabberwocky*, by Lewis Carroll, included in his 1871 *Through the Looking-Glass, and What Alice Found There*— with "snapdragon" being a flower that "speaks" the language of children at play (it can be manipulated with one's fingers to produce sound). Miller constructs a world through additive repetition, with each layer (or expansion) returning to "still," employed in a triune meaning: *still* as quietude, *still* as opposed to motion, and *still* as in remaining. In this way, referents may be drawn through repetition reminiscent of a chant—recalling the Dao of Lao Tzu, or woods of Thoreau—through inferential reference the constructed world encompasses the surface images overtly given.

Lilly constructs through spatial layout, building a world from "seldom" to "moon hooked" to "birds"—under-world references over-world; moon references sun—the poem as a whole perhaps referencing the Demeter-Persephone myth. McDonald's scathing and socially-potent haiku weaves together personal identity and racial history, evoking a steampunk science-fictional landscape: a "shipwreck" brings to mind slave-ship horrors of the age of sail, washing through waves of history to the near-present, with "lunar landing" a reference that recalls Neil Armstrong's Apollo 11 proclamation, "One small step ... one giant leap..."—reverberating against the history of racism and slavery in the US (and elsewhere). Brickley references popular cinema, the "men in black" of yore; and Yovu unites starfish with stars, humorously referencing domestic aquaculture, with some surprise.

22. Temenos

The notion of *temenos*, a term from Jung's lexicon, is "a means of protecting the centre of the personality from being drawn out and from being influenced from outside." Poems exemplifying the quality of *temenos* infer a *ground* from which psychological risk can be explored, within protected space. In these haiku, aspects of protection and the allowance of risk provided by sanctuary are presented with a sense of illumination, of "making the darkness conscious."

> dawn frost
> a blood-streaked
> bowl

blue swallowtail corner of the psyche

not
from here
how nothing is

autumn rain
two spaces
after the period

scattered stars
the space between us
tastes of pine

mountain
the spring sun
in its depths

(Helen Buckingham *H16*; Lee Gurga *H14*; John Martone *H14*; Christina Nguyen *LHA* 2012; Peggy Willis Lyles *LHA* 2003; Ted van Zutphen *LHA* 2011.)[78]

Within dawn's circle of frost "a blood streaked bowl" speaks to archaic sacrifice, in Buckingham; from Gurga, the "blue swallowtail corner" of psyche reflects the poet's inner work and intelligent heart; from Martone, the emptiness at the center of *temenos* is expressed in entirety, as a world: "not from here how nothing is"; in Nyugen, an indeterminate, inner space within "two spaces" portends as protection "after the period," taking on several possible meanings; in Lyles space is converted to taste ("of pine") within a *temenos* of woods (of love or loss); and in Zutphen a naturalistic scene is portrayed, in which the openness of the mountain view reveals psychic depth.

23. Precincts

Around the precincts of sanctuary, at its boundaries, are separations from the ordinary world of coming and goings of daily life—zones of safety in which depth-psychological and spiritual work commence. These poems are lent gravitas by blending the ordinary into a penetration of sanctuary reaching deep into bones. "The poem creates an architecture: story becomes stage, as a theatre of dwelling. The poem creates its own center, a 'linking back' (*religio*) to origins of presence, a mimesis of the divine" (*Theatre of the Sacred*).

morning birdsong letting the light silently in

    forest floor once upon all the time in the world

        knife cold swimming into blue bones

                slow dancing
                to Satie
                the pears ripen

spring rain
he puts everything
into words

                eye contact . . .
                we breathe this mist
                in silence

(Ken Sawitri *H16*; Michael Henry Lee *H15*; Susan Constable *H14*; Lorin Ford *H14*; Anna Maris *LHA* 2015; Hansha Teki *LHA* 2011.)[79]

These haiku each demarcate a space of mind within which something intimate, immediate and potently relational begins. Whatever the topical concern, each is framed or contextualized by a precinct, as an atmosphere or nuance. In Sawitri "morning birdsong" defines both an aural and spatial precinct; in Lee the "forest floor" moves into sacred (timeless) time; in Constable, the sudden shock of freezing water penetrates the swimmer—the precincts are dual: water and body—"swimming into" opens this space to a movement between realms; in Ford, "slow dancing to Satie" expresses private, intimate moments within a private space, within a spring garden, within a precinct of moments—perhaps of blooming love; in Maris, the sanctity—"everything"—of a relationship, is trammeled "by [his] words, with tragedy, "spring rain" inferred as tears; in Teki, an immediacy of self and other is presented sharp as a tack, yet held in an extended tension of silence, as "we breathe this mist" within a precinct of knowing and mystery, in full consciousness.

24. Construction — Sacred Construction

Frameworks pertaining to an ancient, abiding sense of the divine have been transmuted in modernity, yet retained is a link to a primordial sense of sacred construction "in bringing the Word to be ... the pure act of illumination itself ... [which] transcends the thing, the [self], the epoch" (Heidegger).

Gita chanting ...
   birds become
the ellipsis

                      cicada
                      ... not a song
                      ... not a cry
                      —just

> after the rain where perfect was holy

> moss in a fold of rock or round woman spring rain

> the wild where we learned our bodies now subdivided

> on this cold
> > spring 1
> > 2 night 3 4
> > kittens
> > wet
> > 5

(Kala Ramesh *LHA* 2016; Keith Woodruff *LHA* 2016; Sarah Rehfeldt *H14*; Mark Harris *H21* 2009; Paul Pfleuger, Jr. *DD* 2013; Marlene Mountain *HIE* 1977.)[80]

The construction of sanctuary often comes unbidden. The winding ellipsis of birds in sacred chanting, in Ramesh; the architectural construction of Woodruff's four lines build a demarked space through layout and ellipsis, creating "just" silence and presence. In Rehfeldt, the sense of sacred presence in her "after ... where perfect was holy"; the intimate world revealed in "moss in a fold of rock," in Harris. In Pfleuger, speaking to *deconstructions* of the sacred, the divided wild becomes "bodies [e.g. property, homes, neighborhoods, the Commons] subdivided." And in Mountain, a contrasting sense of *reconstruction* in the iterative appearances of kittens completing a family, through the poetic construction of time, space and number.

> Every language is secret. And conversely: every secret language ... borders on the sacred. No matter how speech may have originated, specialists seem to agree on the 'primarily mythical nature of all words and forms of language.'

Each word or group of words is a metaphor. And it is also a magical instrument…. The word is a symbol that gives off symbols … A past always susceptible to being today, the myth is a floating reality, always ready to be incarnated again. (Paz, 1956, 24, 33, 51)

25. Notions of Anarchic Sanctuary

The desire for self-authenticity may lead to the seeking out or creation of anarchic sanctuaries, with reference to "the desert of modernity." Indeed, authenticity of the heart may only become a socially shared possibility within alternative societies. Experiences of such societies are hinted at in the poems below. These works were selected out of several hundred appearing in the *LHA*, by popular vote of the respondents appearing in *Beyond the Salon*.

fireflies
& soul
fragments

>winding roads to nowhere rituals

>another home
>stars resting
>in a river

>>numerically speaking the soul sucks

fireflies
beyond
the sarcasm

>sing at dawn sing at dusk when women were birds

(Michelle Tennison *H16*; Stella Pierides *H14*; Adjei Agyei-Baah *LHA* 2016; Stella Pierides *LHA* 2016; John Stevenson *LHA* 2016; Pat Geyer *LHA* 2016.)[81]

In each haiku, two themes intertwine: anarchic society and freedom—both can be seen as transgressive—acts of resistance, regarding normative consensuality. In Tennison, the image of "fireflies" as/and "soul fragments" evokes an ephemeral light: the consciousness of virtual others; in Pierides, life seems but a path of "winding roads to nowhere"—does the poet accept or reject the "rituals" implied, as a last word? In Agyei-Baah, moving into a new home, will the poet find a new sense of community, or become constrained by isolation? In Pierides (in a second appearance), a playfully biting, ironic comment regarding society is inferred: "the soul sucks" numerically (quantitatively), as value. A gentler irony is employed by Stevenson, with "beyond the sarcasm"—whose fireflies, like Tennison's, hint at a sense of soul; in Geyer, a mythic chorus of birdsong evokes an anarchic sanctuary creation-story—women as birds of animate joy, mythical in utterance, and delight in flight.

Thematic strands of freedom, anarchic society, love, and the poem-act are interwoven by Paz, who writes on the importance of transgression. In his view, a stark contrast exists between (eastern) Buddhist and (western) Protestant views: "Unlike transgressions in the West, which are aggressions tending to destroy, or to abolish, [on] the contrary, the transgression of Tantrism has as its aim to reintegrate—again, to *reincorporate*—all substances" (1969).[82] In a study of Paz's poetics, Jason Wilson (1979) comments:

> Paz envisages the poem-act as analogous to the love-act.... because love is such an intense passion it is condemned by all societies. For Paz all acts of what he defines as love are immoral, scandalous; Paz's view of love provokes and challenges society, since it is totally anarchic and natural experience beyond classification, societal morality, or common sense.... To defend love is antisocial, dangerous and revolutionary, and poetry reflects this explosive

love; it too bursts out in strange and pure forms; it too breaks laws: both love and poetry are transgressions. (115-16)

Wilson articulates Paz's insistence concerning the transgressive and (therefore) "scandalous" nature of love—as a means to "to reintegrate ... *reincorporate.*" Paz sees the poetry of love, and the poem itself as an act of love, representing intelligence of the heart, indicating also a resistance to the status quo, as "the poem act ... provokes and challenges society." Love and the poem-act often arise out of collaboratively-alterative societies, via the *himma* of Corbin: "ardently desiring ... [a] vital force, soul, heart, intention, thought, desire." And in Hillman's view, "the lion, the wound and the rose" of the heart are requisite to the discovery of authenticity (*cf. Beyond the Salon*).

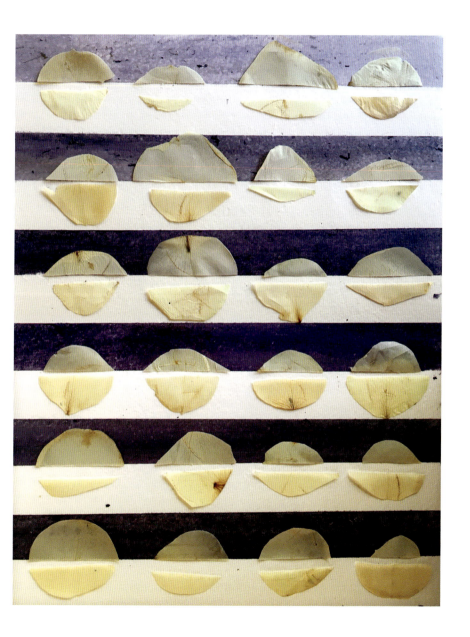

14. "Surface and Depth," 2017

Ambient atmospheres: delicacy of feeling, a resonance which lifts away from gravity; buoyancies, a softening in receptive tone. Hesitancy, gentleness, sadness, longing— distance and intimacies . . .

6) SOUL (Explorative Desire)

26. Soul (as Core Value)

What can be said for poetry? In today's world, something needs to be said, and we could be saying more, concerning which poems we praise. How it is for a soul to find, for however brief a time, novel orientations of landscape, to adopt new shapes and forms of imaginal space through novel surprises, discontinuities and sonorities? And how many ideas change a life? (*Poetry and the Beauty of Distance*).

These haiku address soul directly—within each, an aura of sanctuary is resonant—apart from realism, yet not alienated from it.

fresh snow sadness for the old sadness

                                          incomplete beings
                                          you and me
                                        complete the city

the rain song of our broken machine grief

                                          sunken grinding stone
                                          stories told of herbs
                                          that made us men

deep inside you no more war

                      that we could flower where the earth is so

(John Stevenson *H16*; Kala Ramesh *H14*; Lorin Ford, *H21* 2009; Adjei Agyei-Baah *LHA* 2015; Dietmar Tauchner *HIE* 2006; Peter Yovu, *H21* 2010.)[83]

The term "soul" is meant in a depth-psychological sense (via Hillman) as "that unknown component which makes meaning possible [and] turns events into experiences ... the imaginative possibility in our natures, experiencing through reflective speculation, dream, image, and fantasy" (1975). These haiku attend to a mysterious deepening of images, with soul as a core value.

In Stevenson, the contemplation of "fresh ... sadness for the old sadness" in connection to winter snow. In Ramesh, a dyadic incompleteness "complete[s] the city." In Ford, "rain song"; as a deepening of soul, through the wound of "our broken machine grief." In Agyei-Baah, cultural and ancestral knowledge, largely absented in contemporary life, speak to a loss of soul: those "stories ... that made us men." In Tauchner, the call (or query?) to find "no more war" at the core of self; and similarly in Yovu, the conditional question, "that we could flower" upon a poetic earth where "the earth is so" (revealed, known, evident). Via poetic imagination, soul *deepens*.

27. Remembrance and Distance

Another way that soul finds refulgence through the poem is via distance. In Simone Weil's philopoetic statement (key to Milosz's critical stance), "Distance is the soul of beauty," remembrance also is a form of distance. In these haiku, temembrance and distance are often paired (or opposed) in dialectical tension with intimacy.

I listen to the sea
hoping to catch
where something begins

full moon
I feel my child
and its shadow

their wings like cellophane remember cellophane

                                                harvest moon –
                                                even if that was all
                                                there was

Caprifolium.
In the gray twilight
He awakened to his sex.

                                              moist of rocks lips touch a past

(Jack Galmitz *H15*; Ramesh Anand *H14*; Lorin Ford *H21* 2009; Sondra J. Byrnes *LHA* 2013; Dag Hammarskjöld *DD* 1959, 2006; Johannes S. H. Bjerg *DD* 2011.)[84]

Have we forgotten the elements of the world, those aspects of nature's body that connect us to things on a level more intimate and important than that of simple possession?… It is no long stretch to discern that what happens to the land happens as well to language. Language and landscape are of a psychic and spiritual piece. (Slattery, 2006)

These haiku call to memory: "I listen to the sea hoping to catch …" in Galmitz; to feel under the full moon not only "my child" but "the shadow," in Anand; the mysterious conceptual blending in the simile "wings like cellophane" re-membering (*re-membering*) "cellophane" in Ford; the call, through distance, to memory honored—(if tinged with regret): "even if that was all there was," in Byrnes. The "grey twilight" of distance and remembrance in awakening "to his sex" (sensually portrayed by *Caprifolium*, honeysuckle stamen) in Hammarskjöld. And in Bjerg, the intimate present of one's lips eliding with "moist of rocks" to "touch" (kiss) "a past."

28. Grit, Guts

The idea of *grit* is not usually seen as a qualitative description in literary criticism. This is a determination of spirit—fight—the struggle and power to continue to live and create. Hillman (as with Milosz and Lorca, earlier quoted) muses on the artist's bravery as "a companion of the dead," acting as a bridge between realms of inhabitation:

> Is the mountain emerging from the fog or receding into it? Near and Far, both. Suppose we imagine the dead are partly living and the living are partly dead, inhabitants of both all the time, essentially. Receding and emerging always. Does this account for the romantic fantasy of the artist as courting death. Perhaps, in fact, the artist courts death, must court death. So that his/her living is a living death. Courts death with romanticized "self-destructive tendencies"; illness, drugs, drink, risk and folly. A vibrant life among shades. So that someone with softened or amplified permeability—the artist say—is a companion of the dead and is more with the dead than those who live only on this side of the wall, walled off, merely living—the denial of death. Artist. Resident of bothville. (Hillman & McLean, 2011)

The haiku below speak to this quality of sanctuary, as told by residents of "bothville."

    anorexic river stepping over like love

                            the phantom limb of believing
                            war is over

            clinging to work clinging to home cicadas

                            predator drone the butterfly is yellow

just a shell
this bombed out
child

                          tamarind
                          the bitter sweetness
                          of pregnancy

(Jon Baldwin *H14*; Robert Epstein *H14;* Kate MacQueen *H14*; Johnny Baranski *LHA* 2013; Sara Winteridge *LHA* 2014; Shrikaanth Krishnamurthy *LHA* 2015.) [85]

"It ain't what you do, it's how you do it," Dizzy Gillespie writes[86]; poets sing towards death, as residents of *bothville*. Stepping over the river of anorexia (near to death), in Baldwin; Epstein's amputated limb, a permanent disfigurement as a "phantom"—the gift of war; "clinging to work" with the cutting sense of life's impermanence (as "cicadas"), in MacQueen; the cruel irony of a "predator drone" invisibly bringing death as though a butterfly, in Baranski; the PTSD witnessed in a shell-shocked child, in Winteridge. And the life/death gain and loss implied in the "bitter sweetness" of tamarind in pregnancy, in Krishnamurthy.

29. Desire, Passion

Desire and passion frame our lives, and poetry may arise as forms of *eros*—to those who wander out of love, looking for answers to prayers for love. Perhaps to meet their mate, or *that* tree, *that* poetic angel, *those* moments of unity, harmony, surcease—*that* perfect cup of tea shared with another.

"Metaphor and meaning would remain rational sciences in 'stiff and stubborn, man-locked set' lacking a desire for imaginal inhabitation—these are generally indescribable qualitative experiences, each of individually unique" (*Secrecy*).

desires flicker
on the tips of my fingers
summer stars

        weighing his answer
        to the nearest gram —
        a scent of nutmeg

                inside you
                a black tulip
                cups the evening
                sun

columbine, by any other name

        whatever happens
        the song
        of the river

        red candle i enter your narrative

(Victor Ortiz *H15*; Sandra Simpson *H15*; S. M. Abeles *H14*; David Caruso *H14*; Coralie Berhault-Creuzet *LHA* 2012; Roberta Beary *LHA* 2010.)[87]

These haiku tempt: "desires flicker" in Ortiz, right "on the tips" of his fingers, "summer stars." In Simpson, the "scent of nutmeg" steals the scales, as a weighing of heart. In Abeles, in a more surrealistic mode: "inside you" a dark midnight sun exotically lights "a black tulip"; and in Caruso "by any other name," as an intention, seems to call out, in longing for love. (An alternate interpretation references the Columbine school massacre, 1999.) In Berhault-Creuzet is the beginning of romance ("song of the river") and a willingness, the emotional openness to 'go with it' "whatever happens." And in Beary, another form of desire ("red candle") is expressed minimally with delicacy, in the eloquently nuanced penetration, "i enter your narrative."

30. Emotion

"In valuing uniqueness and finding visibility in socially-alternative societies, one gains soul. In order to let lions roar ..." (*Beyond the Salon*); this journey is difficult as emotional challenges are involved in breaking through social consensus. Too often, Hillman writes "we do not face emotion in honesty and live it consciously. Instead emotion hangs as a negative background." An impasse which poetry and anarchic sanctuaries seek to ameliorate:

> The refusal to meet the challenge of emotion, this *mauvaise foi* [inauthenticity; existential bad faith] of consciousness is fundamental to our "age of anxiety." It is characteristic of—even instrumental in—what has been called "the contemporary failure of nerve." We do not face emotion in honesty and live it consciously. Instead emotion hangs as a negative background shadowing our age with anxiety and erupting in violence. A "therapy" of this condition depends altogether upon a change in the attitude of consciousness toward emotion ... (1989, 274)

The haiku below reveal the potent ability of poetry to pierce the "background shadow" of repressed emotion, bringing difficult issues to the fore.

dotting an i dotting an i death verse

generic sunlight
the broken embryo's
apostrophe

gunfire the length of the playground

> grieving mosquito dead too, dead too

> back from the war
> all his doors
> swollen shut

> I return home
> without an arm, a leg . . .
> drifting clouds

(Lee Gurga *H16*; Roberta Beary *H15*; John McManus *H15*; Ernesto Santiago *H15*; Bill Pauly *HIE* 2011; Dick Whyte *LHA* 2013.)[88]

Working on a written eulogy, through a repetition of language, the poet, "dotting an i dotting an i" (mimetically) impels the reader to empathize with the loss of a loved one, and a need to speak to the authentic heart, in Gurga. The "broken embryo's apostrophe" is the end of a life—it may be the cracking of a breakfast egg, though a human loss more intimate (and painful) is implied by the harshly impersonal "generic sunlight" and disjunctive "apostrophe" of the embryo (as well as literal apostrophe)—inferring a pause or break in life, in Beary. There is present danger and reference to ongoing school killings "gunfire the length of the playground"—these too-familiar emotions of horror and disbelief surrounding this issue, in McManus. In Santiago, the repetition of "dead too" seems likewise referential: the loss of a loved one—the "mosquito dead too" implying needlessness, insignificance and a tragic sense; the double-entendre of "all his doors swollen shut"—both as a physical home long abandoned, and a psychologic state, impel an emotional confrontation for the reader, if not for the war victim unable to handle ongoing trauma, in Pauly. And in Whyte, with "I return home" only the bare facts are given: the reader is left to fill in the emotional blanks of missing limbs in "drifting clouds."

31. With Risk

Without risk there can be no honest passion; no way to meet with what is beyond oneself. With risk often come wounds; a truism of love, if not of bungee-jumping. Below, a few quotes on the topic, drawn from contemporary literature:

> We need people in our lives with whom we can be as open as possible. To have real conversations with people may seem like such a simple, obvious suggestion, but it involves courage and risk. (Moore, 1992)

> Do you want me to tell you something really subversive? Love is everything it's cracked up to be. That's why people are so cynical about it. It really is worth fighting for, being brave for, risking everything for. And the trouble is, if you don't risk anything, you risk even more. (Jong, 1973)

> There is no discovery without risk and what you risk reveals what you value. (Winterson, 1992)

There is no way around risk for those who seek poetic feeling. At the same time, ordinary life is inevitably linked to ordinary death as companion—we might strive to avoid risk, seek defensive shelter through repression of emotional feeling, etc.—though there is another way: sanctuary as *temenos* can function as a space within which one *can* risk. Sometimes out of *conscious darkness* the poet illumines this journey, or echoes it.

    in his buttonhole our forgotten war

                    oncologist's aquarium the goldfish know

cardiogram . . .
this trembling distance
between us

        A small pool of blood—
        Killed in air raid:
        little girl and her huge doll

what swallows me more
this vacant lot
or the baby in my arms

                an i just fine enough to hit a vein

(Fay Aoyagi *H14*; Steven Carter *H14*; Paresh Tiwari *LHA* 2013; Vladimir Devidé *LHA* 1993; Tyrone McDonald *DD* 2012; John Stevenson *DD* 2011.)[89]

"Everything in the Universe is an echo" says Bachelard. "And birds," he says "are the first creators of sound." From their sudden permanence, we learned poetry.... Bachelard: "Imagination is a sound-effects man; it must amplify or soften." That is the agency, that is the willing work: tuning in, turning up, dying down. "Amplify or soften." All things flow ... the oldest insight of Western philosophy. (Hillman, 2016)

The poems here speak of risks taken, communiques from moments in lives—in Milosz's words, there is "a distance achieved" due to the passage of time, in which the poet does "not change events, landscapes, human figures into a tangle of shadows growing paler and paler. On the contrary, [the poet] can show them in full light ..." With risk, the character of life becomes sharply etched.

The remembrance of lives through a "buttonhole" in the war, in Aoyagi; news received of cancer, in Carter. In Tiwari, the heart read by a scientific instrument is the vehicle of shocking news imaged in "the trembling distance between" doctor and patient. Among the most graphic haiku here, Devidé bears witness at the war front: "Killed in air raid: little girl ..."; like Devidé, McDonald presents a desperate situation and a war: "what swallows me more"—if of a different kind. How to care for a baby in dire economic circumstances? And in Stevenson, the sardonic humor of "an i just fine enough" to shoot up (recalling Simon & Garfunkel's, "bridge over troubled water")—empathy for those in pain—the question of social care pierces this reader.

With risk, poetic imagination is linked with distance, death and remembrance—living in risk, poets make the darkness more conscious, so that we may also see.

The Soul's distinct connection
With immortality
Is best disclosed by Danger
Or quick Calamity—

As Lightning on a Landscape
Exhibits Sheets of Place—
Not yet suspected—but for Flash—
And Click—and Suddenness.

(Emily Dickinson, poem 974)

15. "The Spectral City," 2017

*Perhaps a drowning man can be saved, when pulled
into an insolent color by hydrangea, even if maimed—
a revision of consciousness devoutly wished for.*

7) THE "THIRD" ("Hypothetical" Humanity)

This is a "third" place or zone of knowing, neither fictional nor non-fictional: a *mythopoetic* reality. Between chaos and cosmos is a *third thing*, at a distance. How to define this distance? Perhaps as a process of psychological deepening, a discovering or intuiting of "the grain of things." Akin to the *metaxic* realm in depth psychology, as Hillman writes, "this intelligence [of the heart] takes place by means of images which are a third possibility between mind and world": Machado's "third thing" between living and dreaming lies at the heart of the poem, encompassing ideas of *imaginal* poetic space.

32. Distance

Invoking a third. Of the qualities of *thoughtspace*, this one is difficult to describe, though hints are found in the poems below. What lies between realism and imagination, between living and dreaming, is a particular form of sanctuary; a space of *poiesis*. It seems most fragile and nuanced, insignificant and ephemeral—yet it calls or we call, in seeking deeper, more enriching, increasingly multiple, multifarious dimensions of knowing in psyche.

Wallace Stevens refers to this poetical process as "enlargement" (quoted at the end of this Chapter).

two ballerinas in one skin a newborn foal

                        how deer
                        materialize
                        twilight

night of small colour
a part of the underworld
becomes one heron

>   you whisper
>   just your sometimes
>
>   pretty sure my red is your red
>
>   her going in her coming the rain before it falls

(Peter Yovu *H16*; Scott Mason *HIE* 2008; Alan Summers *H15*; Brendan Slater *H14*; John Stevenson *DD* 2009; Jim Kacian *H21* 2008.)[90]

Invoking a "third" reality or poetic space occurs frequently in poetry—though as mythopoesis, is not overtly given in the text; under purview is the phenomenology of reader reception. Each of these examples points to a "third" realm of being in consciousness—at some distance. For instance, the "foal" envisaged by "two ballerinas in one skin" is an existence at some distance between fact and fiction, in Yovu. The space in which deer seem to materialize both *themselves* and/or *twilight itself*, in Mason; the mythopoesis evident in the semantic twist of "small colour" of night, a part of which "*becomes* one heron," in Summers; the whispered and distant "third" space of "just your *sometimes*," in Slater; the intermediate "third" space existing between meaning and unknowing, within intimate relationship, evoked by the idiomatic degree-adverbial "pretty sure" in Stevenson, concerns the perceptual disfluency of "red" within the intimate relations of a couple. And in Kacian, the distance created by paradoxical spatial and temporal removals in "the rain *before* it falls" invokes a quiescence or pause, conceptually juxtaposed with "her coming and going"—an 'as if' hypotheticality—*eventual* action merges with the precience of rain.

33. Forms of Resistance

Here, resistance indicates the poet's resistance to denials of hypothetical reality, and resistance to soul-erasure. Concerning *poiesis*, everything leads to mythopoetic landscape, in psyche. These poems break with levity, cutting through habitual expectation and offering social commentary.

> what's left of us
> caves
> on Mars

> beheading over the edge of space

> BEHEADING
> green light

> cold rain –
> my application
> to become a crab

> nothing rhymes with it Agent Orange

> less and less nature is nature

(Deborah P Kolodji *H16*; Brent Goodman *H15*; Scott Metz *H15*; Fay Aoyagi *H21* 2002; Christina Nguyen *H14*; Marlene Mountain *HIE* 1986.)[91]

Implying a possible-future as a conditional mythopoetic space in which humanity might or might not have survived on our nearby exo-planet, in Kolodji—what lies in that Martian cave might be dust, or bones—in any case, markings of lost dreams and survival-error. In Goodman are reflected terrorist images of barbaric horror ("beheading"), with a twist—as sociopolitical statement, the "third" space of "over the edge" resonates with socioeconomic and cultural issues. Metz addresses a similar theme in his screaming one-word headline "BEHEADING," with "green light" as a response to cut it off—or in consequence, to bomb. Aoyagi addresses the dark mythopoesis of the work-world, projecting the inevitability "to become a crab" via acceptance of her work application. Nguyen poses a conceptual-blend as a semantic puzzle-rhyme-challenge of bio-genocide—the reader is asked to envision its answer: *does* anything rhyme with "Agent Orange"? And in Mountain, iterative worldplay deepens a key contradiction of our era—what is meant by "less nature"? And *how much* "less" will suffice?

Each of these haiku takes a critical stance of resistance regarding social violence, inhumane and ignorant destruction.

34. Inhabitation (Dwelling)

Each sanctuary is a dwelling with borders, boundaries and a center—spaces, precincts and zones—walls, gates, cornices, portholes, and viewpoints. Yet *inhabitation* involves more than entering; more than just existing within a space. Inhabitation is living, breathing, experiencing, animately: *dwelling* in such spaces, through the medium of poiesis. In these haiku selections, inhabitation is evoked as a *sanctity* of absences.

> stolen wombs –
> the wind brings only dust to the
> village well

> > Geiger counter
> > still singing to the radishes –
> > Fukushima Day

> I see through
> you to the rain
> the rain to you

> higgs boson …
> deepening henna pattern –
> on the first night

first poem –
not in a language
mother speaks

> riverside
> a crocodile waits
> in a monkey shadow

(Sonam Choki *H14*; Brent Goodman *H14;* Bill Pauly *DD* 2012; Paresh Tiwari *LHA* 2013; Tzetzka Ilieva *LHA* 2012; Adjei Agyei-Baah *LHA* 2016.)[92]

Missing life as "stolen wombs," a missing culture, missing village, and missing also, its ruined well—Sonam Choki envisions the inhabitation of absence in a living community as it had once been. The fruits of an anniversary of nuclear disaster are *presenced* in Goodman, who propels the reader into a mythopoetic landscape *where no one must go*; Pauly's "see through" well-expresses psyche's 'seeing through' literal form—as a mergence of inhabitation. Tiwari juxtaposes symbolic values of ancient lifeways and the "god particle" of quantum physics on a marriage night, "deepening" mysteriously—the two worlds of ancient tradition and science—do they fruitfully merge, or collide? Evoked is the marriage bed on the first night. In Ilieva is projected the inhabitation of a novel "otherness" of culture through the poem itself, having been written in English—"not in a language mother speaks"—communication between mother and daughter is thus aborted. And in Agyei-Baah, the poet is present on the riverside near his Ghananian home, among the light and shadow of hidden (or absent) animal presences—inhabitations *presencing* a timeless metamorphic abiding.

35. Place

It seems odd to write about place as *hypothetical*. But places often cease to exist, as these poems reveal. Sometimes "place" is a space in mind which only the poem provides—the external space represented has been denied existential presence. Ultimately, "place" is our map of being from which we navigate, towards (and from) which we journey through our days. It's also the environment of civilization (so-called)—or the wilds (so-called). It's this "so-called" which emblematizes the *hypotheticality* of language. Poems such as these allow the resurrection or reconstruction what has been abandoned to obscurity.

> a bag of them
> figs
> without a country

>> nagasaki . . .
>> in her belly, the sound
>> of unopened mail

> bleeding under my skin the American dream

> in the prison graveyard
> just as he was in life –
> convict 14302

>> television light
>> lies on the
>> American lawn

dense fog
a bullock cart
rides into obscurity

(Johannes S. H. Bjerg *H16*; Don Baird *H14*; Eve Luckring *DD* 2010; Johnny Baranski *HIE* 2006; Joseph Massey *HIE* 2005; Mamta Madhavan *LHA* 2013.)[93]

In Bjerg, figs (i.e. people, refugees) "without a country"; in Baird, within the sanctity of the womb, the atomic destruction of all life at Nagasaki; in Luckring, the "third" space of (American) myth bleeds "under my skin"; in Baranski, the ironic humor of what is left of identity, from a death in prison—convict as number. In Massey, the double-entendre of "lies" (on the lawn, or as untruth) of "television light; and in Madhavan, the present obscurely merges with the past as a "bullock cart rides into obscurity."

Place exists at the heart of each poem's mythopoetic landscape. Absences and erasures are recapitulated, remarked upon, and reconstructed as presences.

36. Consciousness — Revisions of World and Self

To revise is to be remade. We are ourselves revising cell-by-cell with each breath. Cognitive science has shown that memory is often more hypothetical then we realize—even the most precious, memorialized images we conjure of the past as real (a past as true as the sense of ourselves); memory has been found to concatenate into iconic gestalts—as a result we remain somewhat mythopoetic, self-storied beings. The ability of literature, as with memory itself, to revision consciousness is here likened to a poem.

> windfall apples
> what I think about
> what I think

> > > fogged into the familiar dying peripheral

> > a drowning man
> > pulled into violet worlds
> > grasping hydrangea

> > > > vast blue sky –
> > > > the freedom that
> > > > never was

> > daydreaming how quickly my mind

> > > > afternoon rain
> > > > emptying a book
> > > > of its words

(Carolyn Hall *HIE* 2009; Susan Diridoni *H14*; Richard Gilbert *HIE* 2004; Kashinath Karmakar; *LHA* 2013; Don Baird *LHA* 2014; Peter Newton *H15*.)[94]

It may be that in windfall apples, "what I think about what I think" is one answer to how a *moment* becomes a *mind*, and how mind takes on gravitas—gravity as Newton's apple measured in its fall—this is what I think about *what I think*, in Hall. Fogged into the familiar; a dying of peripheral vision, the loss of the known, perhaps of a loved one, and a coming to grips with wings that flew and are now memorialized—a resurrection hinted at, in Diridoni. Perhaps a drowning man can be saved, when pulled into an insolent color by hydrangea, even if maimed—a revision of consciousness devoutly wished for, in Gilbert.

The vast blue sky—the freedom *that never was* represents a savage revision, in Karmakar. And in Baird, "daydreaming how quickly my mind" revises the world, and self, within the rapidity of ephemerally imaginal comings and goings. Finally, in Newton the afternoon rain empties a book of words, implying an emptying and revision of self.

> Poet and painter alike live and work in the midst of a generation that is experiencing essential poverty in spite of fortune. The extension of the mind beyond the range of the mind, the projection of reality beyond reality, the determination to cover the ground, whatever it may be, the determination not to be confined, the recapture of excitement and intensity of interest, the enlargement of the spirit at every time, in every way, these are the unities, the relations, to be summarized as paramount now. (Stevens, 1951)

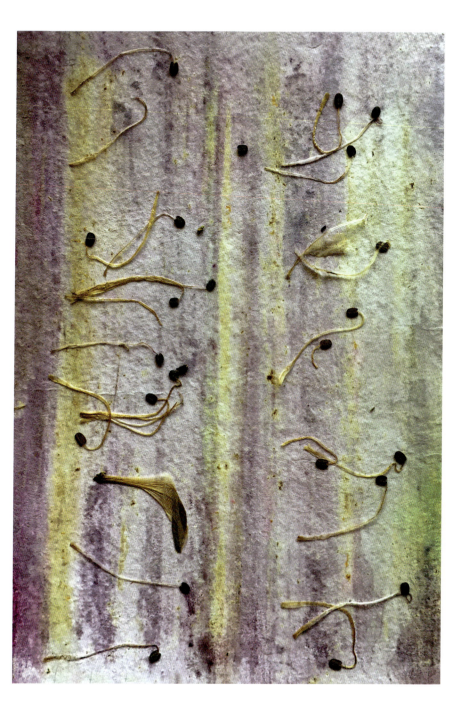

16. "Volitional Formations," 2017

we have to be born again into our uniqueness

Conclusion

Permeability

> Artists work in an imagistic space. A space that has no beginning, no end, no middle. When is an artwork finished? When is a dream finished? The image seems to want to go on. Cézanne said a painting is complete at every stage of the work even if it is never finished. (Mclean in Hillman & McLean, *Permeability*, 2011).

How we dwell has much to do with how we *imagine* we dwell—"in a space that has no beginning, no end, no middle." Depending upon our sense of imagination, how we order the self (self-*meaning*) remains mutable, evolves over a lifetime. Lacking interiority, the space of thought is unable to thrive. In relationship with sanctuary, imaginative space inspires free-thinking, deepening notions of self—a self-educative process of exploration.

We order "self" daily, particularly through language-use—each sentence, however ephemeral, is formed as a *truth* of thought, as self-made story.[95] With Hillman's sense of image in mind, that "images don't stand for anything … they are psyche itself in its imaginative visibility"—and as Weil suggests, "we reconstruct for ourselves the order of the world in an image," the development of personal philosophy as an "order of the world" occurs imaginatively, in ongoing philopoetic reconstructions.

Permeability as shared, collaborative invention is "membranous, osmotic … seducible, seditious"—challenging the status quo via visionary incursion:

> I am concerned, beyond art-making, with the psychology of the incoming… the *invenio*, [which] Catholicism calls the Annunciation—the descent of logos into physical matter, the all-too-solid flesh. I am concerned less with what comes in than with the incurring, the fact of human permeability, the ordinary, quotidian and ubiquitous fact of visionary, ideational, auditory, symptomatic, and personified incursions. Why can fantasy-thinking not be shut out? The composer, the painter, the writer are not special human exceptions. They are the subtle more vulnerable examples—not of "weak ego," but of the essential

nature of the human mind, that it is membranous, osmotic, susceptible, suggestible, seducible, seditious, hysterical. (Hillman, *Permeability*, 2011)

Poetic engagement is an intimate and generally private affair, often requiring extensive periods of non-distraction. In constructing novel mythopoetic architectures, poems as philopoetic enactments inspire psychological nuance and sophistication. From the perspective of thoughtspace, poetic imagination permeates and animates the intelligence of the heart.

Poetic Force and Imaginal Space at Liberty

Concerning "qualities" and "properties" of thought, each poem forges novel permutations—the value of a poem is obviously the poem itself—but there is a different order of value in aggregate, as poetry represents a *collective* livingness, an animating force of humanity invigorating and enriching landscapes of thought and feeling through *presences*.

One act of the poem is to memorialize; another is the evocation of philopoetics. Awakening the sense of what is interior, body, mind and world are brought anew into being. Poetically, one's *dwelling* changes with each new story.

Concerning the haiku genre in particular, poems *infer* properties of thoughtspace. This notion—of distance from objective reality *and* objectively interpretable text—lends haiku a unique value, as such poems often invoke thoughtspace through a "third" sense of psycho-poetic *imaginal space*: modes of ambiguous inference that lie "between living and dreaming." This is a remarkable space to invoke, and artistically definitive.

Temporal compression into "the specious present" produces concentrated effects on consciousness that linger, as the very brief poem requires the reader to complete in imagination partial psychic landscapes and hypothetical possible worlds in the partial stories given. In this way haiku encourage interior, soulful exploration.

When imagination as a value becomes fraught, lacks a precinct, a *temenos* within which to dwell, when the spaces (and places) of sanctity wherein psychological risks can be taken are fragmented and diminished, democratic liberty is in doubt. From this perspective, poetry provides and promotes an ethics of freedom.

An Ethics of Freedom

This book is a manifesto on poetic imagination as soulful inhabitation, and has sought to present a road-map of qualities of engagement through illustrative demonstration—ways to enter and freely explore imaginative spaces. Regarding thoughtspace and poetic value, new forms of philopoetic thinking and volition, how can we nurture and care for these qualities? And more broadly foster greater psychological complexity, enriching presence, in life? Observing the contemporary zeitgeist, novelist and public intellectual Elif Shafak remarks:

> [W]hen things get too confusing, many people crave simplicity. This is a very dangerous crossroads, because it's exactly where the demagogue enters into the picture. The demagogue understands how collective sentiments work and how he—it's usually a he—can benefit from them. He tells us that we all belong in our tribes, and he tells us that we will be safer if we are surrounded by sameness.... All these figures, at first glance—they seem disconnected. But I think they feed each other, and they need each other. And all around the world, when we look at how demagogues talk and how they inspire movements, I think they have one unmistakable quality in common: *they strongly, strongly dislike plurality. They cannot deal with multiplicity.* Adorno used to say, "Intolerance of ambiguity is the sign of an authoritarian personality."... What if [this] same intolerance of ambiguity [is] the mark of our times, of the age we're living in?... So, slowly and systematically, *we are being denied the right to be complex.*
>
> [S]ingular identities [are] also an illusion, because we all have a multiplicity of voices inside.... I think this is what tribalism does to us. It shrinks

our minds, for sure, but it also shrinks our hearts .... I think East and West, *we are losing multiplicity, both within our societies and within ourselves.* (21 September 2017, "The Revolutionary Power of Diverse Thought," *TED*; emphasis added)

Shafak's remarks offer a valuable perspective regarding an ethics of freedom, consisting in part of psychological resistance to "simplicity"—the certainties of literalism—and their incipient, reductive psychologies. She ends her talk, "one should never, ever, remain silent for fear of complexity."

The Latin root of "education" (*E+ducere*) means *to lead or draw out*. Chomsky (in Jones 2012) comments, "the highest goal in life is to inquire and create, to search the riches of the past ... to carry that quest for understanding further, in your own way." To give voice and greater tangibility to poetic imagination, without reducing the inherent mystery of the poetic process is educative in this sense. Poetry promotes self-agency, regarding spiritual and psychological change:

> Soul is intimate, embedded in life, vital and energetic. It seems to constantly want more life and vitality and therefore can be a threat to the status quo.... Soul offers a deep and powerful sense of identity ... It asks that we each become individuals, not so identified with the structures around us ... we have to be born again into our own individuality and uniqueness. (Moore, 2014)

A discussion of identity, authenticity and creativity underscores *Beyond the Salon*, where poets from different walks of life shared experiences of arts-collaborative anarchic sanctuary—social spaces where individual creative thought and expression is seen as a primary value.

Yet the poem becomes distant as life intrudes—how much of the sense of sanctuary is retained, in remembrance? The "necessary angel" of poetic necessity indicates that imagination is only as viable as we are willing to acknowledge these experiences and give them voice—to allow our poetic heart to be contacted, and thereby flower in others.

Poets bring animal presences: the raw, animate *beingness* of language as autonomous psychic creativity. As adults, we often live in our heads, dreaming as animals, finding our greatest freedom in thoughtspace—yet the poem also exists beyond us, a creative gift from another—as an artwork birthing mythopoetic realities. Poems provide a *religio,* linking us back to an ensouled world.

Authenticity is one result of the heart's knowing, arising from an environment of "richly interconnected, interdependent" ecologies of world and thought. Following this logic, poetic insight interweaves aesthetic sensibility throughout factual, fictive and intersubjective realms of knowing. Thinking freely and thinking well, the heart sources its intelligence from a beloved world.

VII. Appendix 1. 36 Qualities of Thoughtspace

Outline: 36 Qualities — 7 Properties of Thoughtspace

Verbose Description

Below are presented connections from: 1) "thoughtspace property" to a 2) "property quality"; each "quality" is then linked to a 3) a textual reference in preceding sections of the book. Exceptions concern three linguistics terms: "neologism," "unusuality" and "alternativity"—citations for these are in the Endnotes (language and figuration are addressed in Chap. 1, Sections 5-7).

1) SPACE

1. **Minimal Creation** ("'Sunny-side up or over-easy' for breakfast may lead to a well of knowing that reaches into the depths of soul for the taste of life incarnate, or be passed by unnoticed as a mere incidental, depending on one's sense of poetry and philosophy." Sunny-side Up); 2. **Novel Worlds** ("We spawn imaginary alternative worlds ..." *Between Meaning and Unknowing*); 3. **Immeasurability** ("Mind is fundamentally poetic in nature: root metaphors of imaginative possibility are 'the poetic basis of mind': there is no ultimate, literal truth or final equation to codify—no last, definitive image or explanation." *Immeasurability*); 4. **Unknown Unknowns** ("There are plenty of unknowns in 'nonvisible and nonliteral inherence.'" *Soul* ; *cf. Endnote 21*).

"Any perceptual surface has the potential to become metaphorically deep if we choose to contemplate it, seeing through mythopoetically." (*Sunny-side Up in Space*)

2) LANGUAGE

5. **Concreta vs Abstracta** (*Abstracta* construct indefinite space; *concreta* can be concrete objects, measurables, tangibles (including language) which provide 'structure preserving functions'; the human face is measureable in this sense—the uniqueness of the human face is not." *Forethought*; *cf. Endnote 11*);

6. **Conceptual Blending** ("Elements and relationships from diverse templates of thought are conceptually 'blended' in a subconscious process which is assumed to be ubiquitous to everyday thought and language." *Immeasurability*);

7. **Neologism** (Collocational unusuality; "fresh images in a poem become origin-points creating imaginal worlds." *Poetry and the Beauty of Distance*);

8. **Possible Worlds** ("Mental spaces are partial structures [that] are dynamically created when we think and talk. They are somewhat similar to possible worlds." *Endnote 23*); 9. **Inferred Narratives** ("In doing so much with so little [haiku] are unique exemplifications of poetic imagination ... and serve as a means to illustrate how the space of thought may be activated or 'performed' by both reader and composer ... haiku mysteriously open us to this space." *Introduction*; *cf*. Turner, 1996); 10. **"Staging" Theatres of Story** ("From altar, to the book and stage—from divine presence to democratic *polis*—the lineage of the sacred as literary tradition persists in the practice and production of contemporary poems and plays." *Theatre of the Sacred*).

"The uniqueness of images can be treated as *poiesis*—the play of metaphoric mind—which may or may not communicate intelligible, extractable meaning but always *displays* itself. Perhaps *we* are the extraterrestrials, experiencing *Arrival* every day as we 'language' imagination ..." (*Space is the Place*)

3) THOUGHTSPACE

11. **Philopoetic Volition** ("Combining the words 'philosophy' and 'poetic,' a zone of the true or real is evoked which need be neither strictly rational nor irrational, scientific nor nonsensical." *Philopoetic Volition*); 12. **Practice**

of Invention ("clinging to concepts as *merely* literal creates functional ignorance, a loss of the intelligence of the heart. When concepts are literalized at the expense of mythopoetic play, imagination is stunted." *Beyond the Salon*); 13. **Spatial Thermoclines** ("From the simplest of notions, complex swum spaces and highly nuanced feeling-tones of spaces are self-generated." *Architectures to Inspire Dwelling*).

"Concerning the subjectivity of modern consciousness: we think ourselves into new forms of subjective selves in a fictive spinning-out of speculation upon speculation (metaphor upon metaphor), applying imaginative logics." (*Immeasurability*)

4) METAPHORICS

14. ***Fantasy Imagery*** ("Stories, dreams, imaginations happen some*where*, and we psychologically exist within these spaces, as much as they do within us." *Soul*); 15. **Paradox** ("I'm going to start the end of my talk." *The Specious Present*); 16. **Alternativity** ("Cognitive estrangement," *cf. Endnote 70*); 17. **Idiosyncrasy** (Fallacy; "words or phrases which cannot be derived by the rules of a language," *cf. Endnote 72*); 18. **Crafting of Presentation** ("The poem creates an architecture: story becomes stage, as a theatre of dwelling. The poem creates its own center, a 'linking back' (*religio*) to origins of presence ..." *Theatre of the Sacred*); 19. **Mimesis** ("The 'shadow of heavenly things'... 'mimes'—brings into being," *Theatre of the Sacred*).

"Metaphors deepen as they propagate, revealing landscapes and story ..." (*Immeasurability*)

5) ARCHITECTURES

20. **Design-architectures** ("Represent the *potential* beginnings of emergent-design architectures in poetic imagination. A 'chaos of creation' implies 'grain' as pattern, rhythm and structure." *Space is the Place*); 21. **World building, Construction** ("How floridly nuanced and passionately creative the space of mind is, and consequently how [it is that] spatial design relates to conceptual architectures of thought." *Architectures to Inspire Dwelling*); 22. **Temenos** ("Anarchic sanctuaries support expressions and invocations of the unique by providing a *temenos*, a sense of sanctity in which novel forms of societal *dwelling* are found, as home." *Beyond the Salon*); 23. **Precincts** ("A zone of the arising of the sacred, a protected space of sanctuary." *Sanctuary, Temenos and Risk*); 24. **Construction, Sacred Construction** ("Sanctuary as bounded space becomes sacred or holy as an animate inhabitation ..." *Sanctuary*); 25. **Notions of Anarchic Sanctuary** ("Authenticity of the heart may only become possible within alternative societies, as the imagination of the heart is held in exile ..." *Beyond the Salon*).

"By 'architectures' of thought is meant, most basically: 1) design-emergent intention: the way thoughts and images conspire to construct notions; and in a further stage, 2) architectures as constructions of landscapes, worlds; and in a deeper sense, 3) architectures as animate places and spaces which inspire dwelling." (*Architectures to Inspire Dwelling*)

6) SOUL

26. **Soul** (As a core value; "we are willing to fight for our need for depth." *The Perception of the Unique*); 27. **Remembrance and Distance** ("Whatever we choose to nourish through creative philopoetic-volition persists for us to inhabit—and so bring to life again." *Remembrance and Distance*); 28. **Grit, Guts** ("The 'intelligence of the heart' relates to self-authenticity, to ways

we may desire to imagine—and re-imagine—self and world more deeply, more essentially." *Beyond the Salon)*; 29. **Desire, Passion** ("The desire for self-authenticity may lead to the seeking out or creation of anarchic sanctuaries." *Cf. Beyond the Salon)*; 30. **Emotion** ("In valuing uniqueness and finding visibility in socially-alternative societies, one gains soul. In order to let lions roar ..." *Beyond the Salon)*; 31. **With Risk** ("A relevant necessity or ground from which psychological risk can be explored." *Sanctuary, Temenos and Risk)*.

"What can be said for poetry? In today's world, something needs to be said, and we could be saying more concerning which poems we praise. How it is for a soul to find, for however brief a time, novel orientations of landscape, to adopt new shapes and forms of imaginal space through novel surprises, discontinuities and sonorities? And how many ideas change a life?" (*Poetry and the Beauty of Distance)*.

7) THE "THIRD"

32. **Distance** (Invoking a "third" reality: "The ego is de-literalized via imaginative experiences. Worlds of imagination arise spontaneously and autonomously—poems re-construct being." *Poetry and the Beauty of Distance)*; 33. **Forms of Resistance** (It becomes possible "to advance an ethics of freedom and resistance in contemporary poetics." *Philopoetic Volition)*; 34. **Inhabitation, Dwelling** ("It seems a rarer thing to dwell, *to inhabit*, when in some manner life is lived beyond oneself, and the world circulates, is illumined, returning to us as from a great distance—remembrance—bringing with it the soul of beauty." *Inhabitation)*; 35. **Place** ("We create novel *spaces* of mind. Lacking dimension, expanse, the landscapes and narratives cannot themselves arise—this is the ground of *thoughtcraft* ..." *Sunny-side Up in Space)*; 36. **Consciousness** (Revisions of world and self: "The development of a living personal philosophy" *Volition: Enactments of Personal Philosophy)*.

"'Distance is the soul of beauty.' ... Only through a distance, in space or time, does reality undergo purification.' Just as notable poetry is unique, its artistry is inseparable from personal philosophy.... 'Distance is the soul of beauty' implores: how vast is the heart, how limitless is our space of thought, how deep the soul of attendance from which we might speak?" (*Volition: Enactments of Personal Philosophy*)

VIII. Appendix 2. Disjunction in Haiku — Strong and Weak

(Excerpted & adapted from *The Disjunctive Dragonfly: A New Approach to English-Language Haiku, 2013; cf. The Living Haiku Anthology. bit.ly/29zNvI5*)

A New Definition

One of the persistent questions asked is "what makes a haiku a haiku"?

In English, as can be seen from the 1000's of examples housed online in the *Living Haiku Anthology*, as well as in noted haiku journals, excellent haiku have long done away with syllable counting, instead incorporating creative metrical styles of rhythm that in various ways articulate (and emulate) haiku sensibility as found in Japan, particularly when the entire oeuvre, contemporary to feudal, is considered. There are a number of reasons—cultural, linguistic, historical, etc., for exploring and utilizing the creative potency and power of each language and literary context evolving from each distinct locale haiku are scribed. That is, haiku in English (in this case) is not likely to achieve excellence by merely copying an imported formula. At the same time, it's necessary to articulate the difference between haiku and epithet, haiku and the nonce phrase, haiku and a quaint if exotic image with a touch of pathos, etc.

While the subject of "genre" elides with sensibility and style (e.g. "traditional," "nature oriented" and "radical," are the kinder terms seen), in taking a broad-minded perspective, Haruo Shirane offers an expansive connotational definition of haiku, meant to benefit poets creatively:

Echoing the spirit of Bashō's own poetry ... haiku in English is a short poem, usually written in one to three lines, that seeks out new and revealing perspectives on the human and physical condition, focusing on the immediate physical world around us, particularly that of nature, and on the workings of the human imagination, memory, literature and history.... this definition is intended both to encourage an existing trend and to affirm new space that goes beyond existing definitions of haiku (2000, 60).

In the above "definition" one is struck not only by what is present, but by what is left out: no haiku "moment," no Zen attributes, no specific linguistic prescriptions or preoccupations. Of particular import is the phrase, "the workings of the human imagination, memory, literature and history." Shirane not only situates the haiku genre within the context of modernity; the limiting sensibility of haiku as a naturalist-realist image-poem is contravened. This new definition of haiku does however present a conundrum: what might be the difference between the haiku and the brief contemporary poem, in English? While it's impossible to draw a precise line in the sand, examining a large number of notable haiku, all play, broadly speaking, with two attributes: disjunction (disjunctive styles), and reader-resistance. In the following excerpt from the book *The Disjunctive Dragonfly* (2013), four ideas are advanced: 1) a poem (or prose phrase, or epithet) lacking disjunction cannot be considered haiku, 2) poems possessing weak disjunction can be excellent haiku, 3) poems possessing strong disjunction can be excellent haiku, and 4) generally the stronger the disjunctive aspect, the more resistant to reader-comprehension the haiku will be.

Disjunctive Modes

One of the questions that has arisen concerning disjunctive modes has to do with their relationship to "traditional" or "mainstream" haiku.... The accepted definition and acceptable range of published haiku in English in the postwar era has generally been delimited by what has come to be termed "traditional haiku": a poem of objective realism composed of two primary, juxtaposed images, associated with nature, and normatively represented in three lines. The terms "traditional" and "mainstream" have increasingly found their way into parlance as a reaction to the burgeoning of diverse disjunctive styles of haiku, over the last decade. As disjunctive concepts are not wedded to syntactical, imagistic or concrete (layout or lineation) concerns, experimental permission is implicitly offered.

Here it is suggested that the force of disjunction acting on the reader's consciousness is the primary motif impelling successful juxtaposition.... From this perspective, all haiku possess disjunction. That said, does it follow that strong disjunction necessarily makes for a strong haiku? And conversely, can an objectively-realist haiku possessing weak disjunction also achieve formal excellence?

Haiku Exhibiting Strong Disjunction

The following examples present "one-image" haiku exhibiting the three styles of strong disjunction (explained in greater detail in the book) in a strong sense—each was published in a *Modern Haiku Journal* (*MH*) issue within 2011-12. (The parenthetical numbers indicate syllable-counts per line.)

> back from the war
> all his doors
> swollen shut
>> Bill Pauly, 2011, *MH 42:1*; *HIE 158* (4-3-3)

> the scent of paradise a dead bird in my hand
>> Lee Gurga, 2011, *MH 42:2* (6-6 | 6-3-3)

> even, if, because
> plum blossoms
> in the courtyard
>> Miriam Sagan, 2011, *MH 42:2* (5-3-4 | 2-1-2-3-4)

Note that in those examples with multiple metrical permutations (syllable-counts), alternate meanings may be divined, as the metrics determine to an extent how the phrases are semantically parsed by the reader.

In Pauly, observe the dual, mutually-exclusive layers of literal versus psychological implication of "doors swollen"; in Gurga, the strong paradox of "paradise," contrasted with the intimate, tragic touch of the dead bird; and in Sagan, the playfully ambiguous linguistic postulations concerning something having to do with those "plum blossoms" of spring.

> sap rising he imagines me completely
> Melissa Allen, 2011, *MH 42:3* (3-8 | 3-5-3 | 8-3)

> sore to the touch his name in my mouth
> Eve Luckring, 2011, *MH 42:3* (4-5)

> a word that takes time defoliation
> Johannes S. H. Bjerg, 2012, *MH 43:1* (5-5)

In Allen, there appears her notion of his notion of her, and her notion of the situation altogether, presented within a scenario of erotic drama—the haiku leaves much to the imagination, inviting misreading; Luckring presents a complex texture of perceptual near-synesthesia, as pain (mixed with bliss?) combines with touch, metaphor and identity—also within an intimate context, yet one given ambivalently, as it may be read with multiple (and mutually exclusive) readings. Bjerg sets up readers by breaking the "fourth wall," addressing us directly from the poem—then caps the set up with multiple implications (linguistic, sociopolitical, ecological) of that single, final word "defoliation": indeed, also a mouthful.

> raven shadow clinging tightly to my victim story
>> Michelle Tennison, 2012, *MH 43:2* (4-10 | 8-6 | 4-4-6 | etc.)

> in tune with its obstacles, rain
>> Eve Luckring, 2012, *MH 43:3* (7-1 | 2-5-1 | 3-4-1)

> quietly in the 21st century
>> dark places
> on a full moon
>> Gary Hotham, 2012, *MH 43:3* (11-3-4)

Tennison begins with an unusual collocation, "raven shadow" and plays with misreadings of syntax, as the haiku can be read "raven shadow clinging tightly," "raven shadow | clinging tightly," and in further alternatives, according to its metric options—metrical multiplicity invites misreading as meaning. Potent and disturbing emotions are evoked, yet paradoxically, as an artwork this haiku is a talisman of clarity and healing, possessing psychological concision. A sense of musical analogy and aural space inhabits Luckring's ku, with the sound of rain shaping the sense of what those obstacles may be: physical, emotional, psychological? The disjunctive paradox of "in tune" offers notions of harmony. Hotham evokes the era by presenting most of what is absent (darkness, silence) as a presence, offering the reader a vision of what lies behind or apart from the noise, whether in a serene or an abandoned sense. This strongly disjunctive aspect propels the sense of reader-paradox, concerning meaning and perception.

Haiku Exhibiting Weak Disjunction

Next, several examples of notable haiku that exhibit weak disjunction are presented, taken from three major haiku anthologies illustrating historical influence: *Haiku in English, 2013 (HIE), The Haiku Anthology, 3rd ed., 1999 (THA),* and *Haiku Moment, 1993 (HM)*:

> Just enough of rain
> To bring the smell of silk
> From umbrellas
>   Richard Wright, c. 1960; *HIE* (5-6-4)

> in morning sun two white horses   the autumn aspen
>   Elizabeth Searle Lamb, 1985; *HM* (8-5)

> JANUARY FIRST
> the fingers of the prostitute cold
>   Bob Boldman, 1981; *THA 15* (5-9)

Richard Wright's haiku seems to possess almost no disjunctive aspect. It is a puzzle-haiku however, with the subject last, and the setup of "just enough" creates psychological suspension, within which develops a cascading contrast from rain, to silk, to umbrellas. Each sequential noun is unexpected in relation to the previous. The poem offers a nuanced observation that plies language with delicacy. The first line also presents unusual or irruptive grammar. Yet if the poem were read as a sentence within a novel (as a narrative muse), most probably wouldn't blink. We know Wright was a long-term expatriate living in Paris, and the umbrellas were indeed made of silk and colorful. "Just enough" here means a mere sprinkle, and one imagines the fashionable women of Paris out on the sidewalk, having suddenly in near-unison opened their varicolored canopies. Wright, a deeply principled man, was around this time justifiably paranoid: "The CIA and FBI had Wright under surveillance starting in 1943, [and he was] blacklisted by Hollywood movie studio executives in the 1950s"

(*Wiki*). Wright lived the last years of his life under "extraordinary pressure" (*ibid*). He sickened in 1957, and in 1960 died in Paris at the age of 52. Biographical knowledge adds sociopolitical and psychological depth to the objective presentation here. (See his poem, "The FB Eye Blues," which contains the lines, "Each time I love my baby, gover'ment knows it all ... Woke up this morning / FB eye under my bed").

In E.S. Lamb is found a minimal application of concrete disjunction (the spatial gap between the two parts of the poem), and a profound sense of quietude is evoked. The elegantly phrased and rhythmically paced description is painterly. An entire mountain valley seems present in its fall season, a nip in the air, the golden aspen quivering in the merest breeze, and shining white horses—offering that rare echo of remembrance: the perfection of a day, an expansive sense of peace extending through paddock, fields and woods. A Rocky Mountain or Sangre de Cristo haiku of the rugged American West.

Boldman begins with what seems like a newspaper headline in "all caps." A new year's haiku, traditional as to "season," yet, a strongly urban haiku as well. As he passes, are her fingers a raw, red-white or even a little blue, ungloved; and he seems to be hanging out in a ratty part of town (or, is the knowledge of cold fingers communicated through touch—a proposition, implied?). The headline scans like an announcement read on a newspaper when passing a newsstand, probably at night, perhaps even New Year's Eve, after midnight; waiting on the street in mid-winter for a john. Concerning disjunction, "semantic register shift" (newspaper headline-to-internal observation) is utilized; however, contrast and topic, rather than disjunctive effect, provide the main poetic force. This is a haiku of social consciousness, presented in a unique style.

The last example is by William Higginson, 1970; *HIE* (3-3-3)

I look up
from writing
to daylight

There is surprise in the disjunctive aspect of overturning expectation, and misreading (writing-to-daylight is also a shift of semantic register). Yet for a writer, it's a familiar experience. This haiku feels real and exact to the author as a being. A poem of *makoto* (verity): it's honest.

These four different styles of excellent haiku each exhibit weak disjunction. Perhaps only Wright's haiku would be considered most "traditional," with its objective realism, three-line form, and genre-median short-long-short syllable count; yet it also has a degree of unusuality in its lack of fragment/phrase. In fact, this compositional style was once labeled (in the pages of North American haiku journals) as the dreaded "one-image" haiku—a haiku lacking two separated imagistic segments. E.S. Lamb's haiku is presented in one line, with a gap, so it's not a traditional form; Boldman has all caps and a prostitute; and Higginson presents a big fat capital "I" as a first word, and is focused on self-experience (said to be a traditional no-no—though it's common enough in Japanese haiku). As with Wright, Higginson's haiku is likewise a "one-image" poem. Each of these works evokes a delicately-nuanced world, and intriguing feelings; each possesses originality and a degree of formal uniqueness. The form (including perceptual disjunction, compression, and surprise as an overturning of semantic expectation) also helps each achieve its poetic power; all are poems of objective realism.

Critical Usefulness: Terminology

What can be drawn from these brief examples is that so-called "non-traditional" haiku do not necessarily equate to poems possessing strong disjunction, or highly unusual genre-deformative experiment; nor must excellent haiku possess strong disjunction, though they must possess intrinsically the three genre-types of disjunction in order be considered haiku, in my opinion: varieties of genre-specific disjunction, 1) perceptual disjunction, 2) overturning semantic expectation, and 3) misreading as meaning—can be observed, but their presence is weak or mild in the examples just above—more of a background effect. Instead, contrast, image, topical surprise, and compression create the potent, foregrounded effects.

Generally speaking, depending upon which examples are selected, it seems possible to locate continua which thread through "traditional" and "non-traditional" haiku. *It may be that the simplistic duality of "traditional" versus "non-traditional" has outlived its critical usefulness, in terms of language characteristics and descriptions of haiku style.*

For those fond of realism in haiku, who eschew language play, metaphor, modes of disjunction and the like, where should these four examples of weak disjunction be placed in the haiku pantheon? Is "traditional" more a matter of weak disjunction, than a hewing to realism? Is there an objection to the use of "I" in Higginson's signature haiku, or the one-line-with-gap "single-line" (monoku) haiku of Lamb? The all-caps and urban theme of Boldman? The lack of fragment/phrase in two of the above examples? It can be noted that Wright's haiku was first anthologized in the significant, posthumous book-length collection, *Haiku: This Other World* (1998), and Bill Higginson was arguably the most significant 20th century critic and scholar of English-language haiku.

Within Japan, similar experiments and topics to those presented above may be found—some from the haiku masters of yore: Bashō, Chiyo-jo, Buson, Issa, and additional works penned by the early 20th century masters. Each of these haiku have certain, so-to-say "traditional" elements, and avoid strong disjunctive action. Yet upon closer examination, these examples as a group depart from those overly restrictive formal requirements once considered a *sine qua non* of English-language haiku in the 20th century: juxtaposition, the two-image poem of fragment/phrase, seasonal reference, *kireji* (an overt "cut" between parts of the haiku), etc.

When comparing and contrasting haiku plying strong versus weak disjunction, qualitative differences of style and presentation are evident—yet in the above examples, similarities outweigh differences. Observed is a range of variation rather than exclusive conceptions of haiku as a genre. Innovation is the lifeblood of haiku as an art-form, and excellent haiku of every stripe exhibit *innovative disjunctive elements*.

Living Haiku

Disjunctive action as an aspect of reader-resistance is fundamental to haiku in English, and provides a means of determining genre, applying the broadest possible brush. By taking into account the aspects of genre-definition provided by Haruo Shirane (2000), and the applied concepts of disjunction (Gilbert, 2013), as observed in all excellent haiku, it becomes possible to delimit the scope of the haiku genre.

IX. Appendix 3: Forethought

Inspiration from Simone Weil, with comments.

Movement Toward a Poetics of Sanctuary

*We reconstruct for ourselves
the order of the world in an image,*

(these are places that we go[96])

*starting from limited, countable,
and strictly defined data.*

(all that is known; data being measureable[97])

*We work out a system for ourselves,
establishing connections and conceiving*

(a poetics of space arises from evolving personal philosophy)

*of relationships between terms that are abstract and
for that reason possible for us to deal with.*

(only abstraction impels generative poetic space[98])

*Thus in an image, and image of which the very existence
hangs upon an act of our attention,*

(lingering, wavering—existence; existent as liminal, attentive creation)

we can contemplate the necessity
which is the substance of the universe

(the "why" of creative desire; to arrive anew)

but which, as such, only manifests
itself to us by the blows it deals.

(Goethe writes, "to die [to suffer] so to grow"[99])

We cannot contemplate
without a certain love.

(*philosophia*: ardent desiring, love of wisdom;
 himma: heart, thought, intention, desire;
the intelligence of the heart[100])

The contemplation of the image of the order of the world
constitutes as certain contact with the beauty of the world.

("To sing beyond the genius of the sea..." our song has
 something to add to the world, to nature, as revelation[101])

The beauty of the world is the order
of the world that is loved.

(this is the poem[102])

(*italic text*, Simone Weil[103])

X. Endnotes

[1] Sabine Miller, floragramist. A Note on the Floragrams (2017):
> For this project, I've limited myself to my favorite medium: flowers (garden or wild, usually wilted) smeared on watercolor paper. Egg whites, pencil, water, Elmer's glue, and/or citrus juice sometimes get layered over the pulp, with dried flower parts and paper for collage. I don't use a paintbrush, but I occasionally use tape for the harder edges.
>
> Many things inform this choice of materials: a longing to be outdoors when I need to be indoors; boredom; a preference for the smell of flowers over that of oil or acrylics; a low-consumption/maximum use ethic; and last but not least, a perverse pleasure in the impossibility of mastery, which is another way of saying a passion for wildness and wild processes. I've been especially inspired by James Elkins in *What Painting Is*, which explores the act of painting as an essentially alchemical process. For the most part, my fidelity has been to the materials and moods, with alignment with theory tending to feel like a happy accident. As Richard's book crystallized, however, some of the images were loosely designed with specific concepts in mind.

[2] Simone Weil. (April 13, 1942). "Attention is the rarest and purest form of generosity." Letter to poet Joë Bousquet (in their collected correspondence). *Correspondance*, Lausanne: Editions l'Age d'Homme, 1982, 18. In *Tough Enough* (2017), Deborah Nelson recounts Weil's influence:
> A short list of those who counted her as an influence includes five winners of the Nobel Prize in Literature (André Gide, T. S. Eliot, Albert Camus, Czesław Miłosz, and Seamus Heaney); philosophers Georges Bataille, Michel Serres, and Iris Murdoch; theologians Reinhold Niebuhr and Paul Tillich; Catholic writers Flannery O'Connor and Thomas Merton; two popes (John XXIII and Paul VI); political activists and writers Dorothy Day, Ignazio Silone, and Adam Michnik; and poets of diverse styles, including George Oppen, Geoffrey Hill, Anne Carson, Stephanie Strickland, Fanny Howe (who has many poems and essays devoted to Weil), and Jorie Graham,

several of whom (Carson, Strickland, and Graham) have written full-length books of poetry devoted to her. (27)

3 Anthologies: *Haiku 21*, Lee Gurga & Scott Metz, 2011 (600 haiku, 2000-2010); *Haiku 2014, Haiku 2015, Haiku 2016* (haiku 2013-2015); *Haiku in English: The First Hundred Years*, Jim Kacian, et al., 2013 (200 authors); *The Living Haiku Anthology*, 2016 (*livinghaikuanthology.com*); *The Disjunctive Dragonfly: A New Approach to English-Language Haiku*, Richard Gilbert, Red Moon Press, 2013 (275 haiku from 120 poets, illustrating 24 disjunctive techniques).

4 "The philosopher David Chalmers, who introduced the term 'hard problem' of consciousness, contrasts this with the 'easy problems' of explaining the ability to discriminate, integrate information, report mental states, focus attention, etc. Easy problems are easy because all that is required for their solution is to specify a mechanism that can perform the function. That is, their proposed solutions, regardless of how complex or poorly understood they may be, can be entirely consistent with the modern materialistic conception of natural phenomena. Chalmers claims that the problem of experience is distinct from this set. He argues that the problem of experience will "persist even when the performance of all the relevant functions is explained." ("Hard problem of consciousness," *Wiki*; *cf*, Chalmers, 1995)

5 "Boden acknowledges that 'we're still a very long way from a plausible understanding of the mind's architecture, never mind computer models of it...' Gilbert Harman, "Mechanical Mind" (book review) *Mind as Machine: A History of Cognitive Science*, Margaret A. Boden, OUP 2006.

6 Wallace Stevens, "Notes Toward a Supreme Fiction" (Part V, line 1). Hillman comments:
"Surprisingly, this desert is not heartless, because the desert is where the lion lives ... if we wish to find the responsive heart again we must go where it seems least present... What is passive, immobile, asleep in the heart cre-

ates a desert that can only be cured by its own parenting principle that shows its awakening by roaring. (*A Blue Fire*, "Eros," 304)

[7] *Cf.* James Hillman, 2015.

[8] *Cf.* Samuel McNerney. (4 Nov 2011). A Brief Guide to Embodied Cognition: Why You Are Not Your Brain. *Scientific American (bit.ly/2jtnsYi)*.

[9] Anil Seth. (1 Feb 2017). The Neuroscience of Consciousness. [Lecture]. *The Royal Institution*.

> ... what we then perceive is the consequence of this joint minimization-prediction error. So you can think of perception as a sort of controlled hallucination, in which our perceptual predictions are being reined in at all points by sensory information, from the world and the body. (Min. 28:00-28:28; *bit.ly/2tr42EZ*)

[10] "Qualia" — "The 'what it's like' character of mental states. The way it feels to have mental states such as pain, seeing red, smelling a rose, etc." (Eliasmith & Mandik, *Dictionary of Philosophy of Mind*; *bit.ly/2tEz3F8*). Consciousness may indeed be a fundamental law of the natural universe. In March 2014, David Chalmers spoke at a Ted Conference summing up the state of scientific understanding of the "hard problem" of consciousness—the "movie in our heads." He presented two main "crazy ideas" as prime research candidates:

> We [now] know that these brain areas go along with certain kinds of conscious experience, but we don't know why they do.... But in a certain sense, those are the easy problems. [They don't] address the real mystery at the core of this subject: why is it that all that physical processing in a brain should be accompanied by consciousness at all? Why is there this inner subjective movie? Right now, we don't really have a bead on that.... [C]onsciousness right now is a kind of anomaly ... Faced with an anomaly like this, radical ideas may be needed, and I think that we may need one or two ideas that initially seem crazy before we can come to grips with consciousness scientifically. The first crazy idea is that consciousness is fundamental.... What we then need is to study the fundamental laws governing consciousness,

the laws that connect consciousness to other fundamentals: space, time, mass, physical processes....

The second crazy idea is that consciousness might be universal. Every system might have some degree of consciousness. This view is sometimes called panpsychism: pan for all, psych for mind, every system is conscious, not just humans, dogs, mice, flies, but even Rob Knight's microbes, elementary particles. Even a photon has some degree of consciousness. The idea is not that photons are intelligent or thinking. It's not that a photon is wracked with angst because it's thinking, "Aww, I'm always buzzing around near the speed of light. I never get to slow down and smell the roses." No, not like that. But the thought is maybe photons might have some element of raw, subjective feeling, some primitive precursor to consciousness. If [consciousness is] fundamental, like space and time and mass, it's natural to suppose that it might be universal too ... although the idea seems counterintuitive to us, it's much less counterintuitive to people from different cultures, where the human mind is seen as much more continuous with nature.... Okay, so this panpsychist vision, it is a radical one, and I don't know that it's correct. I'm actually more confident about the first crazy idea, that consciousness is fundamental, than about the second one, that it's universal.... If we can answer those questions, then I think we're going to be well on our way to a serious theory of consciousness. If not, well, this is the hardest problem perhaps in science and philosophy. We can't expect to solve it overnight. But I do think we're going to figure it out eventually. Understanding consciousness is a real key, I think, both to understanding the universe and to understanding ourselves. It may just take the right crazy idea. (*bit.ly/1X7EO7z*)

[11] Even qualities, the shapeliness of shape, color-sense of color, define themselves as "of a kind" "elements within a range of," "a difference among a spectrum of," others like or unlike: thus likened to. Measure here is meant as a means of discovering and observing the tangible underlying the intangible:

> Measurement, believe it or not, is a widely misunderstood concept. It's often mistaken for a process that produces an exact number. If you are told that something cannot be measured because there is no way to put an exact

number on it, then you know that the problem is a misunderstanding of the measurement concept. The way scientists see it, measurement is the reduction of uncertainty about a quantity through observation. (D. Hubbard, "Everything Is Measurable." (2007; *bit.ly/1UjhuQw*)

"Although this may seem a paradox, all exact science is based on the idea of approximation. If a man tells you he knows a thing exactly then you can be safe in inferring that you are speaking to an inexact man" (Bertrand Russell, "The Scientific Outlook," 1931); "In measure theory, *measurable functions are structure-preserving functions* between measurable spaces; as such, they form a natural context for the theory of integration." ("Measurable function," *Wiki*; *cf. bit.ly/2vPd8jE*)

In terms of this book, data (information) is considered to be *concreta*, measureable in the above sense. "An abstract object is an object which does not exist at any particular time or place, but rather *exists as a type* of thing" [pl. *abstracta*]" (*Wiki*). *Abstracta* construct indefinite space; concreta can be concrete objects, measurables, tangibles (including language) which provide "structure-preserving functions"; the human face is measureable in this sense. The *uniqueness* of the human face is not. Human faces are concreta; uniqueness, being an abstract object, is an immeasurable. In this sense, immeasurables are related to the *perception of the unique*.

[12] "I think our kind of inwardness, which really means our sense of personality, is a Shakespearean invention. He more than prefigured our humanity, its quandaries and dilemmas. Shakespeare so deeply pervades not just Western culture, but so far as I can tell, all the world's culture." (Harold Bloom, in "A Prospero or Lear? Nay, Verily a Falstaff; A Boisterous Tribute to Shakespeare," Mel Gussow, November 16, 1998, *The New York Times*); "In the book I propose that a civil war goes on between Hamlet and his maker ... Shakespeare ... cannot control this most temperamentally capricious and preternaturally intelligent of all his creations." (Yvonne French, "Harold Bloom Interprets 'Hamlet,'" May 2003, *Library of Congress*. (*1.usa.gov/1RXdd3R*)

¹³ "Conceptual blending," *Wiki*. Discussed by cognitive scientist and linguist Mark Turner in *The Origin of Ideas*, OUP, 2014; *The Literary Mind*, OUP, 1996.

¹⁴ In Brahic, C. (3 Dec 2014). "Shell 'art' made 300,000 years before humans evolved"; "Sediment inside them and tiny grains pulled from cracks were dated, to reveal that they had been buried between 430,000 and 540,000 years ago ... One turned out to be a tool, its sharpened edge probably used for scraping. Many were pierced where the clam's muscle attaches to the shell" *New Scientist* (*bit.ly/2toAo7q*). In "Dating the Origin of Language Using Phonemic Diversity," Perrault & Mathew (2012) give an oldest date of 350,000 years ago. *PLoS One 7.4.* (*bit.ly/2uB7sZm*)

¹⁵ Recent neuroscience evidence links creative thought to the "default mode network" (DMN):

> The default mode network is most commonly shown to be active when a person is not focused on the outside world and the brain is at wakeful rest, such as during daydreaming and mind-wandering, but it is also active when the individual is thinking about others, thinking about themselves, remembering the past, and planning for the future. The network activates 'by default' when a person is not involved in a task ... and is sometimes referred to as the task-negative network ... The default mode network is active during passive rest and mind-wandering. Mind-wandering usually involves thinking about others, thinking about one's self, remembering the past, envisioning the future..." [numerous mental functions are also given]. ("Default mode network," *Wiki*)

> [P]sychologists and neuroscientists estimate that we spend [about a third of] waking hours daydreaming—that is, straying away from focused tasks or external stimuli to inner thoughts, fantasies, and feelings. And when our brain has nothing else in particular to do, it turns on and kicks into high intensity a whole neural network dedicated to reviewing what we already know and *imagining possible worlds*... [emphasis added] (Josie Glausiusz, "Devoted to Distraction," 1 Mar 2009, *Psychology Today*)

> One of the most intriguing yet least understood aspects of the human mind is its tendency to spontaneously give rise to words, images, and emotions that flow effortlessly from one topic to another. There is a stunning ubiquity of such spontaneously arising mental content in people's lives: thoughts that occur without our deliberate control take up as much as one-third of our mental experience... (S. Kaufman & C. Gregoire. (2015). *Wired to Create: Unraveling the Mysteries of the Creative Mind*, Tarcher).

[16] *Cf. plato.stanford.edu/entries/language-thought*

[17] "Chaos theory," *Wiki*.

[18] Classicist Victor Ortiz comments:
> Ovid uses two Latin phrases to define Chaos: *"rudis indigestaque moles"* (*Met.* 1.1.7) and *"pondus iners"* (*Met.* 1.1.8). As used by the Greek Hesiod, Chaos refers to a yawn or gap or a void, if you will, but then Ovid goes on to define it as a shapeless mass, a *"moles,"* and this *"moles"* is qualified by the adjectives, *"rudis"* = raw, rough, not worked into shape, and *"indigesta"* = disorganized, confused, unarranged without order, not worked into shape (and apparently our word "undigested" derives from this word), a word which was first coined by Ovid in this passage, as far as scholars like Anderson can tell. *"Pondus"* refers to a weight on a scale, and was also used to refer to a mass or a load of something, while the adjective *"iners"* modifies *"pondus"* and means something like unskilled or without skill (with additional meanings of inert, inactive, and lazy), and very interestingly, *"iners"* also has a meaning of "without digestion" by the stomach. So, I think Anderson has support from the Latin when he writes that *iners* "suggests the need of art to turn this Chaos into form (like a statue, *cf. Fast*.1.108." - William Anderson, *Ovid's Metamorphoses Books 1-5*, Oklahoma UP, 1997, 153. (*Personal communication*, June 2017)

[19] *Cf.* Ethnopharmacology, vol II. (2009). Elaine Elisabetsky & Nina L. Etkin (eds.). "Psychoactive Botanicals in Ritual, Religion and Shamanism," Glen H. Shepard, Jr., National Institute of Amazonian Research (INPA), Brazil. UNESCO, Eoloss Pub. Oxford, UK, 128-182; The Wiley-Blackwell Hand-

book of Transpersonal Psychology. (2015). Harris L. Friedman & Glenn Hartelius, eds. Hoboken, NJ: Wiley-Blackwell.

[20] William James, in "The Experience and Perception of Time," (rev. April 6, 2015) *Stanford Encyclopedia of Philosophy.* (*plato.stanford.edu/entries/time-experience*)

[21] "Is the underlying assumption that language structures thought and reality? If so, how does this tie back into poetry as consciousness, as experiences of consciousness?" (One of this book's editors, Victor Ortiz, asked this question.) To a large extent we repeatedly "story" ourselves into being. This concept is found in cognitive studies, Mark Turner's work in particular (*cf. The Literary Mind*, 1996). In addressing this question, of poetry as consciousness, as experiences of consciousness, the answer must remain illustrative, since we are discussing heuristic notions. Concerning the present work, the reader is invited to examine the 36 qualities illustrated in Chapter 6.

[22] Of these two terms, "meaning" is employed frequently and familarly (as a container for that which is known "means something"), while "unknowing" appears to contain only absence—both terms however represent equally abstract objects. Recall the quip by then-Secretary of Defense Donald Rumsfield: "... because as we know, there are known knowns; there are things we know we know. We also know there are known unknowns; that is to say we know there are some things we do not know. But there are also unknown unknowns – the ones we don't know we don't know." The comment is indicative of the arrow of science—it is from unknowing as a basis that we ponder means and methods (via theory and experiment) to further understand our universe. The Large Hadron Collider, was built not only to "help answer some of the fundamental open questions in physics"; there remains speculation that there are "unknown unknowns" which might be discovered. The idea of unknown unknowns is especially interesting for poetry, as language-use always involves "knowns" (not nonsense) that somewhat paradoxically allow the perception of "unknown unknowns." So "unknowing" is an abstract noun indicating expectancy in relation to discovery, and

discovery as a disclosure of meaning—in haiku, which are are often meaning-indeterminate, it is possible to ponder known unknowns and unknown unknowns as well—a process paralleling that of philosophic and scientific inquiry.

[23] This topic draws on cognitive linguistics, which employs recent concepts such as "conceptual blending," "many worlds theory," "possible worlds theory," "metaphor theory," "mental spaces theory," etc. In her analysis of Bulgakov's *The Master and Margarita*, linguist Olga Gurevich writes:
> Mental spaces are partial structures [that] are dynamically created when we think and talk. They are somewhat similar to possible worlds, without the philosophical implications of whether or not these possible worlds exist. The claim is that mental spaces represent psychological reality and *are essential for constructing meaning, both in everyday situations and in fictionalized contexts*. Mental spaces have been used to analyze descriptions of past and future [Fauconnier 1997], conditional and counterfactual constructions [Sweetser 1996, Fauconnier 1996], literary works [Sweetser, in press], and other questions. Each mental space is structured by a frame with roles that stand in structural relationships with each other... [emphasis added] (*Glossos Journal, Issue 4* (Summer 2003), *The Slavic and East European Language Resource Center*, 7-8).

[24] I thank Sabine Miller for suggesting this term (*personal communication*, 14 June 2016). "Volitional formations" is used in Buddhist studies (a translation of sa☐khāra); as the five *skandhas* ("aggregates"), this "refers to the form-creating faculty of mind." My usage, somewhat related, does not parallel the Buddhist philosophical system. (*Cf.* "Skandha," *Wiki*)

[25] *Cf.* "Theory of Mind," Alvin I. Goldman:
> "Theory of Mind" refers to the cognitive capacity to attribute mental states to self and others. Other terms for the same capacity include "commonsense psychology," "naïve psychology," "folk psychology," "mindreading" and "mentalizing." Mental attributions are commonly made in both verbal and non-verbal forms. Virtually all language communities, it seems, have words or phrases to describe mental states, including perceptions, bodily

> feelings, emotional states, and propositional attitudes (beliefs, desires, hopes, and intentions). People engaged in social life have many thoughts and beliefs about others' (and their own) mental states, even when they don't verbalize them. In cognitive science the core question[s] [which yet remain matters of theory] in this terrain [are]: How do people execute this cognitive capacity? How do they, or their cognitive systems, go about the task of forming beliefs or judgments about others' mental states, states that aren't directly observable? Less frequently discussed in psychology is the question of how people self-ascribe mental states. Is the same method used for both first-person and third-person ascription, or entirely different methods? [continues]. (*The Oxford Handbook of Philosophy of Cognitive Science*, OUP, 2012, pp. 402-24, Introduction. (*bit.ly/1ACfnRQ*)

26 Qtd. in *Soul*; *cf.* Hillman, 1975, *Re-visioning Psychology*.

27 *Cf.* "Simone Weil's Last Journey," Terry Halstead, 9 April 2001, *America Magazine* (*bit.ly/1UeE5UO*):
> Simone Weil reminds us of the importance of attention, of learning to look again in a world where a culture of distraction often dissipates our awareness. She calls upon us not to flee suffering, whether our own or that of others. By being attentive to suffering, we can find the next step as we discover our common humanity with those who suffer.

28 *Cf.* Mark Turner, *The Literary Mind*, OUP, 1996, p. 93: "Conceptual blending is a fundamental instrument of the everyday mind, used in our basic construal of all our realities, from the social to the scientific." "[E]lements and vital relations from diverse scenarios are 'blended' in a subconscious process, which is assumed to be ubiquitous to everyday thought and language." ("Conceptual Blending," *Wiki*)

29 Qtd., "Free Jazz: A Subjective History," Chris Kelsey, *Allmusic* (*bit.ly/28Jo740*). Ornette Coleman died in 2015—he was a bandleader on 50 albums and a sideman on 13.

30 Wallace Stevens, "Angel Surrounded by Paysans," *The Auroras of Autumn*, Knopf, 1950 (extract; concluding poem in his last volume of selected poetry prior to the *Collected Works*; Stevens died in 1955).

31 "Eric Schmidt, who, when asked about all the different ways his company is causing invasions of privacy for hundreds of millions of people around the world, said, 'If you're doing something that you don't want other people to know, maybe you shouldn't be doing it in the first place.'" (in Greenwald, 2014)

32 "America and the Shift in Ages: An Interview with Jungian James Hillman," Pythia Peay (26 Feb 2011) *The Huffington Post*, (*huff.to/1WYkR6d*)

33 Gigi (10 Sept 2015). 45 Texting Statistics That Prove Businesses Need to Take SMS Seriously. *OneReach* (bit.ly/2505PMw). *Cf.* Pew Research Center 2015 statistics. (*pewrsr.ch/1DMho1V*)

34 *Rattle Poetry Group*, Facebook (*http://bit.ly/2a1ALth*); *Rattle Poetry* "About" (*rattle.com/info/about-us*).

35 Mircea Eliade, *Myth of the Eternal Return*, Princeton UP, 2005. Publisher's synopsis:
> This founding work of the history of religions (1954) secured the North American reputation of the Romanian émigré-scholar Mircea Eliade (1907-1986). Making reference to an astonishing number of cultures and drawing on scholarship published in no less than half a dozen European languages, Eliade's *The Myth of the Eternal Return* makes both intelligible and compelling the religious expressions and activities of a wide variety of archaic and "primitive" religious cultures.... Eliade passionately insists on the value of understanding this view in order to enrich our contemporary imagination of what it is to be human. (*press.princeton.edu/titles/8010.html*)

36 *Cf.* Auerbach, *Mimesis: The Representation of Reality in Western Literature*, PUP, 1968. "In many ancient cultures, the inviolability of deities was considered to extend to their religious sanctuaries and all that resided within, whether criminals, debtors, escaped slaves, priests, ordinary people, or, in some cas-

es, passing cattle; biblical scholars suspect that Israelite culture was originally no different." (*bit.ly/28XZgJT*)

37 William Richardson, *Heidegger: Through Phenomenology to Thought*, 2nd ed., Martinus Nijhoff, 1967., 410; Thomas Langan, *The Meaning of Heidegger: A Critical Existentialist Phenomenology*, CUP, 1971, 118.

38 Dudley Young (Ret.), Professor of Literature, University of Essex, also taught Athenian Drama.

39 "Great Dionysia (also called City Dionysia): an ancient dramatic festival in which tragedy, comedy, and satyric drama originated; it was held in Athens in March in honour of Dionysus, the god of wine. Tragedy of some form, probably chiefly the chanting of choral lyrics, was introduced by the tyrant Peisistratus when he refounded the festival (534/531 BCE), but the earliest tragedy that survives, Aeschylus' Persai, dates from 472 BCE. (*Encyclopædia Britannica*)

40 Risk. *Stanford Encyclopedia of Philosophy*, 2007, 2011. (*plato.stanford.edu/entries/risk*)

41 Jung Lexicon. *New York Association for Analytical Psychology.* (*nyaap.org/jung-lexicon/t*)

42 C. G. Jung, *Psychology and Alchemy*, p. 99; *Contributions to Analytical Psychology*, 193; *Psychological Types* (Chap. 1), 82.

43 Qtd. in C. Forrest McDowell (26 May 2011). Sanctuary & Temenos—Sacred Boundary for the Soul. (Blog; *bit.ly/29c3F8A*)

44 Nalanda Translation Committee. (1975, 1980). *The Sutra of the Heart of Transcendent Knowledge.* (pdf) (*bit.ly/2sNcGSb*); *nalandatranslation.org*; cf. Judy Lief. (2016). Atisha's Mind-training System. (Sourcebook). (pdf: *bit.ly/2sNb6zD*)

45 Clayton Beach is a freelance editor and poet, he lives in Portland, Oregon, with his wife and two children. His poetry and haikai are syncretic, drawing from

a wide variety of artistic traditions and disciplines including music, the sciences, philosophy, and literature.

[46] Susan Sontag. (23 Sept 2009). Qtd. in *Against Interpretation*, By Susan Sontag (book review). *Independent* (*ind.pn/2gX1hd0*); *cf. Against Interpretation*, 1964, 1966, FSG, 10 (concluding sentence); *cf.* "Against Interpretation, Summary," *Wiki*. (*bit.ly/2u6KFCi*)

[47] Acronyms and publication information for the sources used. For each haiku cited, the date of first-publication will be given, where known (e.g., "*HIE* 1979"). Additional citation information is found in the accompanying Endnotes.

> **DD**—*The Disjunctive Dragonfly: A New Approach to English-Language Haiku*, Richard Gilbert, Red Moon Press, 2013 (275 haiku illustrating 24 disjunctive techniques).
>
> **H21**—*Haiku 21* (anthology), Lee Gurga & Scott Metz, eds., Modern Haiku Press, 2011 (over 600 haiku, 200 authors, covering 2000-2010).
>
> **H14**—*Haiku 2014* (anthology), Gurga & Metz, *ibid*, 2014 (100 haiku, 100 authors, in 2013).
>
> **H15**—*Haiku 2015* (anthology), Gurga & Metz, *ibid*, 2015 (100 notable haiku, in 2014).
>
> **H16**—*Haiku 2016* (anthology), Gurga & Metz, *ibid*, 2016 (100 notable haiku, in 2015).
>
> **HIE**—*Haiku in English: The First Hundred Years* (anthology), Jim Kacian, et al., eds., Norton, 2013 (800 notable haiku from over 200 authors).
>
> **LHA**—Living Haiku Anthology (online archive), Don Baird, et. al., eds. (*livinghaikuanthology.com*) (thousands of international previously published haiku).
>
> Journals frequently cited: **AC**—Acorn; **AHG**—A Hundred Gourds (2011-16); **FP**—Frogpond; **HN**—The Heron's Nest; **IS**—Is/let (2014-Present); **MH**—Modern Haiku; **NN**—Noon; **RR**—Roadrunner (2004-13); **TW**—Tinywords. Publishing house: **RMP**—Red Moon Press.

[48] An article on "haiku definition" at the LHA online provides additional information: Gilbert, R. (Jan 2016) "Haiku in English – A General Guide to Genre Distinction." *LHA*. (*bit.ly/29zNvI5*)

⁴⁹ Adam Alter, "Disfluency, A Conversation with Adam Alter." (25 Feb 2013). *Edge.org* (*bit.ly/29pWnMR*). Alter is a psychologist and NYU professor; *cf.* "Fortune favors the BOLD (and the Italicized): Effects of disfluency on educational outcomes," Connor Diemand-Yauman, et. al., *Cognition* 2010, PUP (bit.ly/29vT6i8); James Lang. (3 June 2012). The Benefits of Making It Harder to Learn. *Chronicle of Higher Education.*

⁵⁰ "pig" Marlene Mountain, *HIE* 1979; "dust" Patricia Donegan, *HIE* 1998; "just" Michelle Tennison, *MH* 44:1 2013.

⁵¹ "silence" Jack Galmitz, *Y* (ImPress) 2013; "isms" Paul Pfleuger, Jr. *A Zodiac* (RMP) 2013; "anchoritic" Philip Rowland, *HIE* 2009.

⁵² "my life" Sabine Miller *NN* 9 2015; "blue" Peter Yovu *RR 13.1* 2013; "from" John Martone, *RR 12.1* 2012; "first frost" Anna Maris *FP 38:2* 2015;"im-mi-grant" Chen-ou Liu, *7th Kokako Haiku Competition* 2013; "in out" Paul Pfleuger, Jr., *A Zodiac* (RMP) 2013; "first light" Susan Constable *HN 8:3* 2006.

⁵³ "how on" John Martone *so long* (Ornithopter Press) 2015; "between wound" Lee Gurga *MH 45.3* 2014; "bomb nor" Mark Harris *RR 13:2* 2013; "more signs" Gary Hotham *RR 11:3* 2011; "running" Richard Gilbert *RR 12:3* 2012; "beyond" L. A. Davidson, *HIE* 1972.

⁵⁴ "this side" Eve Luckring *HN 52:3* 2015; "if glass" John Stevenson *FP 37:1* 2014; "out of" Jim Kacian palimpsest (RMP) 2011; "dense fog" Kala Ramesh, *Simply Haiku 7:2* 2009; "plum blossom" Fay Aoyagi, *H21* 2009; "swallow flight" Jim Kacian, *Presents of Mind* (RMP) 2006.

⁵⁵ "blue" Joseph Salvatore Aversano *Acorn 35* 2015; "testing" Barbara Snow *bottle rockets 31* 2014; "hiding" Don Wentworth *TW 13:2* 2013; "a word" Johannes S. H. Bjerg, *MH 43:1* 2012; "mosquito" Ajaya Mahala, *Shiki Monthly Kukai* (May) 2014; "lily" Nicholas Virgilio *HIE* 1963.

⁵⁶ Mark Turner, *The Literary Mind*, OUP, 1998, p. 93.

[57] "winter" Don Baird *MH 46:3* 2015; "against" Markeith Chavous *MH 46:3* 2015; "the way" Robert Epstein *moongarlic 2* 2014; "dandelion" Aditya Bahl *Notes from the Gean 17* 2013; "ants" Scott Metz *Simply Haiku 7:2* 2009; "war zone" Dick Whyte *Lakeview International Journal 1:2* 2013.

[58] "c" John Martone *Otoliths 32* 2014; "starfish" Mike Andrelczyk *RR 13:2* 2013; "flash mob" Alan S. Bridges *MH 44:2* 2013; "flown" Barrow Wheary *Bones 1* 2013; "as an and" Richard Gilbert *HIE* 2011; "even, if" Miriam Sagan *MH 42:2* 2011.

[59] "at the window" Joseph Salvatore Aversano *FP 37:3* 2014; "night" Gary Hotham *RR 13.2* 2013; "decisively" Jeffrey Winke *Vexing Laughter* (Yet To Be Named Free Press) 2013; "tunnel" Tyrone McDonald *HIE* 2011; "the river" Jim Kacian *HIE* 1997; "as a window" Scott Metz *RR 13:2* 2013.

[60] "father" Matthew Caretti *MH 46:1* 2015; "waging" John Soules *FP 37:3* 2014; "so greenly" Eve Luckring *RR 13:1* 2013; "morning" Tyrone McDonald *HN 15:1* 2013; "silent" Chen-ou Liu *Lyman Haiku Award* 2011; "Passover" Roman Lyakhovetsky *AHG 3:4* 2014.

[61] "further" Sharon Pretti *Acorn 34* 2015; "blue" Aashika Suresh *Bones 8* 2015; "midnight" Kath Abela Wilson *Notes from the Gean 21* 2013; "sun on" Paul Miller *H21* 2009; "body bag" Jerry Kilbride *HIE* 2003; "whom one" Philip Rowland *RR 12:2* 2012.

[62] Cf. *The Politics of Poetic Form: Poetry and Public Policy*, Bernstein, ed. (1990). Roof Books; online at ISSUU (*bit.ly/2a4ZmAt*); "The Politics of Poetic Form," *Syllabus*, U. Buffalo, 1998. (*bit.ly/2a6YkxK*)

[63] Cf. Simon Critchley. (31 Mar 2011). *Politics, Nihilism, and the Philosophy of Disappointment* [lecture]. (*bit.ly/2tUqc26*)

[64] "crucifixion" Joy MacVane *Bones 6* 2015; "leaves" Jeffrey Stillman *Acorn 33* 2014; "spring dawn" David Lanoue *MH 44:3* 2013; "impossible" Peter New-

ton B*ones 3* 2013; "between what" George Swede *RR 13:1* 2013; "horizon" Rajiv Lather, *HIE* 2003.

65 "hold your" Cherie Hunter Day *IS* 2015; "Do you" David McCann *Acorn 32* 2014; "old black" Paul Pfleuger, Jr. *IS* 2014; "a love letter" Chris Gordon Cucumbers Are Related To Lemons (antantantantant) 2011; "where the lines" Chris Gordon *HIE* 2002; "my fingerprints" Jim Kacian *Kusamakura International Haiku Contest* 2003.

66 "inside" Rob Cook *MH 45:2* 2014; "blossoming" Rebecca Drouilhet *AHG 3:4* 2014; "moon beggar" Alegria Imperial *Notes from the Gean 20* 2013; "monologue" Fay Aoyagi *HIE* 2002; "autumn mist" Marlene Mountain, *H21* 2003; "just enough" Richard Wright *HIE* c. 1960.

67 "Linguistics in Literature," *Linguistic Society of America* [LSA]. (*bit.ly/29UtNrI*)

68 "turn the record" Melissa Allen *Red Dragonfly* (November 24) 2015; "through eyes" Ann K. Schwader *TW* (June 5) 2014; "another bird" Melissa Allen *FP 36:1* 2013; "meadow speaking" Scott Metz *HIE* 2009; "salt wind" Cherie Hunter Day *HIE* 2010; "without child" Scott Metz *lakes & now wolves* (Modern Haiku Press) 2012.

69 "touch-move" Ramona Linke *Bones 5* 2014; "wormhole" Jack Galmitz *Blow Out* (Yet to be Named Press) 2013; "inside a batYs ear" Eve Luckring *RR 11:3* 2011; "carpentry" Hélène Duc *The Quadrille of the dragonflies, collection Solstice*, (*AFH*) 2012; "out of nowhere" Marlene Mountain *H21* 2007; "nothing matters" John Stevenson *HIE* 2007.

70 Qtd. from an exegesis of "alternativity," given in Gilbert, R. (2007, 2009). *Plausible deniability: Nature as hypothesis in English-language haiku*, "Section 2.1 'Alternativity.'" For a more detailed description of this "quality" please refer to the full article. (*research.gendaihaiku.com/plausible*)

71 "white breath" Fay Aoyagi *MH 45:2* 2014; "raw umber" Cherie Hunter Day *THF HaikuNow! Award* 2014; "at seven" Helen Buckingham *Bones 2* 2013; "pain

fading" Jim Kacian *HIE* 2007; "forgotten" Lee Gurga, *H21* 2003; "the government" Peter Yovu *RR 11.3* 2011.

72 "Idiosyncrasy," *Wiki. Lexicon of Linguistics*, "I": "A property of words or phrases which cannot be derived by the rules of a language. Words can be idiosyncratic in a variety of ways: (a) semantically (by having some unpredictable aspect to their meaning), (b) phonologically (by being an exception to a phonological rule), or (c) morphologically (by being an exception to a word formation rule)." (*bit.ly/2tZh3ZM*)

73 "photon" Fay Aoyagi *FP* 38:1 2015; "blind" Christopher Patchel *MH* 46:2 2015; "lettuce" Jim Westenhaver *MH* 44:3 2013; "whale" Michelle Tennison *Acorn 32* 2013; "this morning" Michele Root-Bernstein *Acorn 31* 2013; "sweet smell" Kai Falkman *Ginyu 21 (Ginyu Journal)* 2004.

74 "only a drawing" Mark Harris *NN 8* 2014; "cosmos" Michael Nickels-Wisdom *Bones 5* 2014; "drinking" Paul Reps *Zen Telegrams* (Tuttle) 1959; "Gettysburg" Gregory Longenecker *World Haiku Review* 2012; "a long hard lie" Eve Luckring *RR 12:2* 2012; "deep snow" Mark Harris *HIE* 2011.

75 "mimesis" Sabine Miller *IS* (August 19) 2014; "take it off" Donna Fleischer *Bones 2* 2013; "in the incandescence" Paul Pfleuger, Jr., *RR 11:2* 2011; "silence" Joseph Salvatore Aversano *FP 36:3* 2013; "she slips" Peter Yovu *HIE* 2009; "one by one" George Swede *HIE* 1980.

76 "a word" Hansha Teki *Bones 8* 2015; "the beach" Adan Breare *MH* 45:1 2014; "jasmine" Roberta Beary *MH 44:1* 2013; "strawberry" Carlos Colón *RAW NerVZ 7:2* 2001; "spring wind" Carmen Sterba *Whirligig* (April) 2011; "a seed" John Martone *RR 12:2* 2012.

77 "mimsy borogoves" Michele Root-Bernstein *Haiku Canada Review 9:1* 2015; "still river" Don Miller *FP 37:1* 2014; "seldom" Rebecca Lilly *RR 13:1* 2013; "lunar" Tyrone McDonald *RR 12:2* 2012; "manhole" Chuck Brickley *HIE* 2009; "the galactic" Peter Yovu *Sunrise* (RMP) 2010.

78 "dawn" Helen Buckingham *Bones 7* 2015; "blue swallowtail" Lee Gurga *RR 13:2* 2013; John Martone *bheid* (samuddo/ocean) 2013; "autumn rain" Christina Nguyen *Bones 1* (December) 2012; "scattered" Peggy Willis Lyles *Brocade of Leaves* (HNA Conference Anthology) 2003; "mountain" Ted van Zutphen *Simply Haiku 9:1* (July) 2011.

79 "morning" Ken Sawitri *AHG 4:3* 2015; "forest" Michael Henry Lee *FP 37.2* 2014; "knife cold" Susan Constable *MH 44:1* 2013; "slow dancing" Lorin Ford *MH 44:1* 2013; "spring rain" Anna Maris *Acorn 34* (Spring) 2015; "eye contact" Hansha Teki *Simply Haiku 9:3-4* (Autumn-Winter) 2011.

80 "Gita" Kala Ramesh *Akita International Haiku Award* (Sept.) 2014; "cicada" Keith Woodruff *Presence 54* 2016; "after the rain" Sarah Rehfeldt *AHG 2:2* 2013; "moss" Mark Harris *H21* 2009; "the wild" Paul Pfleuger, Jr. *A Zodiac (RMP)* 2013; "on this cold" Marlene Mountain *HIE* 1977.

81 "fireflies" Michelle Tennison *IS* (January 29) 2015; "winding" Stella Pierides *Blithe Spirit 23:2* 2013; "another home" Adjei Agyei-Baah, *Paper Wasp 22:2* 2016; "numerically speaking" Stella Pierides *Bones 7* 2015; "fireflies beyond" John Stevenson *MH* 35:3 2004; "sing at dawn" Pat Geyer *Brass Bell*: March 2016.

82 "Transgression," explicated in *Conjunctions and Disjunctions*. (1969). Seaver Books (excerpt):
> The extreme immateriality of the Protestant sacrament emphasizes the separation between spirit and matter, man and the world, soul and body; the Tantric feast is a deliberate transgression, a breaking of the rules, the object of which is to attain the *reunion* of all the elements and all substances, to tear down walls, to go beyond limits, to erase the differences between the horrible and the divine, the animal and the human, dead flesh and living bodies, to experience samarasa, the identical flavor of all substances.... Protestant communion is individual, and as I have already said, it has retained only the barest trace of the material, corporeal nature of the sacrament.... Purity is separation, impurity is union. The Tantric ceremony

subverts the social order but it does so not for revolutionary but for ritual purposes: it affirms with even more emphasis than the official religions the primacy of the sacred over the profane. Protestantism was also a subversion of the social and religious order; however, it did not turn the old hierarchies upside down in order to return to the primordial mingling of all with all, but in order to proclaim the freedom and responsibility of the individual. It separated, it distinguished, it traced limits intended to preserve personal awareness and privacy. For the one the result was communality; for the other, individualism. ("Eve and Prajnaparamita," *The Judgment of God and the Games of Gods*, 61-62)

[83] "fresh snow" John Stevenson *MH 46.2* 2015; "incomplete beings" Kala Ramesh *RR 13:2* 2013; "the rain song" Lorin Ford, *H21* 2009; "sunken" Adjei Agyei-Baah *Heart Journal Online* (June 8) 2015; "deep inside "Dietmar Tauchner *HIE* 2006; "that we could" Peter Yovu, *H21* 2010.

[84] "I listen" Jack Galmitz *FP 37:2* 2014; "full moon" Ramesh Anand *Mainichi Daily News* (April 14) 2013; "their wings" Lorin Ford *H21* 2009; "harvest moon" Sondra J. Byrnes *European Kukai* (Autumn) 2013; "Caprifolium" Dag Hammarskjöld *A String Untouched* (Kai Falkman, trans., RMP) 2006; "moist" Johannes S. H. Bjerg *RR 11:2* 2011.

[85] "anorexic" Jon Baldwin *Bones 1* 2013; "the phantom" Robert Epstein *Notes from the Gean 17* 2013; "clinging" Kate MacQueen *TW 13:1* 2013; "predator" Johnny Baranski *Bones 3* (December) 2013; "just a shell" Sara Winteridge *LHA* 2014; "tamarind" Shrikaanth Krishnamurthy *FP 38:1* (Winter) 2015.

[86] *Jazz Legends in Their Own Words*. (2014). BBC. (*bit.ly/2v5okW5*)

[87] "desires" Victor Ortiz *AHG 4:1* 2014; "weighing" Sandra Simpson *MH 45:1* 2014; "inside you" S. M. Abeles moongarlic 1 2013; "columbine" David Caruso *Monostich* (April 8) 2013; "whatever happens" Coralie Berhault-Creuzet *L'Eau des nuages* (The Book Edition) 2012; "red candle" Roberta Beary *THF Facebook Haiku Contest* 2010.

⁸⁸ "dotting an i" Lee Gurga *FP 38:2* 2015; "generic sunlight" Roberta Beary *MH 45:3* 2014; "gunfire" John McManus *MH 45:1* 2014; "grieving" Ernesto Santiago *Bones 5* 2014; "back from" Bill Pauly *HIE* 2011; "I return" Dick Whyte *Lakeview International Journal 1:2* 2013.

⁸⁹ "in his buttonhole" Fay Aoyagi *Haiku North America* (Conference Handout) 2013; "oncologist's" Steven Carter *AHG 2:4* 2013; "cardiogram" Paresh Tiwari *Shiki Monthly Kukai* (December) 2013; "A small pool" Vladimir Devidé *A Thousand Hummingbirds* (in Belgium) 1993; "what swallows" Tyrone McDonald *MH 43:2* 2012; "an i" John Stevenson *RR 11:2* 2011. Hailing from Croatia, Vladimir Devidé holds an esteemed place in international haiku history. (Cf. bit.ly/2uOGCcP & bit.ly/2uwYcXx)

⁹⁰ "two ballerinas" Peter Yovu *FP 38:1* 2015; "how deer" Scott Mason *HIE* 2008; "night of small" Alan Summers *MH 45:2* 2014; "you whisper" Brendan Slater *Notes from the Gean 17* 2013; "pretty sure" John Stevenson *RR 9:1* 2009; "her going" Jim Kacian *H21* 2008.

⁹¹ "what's left" Deborah P Kolodji *MH 46:3* 2015; "beheading over" Brent Goodman *Bones 5* 2014; "BEHEADING" Scott Metz *IS* (September 11) 2014; "cold rain" Fay Aoyagi *H21* 2002; "nothing rhymes" Christina Nguyen *FP 36:1* 2013; "less and less" Marlene Mountain *HIE* 1986.

⁹² "stolen wombs" Sonam Choki *Haiku News 2:8* 2013; "Geiger counter" Brent Goodman *FP 36:3* 2013; "I see through" Bill Pauly *RR 12:1* 2012; "higgs boson" Paresh Tiwari *Bones 3* (December) 2013; "first poem" Tzetzka Ilieva *Asahi Shimbun* (2 November) 2012; "riverside" Adjei Agyei-Baah *Asahi Shimbun* (1 January) 2016.

⁹³ Johannes S. H. Bjerg *moongarlic 4* 2015; "Nagasaki" Don Baird *THF HaikuNow! Award* 2013; "bleeding under" Eve Luckring *RR 10:1* 2010; "in the prison" Johnny Baranski *HIE* 2006; "television" Joseph Massey *HIE* 2005; "dense fog" Mamta Madhavan *Lakeview International Journal of Literature and Arts (August)* 2013.

[94] "windfall" Carolyn Hall *HIE* 2009; "fogged into" Susan Diridoni Bones 1 2013; "a drowning" Richard Gilbert *HIE* 2004; "vast blue" *Kashinath Karmakar International Kukai 14* ("elephant" photo) May, 2013; "day-dreaming" Don Baird *Haiku—the Interior and Exterior of Being (Little Buddha Press)* 2014; "afternoon rain" Peter Newton *FP 37:3* 2014.

[95] "Individuals form an identity by integrating their life experiences into an internalized, evolving story of the self that provides the individual with a sense of unity and purpose in life." McAdams, D. (2001). The psychology of life stories. *Review of General Psychology 5:2*, 100–122.

[96] "We reconstruct for ourselves the order of the world in an image" (Weil), expresses a fundamental notion of depth psychology, definitional of reflective consciousness: "image *is* psyche" (C. G. Jung, *CW 13*, p.75); James Hillman (2004) in the section "Image and Soul: The Poetic Basis of Mind," writes:

…nor does 'image' mean a mental construct that represents in symbolic form certain ideas and feelings which it expresses. In fact, the image has no referents beyond itself, neither proprioceptive, external, nor semantic: 'images don't stand for anything.' They are psyche itself in its imaginative visibility; as primary datum, image is irreducible. Visibility, however, does not mean that an image must be visually seen. It does not have to have hallucinatory properties which confuse the act of perceiving images with imagining them. (18)

With Hillman's sense of "image" in mind, "We reconstruct for ourselves the order of the world in an image" suggests that the development of one's personal philosophy "as the order[ing] of the world" occurs both imaginatively and as reconstruction. How we dwell has much to do with how we imagine we dwell, depending on one's own sense of imagining. How we "order" self and self-meaning is evolutional, mutable. And we do this daily—particularly through language-use. Each sentence is formed as a truth of thought, so to speak. This idea of self as self-made story is a paradigm now commonly found in schools of personal and social psychology, with broad application. (*Cf,* "Narrative identity," *Wiki*)

⁹⁷ *Cf.* Endnote 11.

⁹⁸ *Cf.* Endnote 11.

⁹⁹ "And so long as you haven't experienced this: to die and so to grow, you remain but a troubled guest on the dark earth" (*cf.* Goethe, "The Holy Longing"); C. G. Jung: ". . . every psychic advance of man arises from the suffering of the soul...." ("Psychotherapists or the Clergy," *CW* 11: §497);
> Originating out of the poetic mind of John Keats, the term soul-making as applied by [James] Hillman refers to a practice through which individuals: slow down and deepen their connectedness to themselves, others, and the world; emphasize being over doing and the present moment over future aspirations; embrace and prioritize one's woundedness, humanity, and limitations over a quest for perfection, transcendence, and transformation. (Christopher Miller, "James Hillman's Shift to Soul-Making"; *bit.ly/2u6g2vv*)

¹⁰⁰ "[Philosophical] problems are solved, not through the contribution of new knowledge, rather through the arrangement of things long familiar. Philosophy is a struggle against the bewitchment (*Verhexung*) of our understanding by the resources of our language" (Wittgenstein, *Philosophical Investigations*, 1953); "Certainely a litle Philosophie inclineth mans minde to Atheisme, but depth in Philosophie bringeth Men about to Religion" (Francis Bacon, "Essay XVI. Of Atheism," *Essays, Civil and Moral*, 1612, *OED*).

¹⁰¹ "'To sing beyond the genius of the sea...' was how Wallace Stevens put it, in part ['genius'; Latin, *'genius loci'*: the protective spirit of a place], meaning, our song has something to add to the world, to nature, as revelation, in imparting new realizations and disclosures" (R. Gilbert, to Timothy Green, "Asking about the Composition of Poetry," 30 May 2016 (Facebook; *bit.ly/1XRWBS8*)

¹⁰² "Following this train of thought, there is an infinite demand ethically (*cf.* Simon Critchley, *Infinitely Demanding*, 2007), which cannot be met: exploration is enmeshed in the impermanence, exploration and changeability of life. This is what it is to live inconclusively and critically, with faith (*cf. The Faith of the Faithless*, 2012, *ibid*), when poetry is a calling. For Critchley, faith here is

not related to a God or abstract notion of divinity, but lies in how truth as "the beauty of the world is the order of the world that is loved" touches the word of utterance, of "song," in Stevens's sense, in creating psychologically enriching landscapes.

[103] Simone Weil. (1950). *Waiting for God* [*Attente de Dieu*]. "Forms of the Implicit Love of God." (Emma Craufurd, trans.). Putnam, 1951, 169-170. (Routledge Revivals, 2009, 62-63; *bit.ly/1WQad0T*). Frontispiece quotation: "Attention is the rarest and purest form of generosity." [*L'attention est la forme la plus rare et la plus pure de la générosité*] Simone Weil (in a 13 April, 1942 letter to poet Joë Bousquet). *Correspondance* (French), Lausanne: Editions l'Age d'Homme, 1982, 18. Cf. *An Encounter with Simone Weil*, Julia Haslett (writer, director), 85 min., Line Street Productions, 2010.

XI. References

Alter, Adam. (25 Feb 2013). Disfluency: A Conversation with Adam Alter. *Edge.org* (*bit.ly/29pWnMR*).

Auerbach, Eric. (1968). *Mimesis: The Representation of Reality in Western Literature*. NJ: Princeton UP.

Bachelard, Gaston. (1969). *The Poetics of Reverie* (Daniel Russell, trans.). NY: Orion Press, 16.

Bacon, Francis. (1612). Essay XVI. Of Atheism. In *Essays, Civil and Moral*. London: OUP.

Baird, Don, et al. (2016). Living Haiku Anthology (*livinghaikuanthology.com*).

Bernstein, C. (1986). *Content's Dream: Essays 1975-1984*. Sun & Moon Press, 247.

_____. (1999). *My Way: Speeches and Poems*. U Chicago, 57, 15-16.

Bloom, Harold. (1999). *Emily Dickinson*. NY: Chelsea House Publications, 205.

Chalmers, David. (1995). Facing Up to the Problem of Consciousness. *Journal of Consciousness Studies 2:3*, 200-13 (*consc.net/papers/facing.pdf*).

_____. (2014). How do you explain consciousness? (Ted Talk, min. 18:37). *TED2014* (*bit.ly/1X7EO7z*).

Corbin, H. (1969). *Creative Imagination in the Sufism of Ibn 'Arabi*. PUP.

_____. (1977). *Spiritual Body and Celestial Earth*. PUP.

_____. (1978). *The Man of Light in Iranian Sufism*. Boulder: Shambala.

Critchley, S. & Catapano, P. (2015). *The Stone Reader: Modern Philosophy in 133 Arguments*. NY: Liveright.

Critchley, Simon. (2007). *Infinitely Demanding: Ethics of Commitment, Politics of Resistance*. NY: Verso.

————————. (2014). *The Faith of the Faithless: Experiments in Political Theology*. NY: Verso.

Delany, S. (1996, 2001). *Dhalgren*. (William Gibson, Introduction). Wesleyan UP & Vintage/Random House.

Diemand-Yauman, Conner, et al. (Jan 2011). Fortune favors the BOLD (and the Italicized): Effects of disfluency on educational outcomes. *Cognition 118:1*. NJ: PUP, 111-15 (*bit.ly/29vT6i8*).

Eliade, Mircea. (1959). Sacred Space and Making the World Sacred. In *The Sacred and the Profane: The Nature of Religion* (W. Trask, trans.). NY: Harcourt Brace, 57.

————————. (2005). *Myth of the Eternal Return*. NJ: Princeton UP.

Ellamil, Melissa, et al. (1 Aug 2016). Dynamics of neural recruitment surrounding the spontaneous arising of thoughts in experienced mindfulness practitioners. *Neuroimage 136*, 186-96 (*1.usa.gov/1UVtHhy*).

French, Yvonne. (2003). *Harold Bloom Interprets "Hamlet."* Washington, D.C.: Library of Congress.

Gilbert, R. (2009). *Plausible Deniability: Nature as Hypothesis in English-language Haiku. Stylistic Studies of Literature*. M. Hori, T. Tabata, & S. Kumamoto, eds. Bern: Peter Lang (*bit.ly/2t0VvI0*).

————————. (2013). *The Disjunctive Dragonfly: A New Approach to English-Language Haiku*. Winchester, VA: Red Moon Press.

————————. (January 2016). *Haiku in English – A General Guide to Genre Distinction*. The Living Haiku Anthology (*bit.ly/29zNvI5*).

Gilbert, Richard, et al. (2011). *The Future of Haiku—Interview with Kaneko Tohta*. Winchester, VA: Red Moon Press, 17-19.

Glausiusz, Jose. (2009, March 1). Devoted to Distraction. *Psychology Today*.

Goldman, Alvin. (2012). *The Oxford Handbook of Philosophy of Cognitive Science*. Oxford: OUP, 402-24.

Greenwald, Glenn. (Oct 2014). Why privacy matters. *TEDGlobal2014 (bit.ly/1RHcgz6)*.

Gurevich, Olga. (Summer 2003). Bulgakov's *The Master and Margarita. Glossos Journal 4*. The Slavic and East European Language Resource Center, 7-8.

Gurga, L., & Metz, S. (2011). *Haiku 21*. Lincoln, IL: Modern Haiku Press.

_____. (2013). *Haiku 2014*. Lincoln, IL: Modern Haiku Press.

_____. (2014). *Haiku 2015*. Lincoln, IL: Modern Haiku Press.

_____. (2015). *Haiku 2016*. Lincoln, IL: Modern Haiku Press.

Gussow, Mel. (16 Nov 1998). A Prospero or Lear? Nay, Verily a Falstaff; A Boisterous Tribute to Shakespeare. [Book review of *Shakespeare: The Invention of the Human* by Harold Bloom]. NY: The New York Times.

Halstead, Terry. (9 Apr 2001). Simone Weil's Last Journey. *America Magazine (bit.ly/1UeE5UO)*.

Harari, Yuval. (2017). *Homo Deus: A Brief History of Tomorrow*. NY: Harper, 168, 206-07.

_____. (2015). *Sapiens: A Brief History of Humankind*. NY. Harper.

Harman, Gilbert. (2006). Mechanical Mind [Book review.] *Mind as Machine: A History of Cognitive Science*, Margaret A. Boden. Oxford: OUP.

Harris, Tristan. (Dec 2014). How better tech could protect us from distraction. *TEDxBrussels (bit.ly/1YC5Ia5)*; *cf., Time Well Spent (timewellspent.io)*.

Heidegger, Martin. (2001). *Poetry, Language, Thought*. (Albert Hofstadter, trans.). NY: Harper Collins. (*Cf.* within, "Poetically Man Dwells").

Hillman, James. (1975). *Re-visioning Psychology*. NY: Harper & Row, Intro., 173.

———————. (1980). *Egalitarian Typologies Versus the Perception of the Unique*. Dallas: Spring Pub.

———————. (1989). *A Blue Fire*. NY: Routledge.

———————. (1992). *The Thought of the Heart & the Soul of the World*. Dallas: Spring Pub., 4.

———————. (2004). *Archetypal Psychology*, Spring Pub., 18-22.

———————. (2015). *Archetypal Psychology*. (Uniform Edition, Volume 1). Spring Pub.

Hillman & McLean. (2011). *Permeability*. The Archive for Research in Archetypal Symbolism (*bit.ly/2tQTTWu*).

James, William. (2015). The Experience and Perception of Time. *The Stanford Encyclopedia of Philosophy*. CA: Stanford UP (*plato.stanford.edu/entries/time-experience*).

Jones, J. (8 Nov 2012). Noam Chomsky Spells Out the Purpose of Education. *Open Culture* (*bit.ly/1rfTLXw*).

Jong, E. (1973). *Fear of Flying*. NY: Holt, Rinehart & Winston.

Jung, C. G. (1921). *Psychological Types, or, The Psychology of Individuation*. [Collected Works of C. G. Jung, 6]. London: Kegan Paul.

———————. (1928). *Contributions to Analytical Psychology*. London: Routledge & Kegan Paul.

———————. (1928, 1969). *Psychotherapists or the Clergy*. [Collected Works of C. G. Jung, 11]. NJ: Princeton UP.

———————. (1929, 1968). Commentary on The Secret of the Golden Flower. *Alchemical Studies*. [Collected Works of C. G. Jung, 13]. NJ: Princeton UP, para. 54.

_____. (1939, 1968). Psychological Aspects of the Mother Archetype. *Part I: The Archetypes and the Collective Unconscious.* [Collected Works of C. G. Jung, 9]. NJ: Princeton UP, 179.

_____. (1961, 1989). *Memories, Dreams, Reflections.* (Richard & Clara Winston, trans.). NY: Random House, 411, 427.

_____. (1968). *Psychology and Alchemy.* [Collected Works of C. G. Jung, 12]. NJ: Princeton UP.

Kacian, J. et al., eds. (2013). *Haiku in English: The First Hundred Years.* NY: Norton.

Kaufman, S. & Gregoire, C. (2015). *Wired to Create: Unraveling the Mysteries of the Creative Mind.* NY: Tarcher.

Kelsey, Chris. (2011). Free Jazz: A Subjective History. *Allmusic (bit.ly/28Jo740).*

Kühl, Tim. (2016). Effects of disfluency on cognitive and metacognitive processes and outcomes. *Metacognition and Learning 11:1.* NY: Springer Science, 1-13 *(bit.ly/2fW0yqJ).*

Lakoff, G. & Johnson, M. (1980). *Metaphors We Live By.* U Chicago Press.

_____. (1981). Conceptual Metaphor in Everyday Language, In *Philosophical Perspectives on Metaphor.* U Minnesota Press.

Lang, James. (3 Jun 2012). The Benefits of Making It Harder to Learn. *Chronicle of Higher Education (bit.ly/2fUs1FA).*

Langan, Thomas. (1971). *The Meaning of Heidegger: A Critical Existentialist Phenomenology.* CUP, 118.

Le Guin, U. (1974). *The Dispossessed.* NY: Harper & Row, Chap. 3, 72; Chap. 2, 55.

Levertov, Denise. (1973). Some Notes on Organic Form. In *New & Selected Essays.* CA: New Directions, 68-69; first published in *Poetry, Vol. 106, No.6,* September 1965.

Longinus. (2012). On the Sublime (G. M. A. Graube; Tanke & McQuillan, trans., eds.). *The Bloomsbury Anthology of Aesthetics*. London: Bloomsbury Academic, 62, 73.

Lorca, F. (1933). Qtd. in *Lorca—A Dream of a Life*. Leslie Stainton. (1999). NY: FS&G.

Machado, Anthony. (1983). *Times Alone: Selected Poems of Antonio Machado*. (Robert Bly, trans.). CT: Wesleyan UP, 143. (*bit.ly/28UodTq*)

McDowell, Forrest. (26 May 2011). Sanctuary & Temenos—Sacred Boundary for the Soul. *Weblog* (*bit.ly/29c3F8A*).

McLuhan, Marshall. (1964, 1966). *Understanding Media—The Extensions of Man*. New York: McGraw-Hill, 73.

Moore, T. (1992). *Care of the Soul: A Guide for Cultivating Depth and Sacredness in Everyday Life*. NY: Harper Collins.

_____. (2014). Psychotherapy and the Care of Souls. p*sychotherapy.net* (*bit.ly/2v9S6vM*).

Nagel, T. (October 1974). "What is it like to be a bat?" *The Philosophical Review 83:4*. Duke UP, 435–450.

Nelson, D. (2017). *Tough Enough: Arbus, Arendt, Didion, McCarthy, Sontag, Weil*. U Chicago Press.

New York Association for Analytical Psychology. (2016). *Jung Lexicon*.

Nietzsche, Friedrich. (1888, 2005). *Ecce Homo*. In *The Anti-Christ, Ecce Homo, Twilight of the Idols, and Other Writings* (Ridley & Norman, trans., eds.). Judith Norman, London: CUP, 96.

Ovid. (1995). *The Metamorphoses of Ovid* (Allen Mandelbaum, trans.). NY: Harcourt Brace.

Paz, O. (1956, 1973). *The Bow and the Lyre* (Ruth Simms, trans.). U Texas.

———————. (1969, 2011). *Conjunctions and Disjunctions* (Helen Lane, trans.). Viking/Seaver Books, 61-62.

Peay, Pythia. (2011, February 26). America and the Shift in Ages: An Interview with Jungian James Hillman. *The Huffington Post* (*huff.to/1WYkR6d*).

Pinker, Steven. (2007). *The Stuff of Thought: Language as a Window into Human Nature*. NY: Viking.

———————. (4 Feb 2010). The Stuff of Thought: Language as a Window into Human Nature. [Lecture]. *Royal Society for the Encouragement of the Arts, Manufactures & Commerce*, London (*bit.ly/1UrlVMp*).

Plant, Stephen. (3 Oct 2014). Simone Weil—In Our Time [Lecture]. *BBC Radio 4* (bit.ly/29Z6FU4).

Richardson, William. (1967). *Heidegger: Through Phenomenology to Thought* (2nd ed.). Boston: Martinus Nijhoff, 410.

Root-Bernstein, M. (2014). *Inventing Imaginary Worlds*. MD: Rowman & Littlefield.

Shirane, H. (2000). "Beyond the Haiku Moment: Bashō, Buson, and Modern Haiku Myths." *Modern Haiku, 31:1* (Winter-Spring).

Slattery, D. (2006). *Harvesting Darkness: Essays on Literature, Myth, Film and Culture*. Lincoln, NE: iUniverse Inc., 63.

Sontag, Susan. (1 Feb 1963). Simone Weil. *The New York Review of Books*.

———————. (1964, 1966). *Against Interpretation*. Farrar, Strauss and Giroux, 10.

Snyder, Gary. (1980). *The Real Work: Interviews and Talks, 1964-1979*. New Directions.

———————. (1996). *A Place in Space: Ethics, Aesthetics, And Watersheds*. Berkeley, CA: Counterpoint, 163-72.

Stanford Encyclopedia of Philosophy. (2007, 2011). Risk. *The Stanford Encyclopedia of Philosophy.* CA: Stanford UP (*plato.stanford.edu/entries/risk*).

Stevens, Wallace. (1942). *Notes Toward a Supreme Fiction.* MA: The Cummington Press.

_____. (1951). *The Necessary Angel: Essays on Reality and the Imagination.* NY: Knopf, 171.

_____. (1950). *The Auroras of Autumn.* NY: Knopf.

Tacey, D. (2009). *Edge of the Sacred: Jung, Psyche, Earth.* Germany: Daimon Verlag.

Turner, Mark. (1996). *The Literary Mind.* Oxford: OUP.

_____. (2014). *The Origin of Ideas.* Oxford: OUP.

Weil, Simone. (1950). Forms of the Implicit Love of God. *Waiting for God* [Attente de Dieu] (Emma Craufurd, trans.). NY: Putnam, 169-170.

Wilson, J. (1979). *Octavio Paz: A Study of His Poetics.* CUP (*bit.ly/2tWkU7D*).

Winterson, J. (1992). *Written on the Body.* London: Jonathan Cape.

Wittgenstein, L. (1953). *Philosophical Investigations* (GEM Anscombe, trans.). Oxford: Blackwell.

_____. (1982). *Correspondance.* Lausanne: Editions l'Age d'Homme.

Young, Dudley. (1991). *Origins of the Sacred: The Ecstasies of Love and War.* NY: St. Martin's Press, 269, 271.

Richard Gilbert (リチャード・ギルバート)

熊本大学大学院社会文化科学研究科・米文学教授。1980年代にナロパ大学（Naropa University, Boulder, Colorado）にてアレン・ギンズバーグ、ゲイリー・スナイダーらビート詩人とともに学び、瞑想心理学（Contemplative Psychology）の修士号を取得。臨床心理士として勤務。ユニオン大学（The Union Institute & University）にて元型心理学の創始者 James Hillman に学び、詩学・深層心理学の博士号（Ph.D. in Poetics and Depth Psychology）を取得。主な著書に *Poems of Consciousness: Contemporary Japanese & English-language Haiku in Cross-cultural Perspective* (HSA 2009 Mildred Kanterman Award 受賞作、2008) *The Disjunctive Dragonfly: A New Theory of English-language Haiku* (the Touchstone Prize 受賞作、2013) など。主な共著に *Earth in Sunrise: A Course for English-Language Haiku Study* (2017) など。

Richard Gilbert is a tenured Professor of American Literature at the Graduate School of Social and Cultural Sciences, Kumamoto University. In the 1980s, he studied with Beat poets Allen Ginsberg, Gary Snyder, and others at Naropa University (Boulder, Colorado). After receiving an MA in Contemplative Psychology he worked as an clinical outpatient psychotherapist; he received his Ph.D. in Poetics and Depth Psychology in 1990, studying Archetypal Psychology with James Hillman at The Union Institute & University. His book, *Poems of Consciousness: Contemporary Japanese & English-language Haiku in Cross-cultural Perspective* (2008), was awarded the HSA 2009 Mildred Kanterman Award for Haiku Criticism and Theory. In August 2013, *The Disjunctive Dragonfly: A New Theory of English-language Haiku* was awarded the Touchstone Prize in criticism. In 2017, he co-authored *Earth in Sunrise: A Course for English-Language Haiku Study*.

本書は平成29年度熊本大学学術出版助成、および平成27〜29年度・採択日本学術振興会　科学研究費補助金　基盤研究（C）「俳句の国際教育への活用とネットワーク構築：現代俳句の文化的多様性の双方向的発信」（課題番号：15K02755、研究代表者：リチャード・ギルバート）の助成を受けたものです。

This work has been supported by The Japan Society for the Promotion of Science (JSPS) Grant-in-Aid for Scientific Research *Kakenhi* 15K02755 (2015-2018). Book publication has been supported by a Kumamoto University Academic Publication Subsidy.

Poetry as Consciousness
Haiku Forests, Space of Mind, and an Ethics of Freedom

平成30年2月28日初版第一刷発行
著　者：Richard Gilbert
発行者：中野　淳
発行所：株式会社 慧文社(けいぶんしゃ)
　　　　〒174-0063
　　　　東京都板橋区前野町4-49-3
　　　　〈TEL〉03-5392-6069
　　　　〈FAX〉03-5392-6078
　　　　E-mail:info@keibunsha.jp
　　　　http://www.keibunsha.jp/
〈印刷所〉慧文社印刷部
〈製本所〉東和製本株式会社
ISBN978-4-86330-189-4

落丁本・乱丁本はお取替えいたします。

本書は環境にやさしい大豆から作られたSOYインクを使用しております。

千宗旦

田中 稔―著　A5判・並製・カバー装

千利休の孫にして茶道三千家の祖・千宗旦。史料・史実重視の立場で二五〇通を超える宗旦の手紙を丹念に解読し、従来「伝説」「定説」として伝えられてきた虚像を覆して、本当の「人間宗旦」を浮き彫りにする。宗旦と茶道に関する研究史に一石を投じる快著。

定価：本体三三〇〇円＋税

ISBN978-4-905849-87-2

現代語訳 宗旦文書

田中 稔 編　A5判・並製・カバー装

かくして三千家は誕生した！ 元伯千宗旦が書き遺した二五〇通もの手紙を分かりやすく現代語に訳し、一つ一つに解説を付した本邦初、画期的歴史史料！ さらに「宗旦文書年譜」や「登場人物名簿」等を掲載し、読者の便宜を図った。茶道三千家必携――！

定価：本体六〇〇〇円＋税

ISBN978-4-905849-20-9

近現代における茶の湯家元の研究

廣田 吉崇―著　A5判・上製・カバー装

茶の湯などの伝統文化に欠かせない存在である「家元」。このような家元のあり方は、いつの時代にはじまるのか。家元と天皇・皇族との間には、どのような歴史があったのか。本書は、近現代の茶の湯に焦点をあてて、茶の湯家元が現代の姿に至る歴史的変遷を明らかにする。

定価：本体四〇〇〇円＋税

ISBN978-4-86330-059-0

増補版 朝鮮上代建築の研究

米田 美代治―著／芹生 春菜―解説

A5判・上製・クロス装・函入

定価：本体10000円＋税

ISBN978-4-905849-85-8

戦前・日本統治下の朝鮮にあって、、現在でも韓国の学会で高い評価を受ける夭折の学者・米田美代治。彼の研究成果の粋である名著に、原本未掲載の遺文および、芹生春菜氏書き下ろしの解説・著者略伝、年譜を新たに加えた増補新訂版！

茶道研究 茶器の見方

今泉雄作―著　A5判・上製・クロス装・函入

定価：本体8000円＋税

ISBN978-4-905849-60-5

岡倉天心らと東京美術学校を設立した美術史家・今泉雄作が、茶器の良し悪しの見分け方（鑑定法）・鑑賞の仕方（鑑賞法）を、日本古来の様々の名器を例にとり徹底解説。身近な茶碗などの鑑定から、茶道具の揃え方などまで解説する一冊。茶器鑑定、茶器鑑賞、茶人必携の書！

日本画の知識及び鑑定法

今泉雄作―著　A5判・上製・クロス装・函入

定価：本体9000円＋税

ISBN978-4-905849-68-1

日本美術界の先駆者・今泉雄作による不朽の名著を、体裁を一新して復刊！古代から明治初年までの一千余年におよぶ日本画の通史と、実践的な鑑賞・鑑定法を、平易明快に、かつ細大漏らさず解説する。日本画の基礎知識全般を一冊に凝縮した、日本画愛好家、美術史研究者に必携の書！

異文化コミュニケーションを考える
50歳英語教師の米国留学体験から

堀口 君子―著　四六判・並製・カバー装

公立中学校の英語教師を長く務めた著者が、五十歳でアメリカに修士留学！　米国の大学で経験した悲喜こもごも、ホームシック、人との出会いや別れ……。文化の違いによるコミュニケーションの相違を研究する著者ならではの卓越した洞察を、情趣溢れる文章で綴った好著。

定価：本体二〇〇〇円+税　　ISBN978-4-905849-40-7

詳説 普遍文法解析

加藤 義之―著　B5判・並製・カバー装

言語学に必携の普遍的な構文解析表示法！　英文の文構造を詳細に解析し、日本語・フランス語・ドイツ語・スペイン語他、あらゆる言語にも応用できる文法解析表示法を提唱。三十八年の高等学校における英語教育の経験が存分に生かされた著者渾身の画期的文法論。

定価：本体三三〇〇円+税　　ISBN978-4-905849-21-6

「XはYが+述語形容詞」構文の認知論的意味分析

豊地 正枝―著　A5判・上製・カバー装

えっ、「花」に十六種類もの意味があった？　認知意味論に基づいて、「XはYがZ」構文の表す多元性に、初めて意味的な側面からメスを入れた画期的な構文論。文法研究者・国語、日本語研究者必携、門外漢でも一気に読めるおもしろさ！　目から鱗の、革新的な日本語論＝文法理論！

定価：本体三八〇〇円+税　　ISBN978-4-905849-11-7

増田 弘・大野 敏明―共著　Ｂ５判・上製・クロス装・函入

古今各国「漢字音」対照辞典

定価：本体二〇〇〇〇円＋税

上古音から現代北京語までの中国歴代と、日本語の呉音・漢音、韓国音、ベトナム音、門南話（福建・台湾・呉楽（上海）という、ある時（時系列）、ある場所（地域・国）で、漢字は「どのように発音されていた（いる）のか？」を、約六万音の膨大な「対照表」で網羅した、他に類書のない画期的辞典！

ISBN978-4-905849-53-7

張　福武―著　Ａ５判・上製・クロス装・函入
日本語・英語・フランス語・ドイツ語・イタリア語・スペイン語対照

六カ国語共通のことわざ集

定価：本体五〇〇〇円＋税

日本語、英語、フランス語、ドイツ語、イタリア語、スペイン語の六カ国語で意味の共通する約三〇〇の「諺」・「慣用句」を集めて、それぞれ原文を掲載・対比させ、ひとつひとつにわかりやすい解説を付けました。各言語を学ぶ方はもちろん、国際的業務に携わる方、留学生等にも必携！　楽しく読めてためになる、活用自在、レファレンスブック！

ISBN978-4-86330-072-9

張　福武―著　Ａ５判・上製・クロス装・函入
日本語・台湾語・英語・中国語・韓国語対照

五カ国語共通のことわざ辞典

定価：本体七〇〇〇円＋税

日本語、台湾語（ホーロー語）、英語、中国語、韓国語の五カ国語で意味の共通する二五〇以上の「諺」・「慣用句」を集めて、それぞれ原文を掲載・対比させ、一つ一つにわかりやすい解説を付けました。各言語を学ぶ方はもちろん、外国人留学生等にも必携！　楽しく読めてためになる、活用自在ことわざ辞典！

ISBN978-4-905849-86-5

スティーヴン・クレインの「全」作品解説

久我俊二 著　A5判・並製・カバー装

クレインの代表作『赤い武勲章』やアメリカ自然主義最初の中編『マギー』、世紀を代表する短編「オープン・ボート」他、従軍記者として名を馳せた寄稿記事、イマジストの先駆的詩など、クレイン作と言われる全ての作品を執筆時期や内容によって分類し、詳説！

定価：本体四〇〇〇円＋税

ISBN978-4-86330-068-2

ハロルド・フレデリックの人生と長編小説 ——詐欺師の系譜

久我俊二 編　A5判・並製・カバー装

作家兼ジャーナリストとして英・米を舞台に一九世紀末に活躍したハロルド・フレデリック邦初の本格的作家論・作品論！スタインベックなどに大きな影響を与え、ジョイス・キャロル・オーツも激賞した名作『セロン・ウェア』他、主要八作品を紹介し、その生涯と思想を辿る。

定価：本体二五〇〇円＋税

ISBN978-4-905849-32-2

セロン・ウェアの破滅

ハロルド・フレデリック 著／久我俊二 訳
A5判・上製・カバー装

「啓蒙」と「堕落」……。南北戦争後の宗教事情、アイルランド移民の状況など当時の世相をリアルに描きつつ、近代化を突き進む一九世紀末の米国社会の葛藤を象徴的に描き出した古典的名著。イギリス版の訳も脚注に付記、訳注も充実！

定価：本体三〇〇〇円＋税

ISBN978-4-86330-001-9

「ユリシーズ」大全

北村富治―著　B5判・上製・クロス装・函入

定価：本体二〇〇〇〇円＋税　ISBN978-4-86330-065-1

歴史、地理、民俗学、哲学、神学そしてカトリック典礼など、多角的視野から『ユリシーズ』に迫る―詳細な解説だけでなく、写真、地図、建物の構造や見取図、新聞・雑誌に掲載された記事や広告なども豊富に。待望の『ユリシーズ』完全註解Book！

マイ・フェア・レディーズ
バーナード・ショーの飼い慣らされないヒロインたち

大江麻里子―編　A5判・並製・カバー装

定価：本体二五〇〇円＋税　ISBN978-4-905849-24-7

『マイ・フェア・レディー』の原作者として知られるジョージ・バーナード・ショー。イライザやジャンヌ・ダルクなど、彼の演劇作品に登場する、闊達で機知に富み、しばしば「女らしくない女」と評されるヒロインたちの分析を通じて、ショーの理想とした男女関係や社会のあり方を探る。

新版 D・H・ロレンス文学論集

D・H・ロレンス―著／羽矢謙一―訳　四六判・上製・カバー装

定価：本体三五〇〇円＋税　ISBN978-4-905849-14-8

ロレンスの著した代表的な17篇の「文学論」を掲載。英文学研究・ロレンス研究に必携の名著が、新装・新訂版で、数十年ぶりによみがえる！　旧版の内容・表記に大幅な加筆・修正を加え、現代の読者にも読みやすくなった本邦唯一のロレンス文学論集！日本図書館協会選定図書

江藤淳氏の批評とアメリカ
――『アメリカと私』をめぐって

廣木寧・著　四六判・並製・カバー装

江藤淳著『アメリカと私』を深く読み解きながら、そこにせつつ、文学者のみならず「戦後日本」にとっての「アメリカ」の存在と意味を深く追究する。著者渾身の作家論・文学論・東西比較文化論にして、戦後史論ともいえる快著！

定価：本体三〇〇〇円＋税

ISBN978-4-86330-040-8

天下なんぞ狂える
――夏目漱石の『こころ』をめぐって
（上）（下）

廣木寧・著　A5判・上製・カバー装

日本という国が世界史に無理往生に急遽接ぎ木された明治という時代に生きた夏目漱石。彼がその時代の中で追い求めたものは何だったのか。『こころ』を軸に、激動の時代の中で漱石が見つめたものと、近代日本人に宿命の悲しみを明らかにする。

定価：各巻本体二〇〇〇円＋税

上 ISBN978-4-86330-170-2
下 ISBN978-4-86330-171-9

北米で読み解く近代日本文学
――東西比較文化のこころみ――

萩原孝雄・著　A5判・上製・カバー装

森鷗外から宮崎駿まで――日本文学に通底する「子宮の感性」を説き明かす。北米の大学で日本文学の教鞭をとる著者が、海外から見た日本文学という独特の視座で、「子宮の感性」に貫かれた日本文学・文化の特色を描き出す。近代・現代文化論に必携！

定価：本体四〇〇〇円＋税

ISBN978-4-905849-91-9